Up in Flames

EDEN FINLEY
SAXON JAMES

Content Warning

Content warnings include emotional manipulation, domestic abuse recovery, death of a child (referenced of page), and any situation the fire department might respond to (car crashes, fires, dead bodies etc)

Names, characters, businesses, places, events, and incidents are either the products of the authors' imaginations or used in a fictitious manner. Any resemblance to actual persons, living or dead, or actual events is purely coincidental.

One

REMY

The only thing stopping my stomach from upending itself is the constant noise and motion around me. I try to focus on that instead of my swirling thoughts, but it's a losing battle. One I'm not even sure I want to win.

I'm having *big* thoughts for my wedding day, and while my family and best friend are toasting and polishing off the champagne, I'm struggling to keep this smile on my face.

"You okay?" my cousin Wren asks, pausing right beside me. "You're not normally this green."

"He's *nervous*," Mom jumps in before I can answer. She staggers tipsily closer to wrap an arm around my shoulders, and since I'm sitting, it's way easier for her to do than it usually is. I'm considered short at five seven, but Mom is barely five feet. "It's a perfectly normal thing to feel on your wedding day."

Then she sniffs.

Ah, fuck. Here come the tears.

Her body shakes on a repressed sob. "I'm so proud of you, baby. Your dream job, your dream holiday, and your dream man. You've always done what makes you happy, and I'm so blessed to be your mother."

I almost wilt on the spot. We've got everyone's attention now, and this impromptu speech is not what I need before saying "I do" in front of a hundred or so people.

Suddenly, all the company that was reassuring before is suffocating now.

"Hear, hear," Dad chimes in.

"To Remy!" Tig cries, and I narrow my eyes at my so-called friend.

For the first time all day, apparently, the universe is on my side because he reads the look I'm giving him.

"And with that love fest, everyone out. Yep, you too, Mrs. P."

Mom waves Tig away. "Remy needs me."

"Actually, a minute to myself would be awesome." I give her my best puppy dog eyes, and she instantly relents.

"Okay, but no runaway bride attempts," she jokes, taking Wren's arm. "I'll hunt you down myself."

They all leave, chuckling over the thought, when ...

I'm actually fucking considering it.

The door clicks closed, and I sag, fake smile gone in a flash.

Holy shit, what am I doing?

It's not the first time I've thought that today. Or this week or even this month. My gut is in knots as I pace the hotel room, doing everything I can to resist pulling my hair with frustration. Eman hates when I do that.

In fact, he hates a lot of things about me lately.

And yet ... there are moments. Glimpses of the man I fell in love with. The man I said yes to marrying.

The incredible part is I wasn't even looking to settle down when I met him. It was a whirlwind, and he literally swept me off my feet. He's hot, confident, and always goes after what he wants.

I never stood a chance.

Since he proposed though ... I can't shake the feeling things have changed. His confidence has shifted from hot to pushy. Almost demanding. He goes out with his friends all the time, but whenever I do anything with mine, he invites himself along and sticks to my side. He's squared off with more than one of my friends over looking at me "wrong." I know Eman cares about me, and he brushes it off as having had too much to drink, but there's *something* in my ear warning me to be careful.

I'm not a pushover. I'm not helpless either. I have no issues with putting Eman in his place, but sometimes the issue isn't worth the argument. My energy is waning, and when we do argue, it can last all day, but then it leads to makeup fucking, and by the next day, he's my sweet fiancé again.

Until last week. Our fight was ... huge. All because he'd

come to an open day at the station, and I'd been called out on an emergency.

Apparently, that meant I didn't want to spend time with him, other than, you know, doing my fucking job.

He'd said he felt neglected.

Neglected.

By me.

Though, in his defense, I *have* been working a lot of overtime to try and save money for our honeymoon. Then Tig threw a weekend-long bachelor party. And ... okay, seeing things from his side ... fuck.

Is that why he's been so clingy? So next-level? Am *I* the reason for all the changes I've been noticing?

The irritation seeps out of me, and I'm more confused than ever.

He left me all night after that fight. An *entire* night right before our wedding, and even now, I haven't been able to get a straight answer about where he'd been.

Was he showing me how it felt to be so neglected?

I give in to the urge to grip my hair. My head hangs back, eyes screwed closed, a million and one thoughts chasing themselves around my mind.

What do I do?

A few months ago, I would have been here laughing and drinking, excited to marry the man.

Now, the thought fills me with dread.

But if it really is *my* doing, we can fix it. If I'm more aware, I can make sure that I'm as attentive as I was when we were first together, and Eman will be *my* Eman again.

That thought doesn't comfort me like it should.

Don't marry him.

The relief that hits with those words is sudden and overwhelming. I picture it, just for a second, going out there and asking him to talk in private. To tell him that we can't go through with this. To apologize. The image of his face is vivid, and I know exactly how his eyes would look as they filled with disappointment. As he begged. As he reminded me again and again that he loves me. And what if he gets angry instead? Would he try to fight someone again? Would he try to fight *me*?

My eyes snap open, and I sigh.

No matter what, I could never do that to him.

We're here now. I committed. The problems we're having are temporary, a rough patch for us to work through together. Couples have them all the time, and with the stress of the wedding, it shouldn't be this much of a surprise that things have started to unravel.

"*Ahh.*" My arms feel like jelly as I shake them out, then scrub my damp palms over my pant legs. The hotel ballroom wedding wasn't my idea, but he likes fancier things than I do. And our compromise was that I got to choose the honeymoon location.

Compromise.

Trust.

Love.

All things we've had in the past and all things we can get back again so long as I pull my head out of my ass. If he'd been the one neglecting me, I'd probably feel the same way he does. If it's my fault, it's up to me to fix it.

I can do this.

The first real-ish smile slips onto my face, and I open the door to find my parents, Wren, and Tig waiting.

"I'm ready."

Their excitement almost convinces me that I'm making the right choice.

When we walk into the ceremony, there are a lot more people here than I'm expecting. Almost my whole station has shown up, whether on their day off or taking a quick break from their shifts while our sister station covers things. We agreed I'd show up first, but now I really wish I at least had a familiar face waiting down the end to distract me from all these people.

Eman's and my families fill both sides, along with our friends and ... *friends* of friends. I don't think Eman's shut up about having famous hockey players at his wedding since Aleks and Gabe RSVP'd. Gabe's a colleague from another firehouse and recently started dating an NHL star, so Eman invited nearly all of Aleks's team. To our wedding. Even though Gabe and I aren't close. Eman is close to Sanden though, who we joke is Gabe's work husband. So it all works out, in a roundabout way. Six degrees of separation and all that stuff.

Given how Eman's obsessed with becoming an influencer, I think he invited the hockey players because he's under the impression it'll get him some kind of social media boost.

My future husband has goals. That's another good thing about him.

My nerves ramp up again at the sight of all these people. I'd always imagined my wedding would be simple and small, outdoors—I shake that thought off. I'm falling into the habit Eman's always pointing out: I'm looking for things to pick at. I have to admit that he's done good. Everything looks amazing.

When we get to the front, Mom and Dad hug me and take their seats, and Tig and Wren follow me up the two stairs to where the officiant is standing. She gives me a warm welcome, and then I take a deep breath and face the room.

I try to block out all the faces pointed my way and focus on the doors at the end.

I'm anxious to see him. Hope he doesn't keep me waiting too long. Tig tries to talk to me, but I'm in this echoey kind of haze where the best I can do is force a laugh now and then.

A few minutes pass. I wipe my clammy palms off on my pants.

Then a few more. The knot in my gut tightens.

Time seems to drag on, and I don't know whether it feels like forever because I'm sweating like I'm performing a resus or if the universe has decided it's against me again.

When I can't take the waiting anymore, I turn back to Tig to ask for the time just as the sound of a door opening fills the room.

My gut flips violently as I look back down the aisle, but it's empty.

Then Sanden, one of the groomsmen, steps through a door on the side of the room.

He walks quickly, head down, avoiding eye contact with anyone. At first, I'm confused before he jogs up the two stairs, and when he finally looks up, his big blue eyes collide with mine, and all I can see is regret.

He's close, too close, his aftershave making my head swim as he leans in to whisper, "Remy, I ... I'm ..." He clears a frustrated growl from his throat. "He's gone. Eman left."

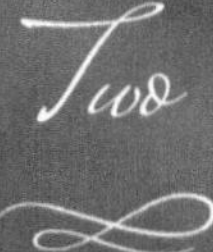

Two

SANDEN

Remy bolts, and I don't blame him. I could fucking kill Eman for doing this to him. And to me since I'm the one who gets to break the news, not only to Remy but to *everyone*. I'm a measly groomsman. The one who stands on the very end and was only asked to be involved because Eman and I have known each other since junior high. This shouldn't be my job, but apparently, I'm the only one who gives enough of a shit to let Remy know. The only person who should be doing this is Eman.

As I turn to the full ballroom, expectant faces staring up at me, I don't have the heart to do it. But I don't want to make Remy do it either.

I force an easygoing smile. "Uh, we'll be right back."

I run after Remy, going in the direction of the suite he

was assigned to get ready in. The door is locked when I get there, giving a good sign that my guess for where he fled to is accurate. I knock a couple of times, but he doesn't answer, even though I know he's in there. He's just pretending he's not.

"I can hear you moving around. Please let me in?"

I get no response.

Okay, fine. I'm going to have to get creative. The function center is on the second floor, and I know the suites have balconies. If only I had my rig and ladder with me. Oh well. Going to have to old-school it.

I exit to the courtyard of the events area. As I head down the steps, I lose my jacket and undo my cufflinks on the way. My tie goes next.

"I can do this." Like some parkour champion, I run at the building, use the side of the concrete steps to launch off, and jump in the direction of Remy's room.

Gripping the bottom of the balcony, I use all my strength to pull myself up, holding tight to the metal pole in between the glass panels of the balcony. Once I get my feet onto the ledge, it's easy to haul myself the rest of the way up and over the railing.

My landing could do with some work though. I hit the ground with a thud, and then Remy appears above me.

"What the fuck? How did you ..." He looks around. "Did you climb up here?"

I stand and shrug off the twinge in my arm. "Easy as. I'm big and tough. You should know that by now."

Remy looks between the balcony and the ground below. "You could've hurt yourself."

I did. I don't say that though. Nothing could hurt more than the pain he's going through right now. "Are you okay?"

"Do you really care?"

I pull back in shock. "What? Of course I do."

Remy cocks his head. "Did Eman send you to make sure I don't cause a scene or have a breakdown that'll embarrass him? Because, you know, that would be the embarrassing part *for him*. Me flipping out over him leaving me. At the fucking altar."

No way am I going to point out Eman isn't sensitive enough for something like that.

Remy's raised voice is something I'm not used to coming from him.

He's sweet and kind, and from the beginning of Eman's and his relationship, I knew Remy was too good for my friend. I've always felt guilty for being the reason they met but told myself if Eman is what made Remy happy, then that's all I needed.

If I'd known ... Fuck, if I knew Eman was going to do this to him, I would've told Remy a year ago that I'm hopelessly, stupidly in love with him and he should leave the guy who never grew up.

Okay, maybe I'm not in love with him, but considering there isn't a day that's gone by where I haven't regretted taking Eman as my "date" to a work function, I'd say it's as close as possible to being in love with someone I've never dated. I didn't even want to see Eman the night they met. Or at all. But he'd been bugging me about catching up, said we were drifting apart—which is true.

On purpose—so I figured taking him to the fireman's ball would get him off my case and distract him with an open bar.

If I'd known it would result in Eman meeting Remy and sweeping my crush off his feet, I never would've done it.

Remy's a paramedic for Station 21, the nearest firehouse to Station 40, where I work, so our paths cross often. I've always thought he was cute, and in the beginning, we'd even flirt. Then he went and fell in love with the guy I'd been trying desperately to cut ties with.

Once upon a time, Eman was all that I had and vice versa. Being the only two out kids throughout high school, we formed a bond. A bond that has been hard to break even as I've grown up and he never moved on from adolescence. He was there for me through the hardest moment of my life, and I hate knowing I've grown apart from that person. It's not the immaturity that gets me but the caring about what everyone else thinks of him. Wanting to be popular. *An influencer.*

It's tiring.

I wonder, not for the first time, if he was only interested in Remy because of his family's money. Remy's parents are all over those late-night lawyer ads. The ones asking if someone has ever wronged you because you could be entitled to compensation type things.

"Oh my God," Remy says. "Eman didn't send you, did he? He doesn't even fucking care if I'm all right."

Color drains from his face, and that murderous feeling creeps over me again. I grip Remy's bicep and pull him inside the room, guiding him to the plush couch that takes up one wall of the suite.

"Breathe," I coax and sit next to him. Both Remy and I have training in these kinds of situations. Where people are on the brink of a panic attack after losing their homes to a fire, their loved ones in a car accident, or any other tragedy we face as first responders. "Eman is not worthy of you. He never was."

Remy scoffs. "That's rich coming from you."

I frown. "What do you mean?"

"Why did you even follow me here? You fucking hate me."

"Whoa, wait, *what*?"

"I thought we were friends when we first met, but then I started dating Eman, and you turned on me because you were jealous. Because you'd always had a thing for him."

I can barely contain my laughter. "A thing? For *him*? Eman. As in Eman Faile." I laugh some more.

"That's ... funny to you?"

"It really, really is. When you two first got together, I was trying to ghost him. I don't know what happened to the guy, but he was this amazing, down-to-earth best friend when we were in high school, and then we grew up, and ... it's like the guy I was friends with wasn't there anymore."

Remy gapes at me. "I felt the same way! This morning, I was in this very room thinking how he'd changed, but I thought it was the stress of the wedding. I put it down to 'having a rough patch.'"

I nod. "I told myself that for years too. He was going through a phase. He'd eventually grow up."

Suddenly, a large breath that sounds a lot like relief leaves his body, and he sinks into the couch. "Holy fuck."

"What?"

"I just dodged a massive bullet."

"You really, really did. I am curious though. Who told you I had a thing for him?"

His eyes cut to me and away again. "Eman. Said you always had."

Of course he did. I can't be certain, but I'm almost sure Eman knew I had a crush on Remy when they met. What better way to make sure Remy and I stayed firmly away from each other than to tell Remy I was trying to steal his man?

Remy's short-lived relief dies, as if realization is a late guest to the party. "The wedding. Everyone's out there. Waiting. And—"

"I'll take care of it if you want me to." I give his shoulder a squeeze but ignore the urge to wrap him in a hug. I'm sure he'd fit against me nicely. He's short and lean, with light brown hair that looks orange in some lights—exactly the type of guy I go for.

Remy bites his bottom lip, and I have to blink away the heat I'm sure is filling my gaze as I watch. "I should do it myself. It's the respectful thing to do. If I don't go out there, I'm just as bad as Eman."

"Or, if you're up for it, we could do this thing I saw on a viral video."

"What's that?"

"This woman was left at the altar, and instead of canceling everything, she threw a huge celebration instead of a reception. Said, 'Fuck the groom, I'm still gonna have a good time.'"

Remy thinks about it, seems hesitant, but then an almost imperceptible smile takes over his face.

"You're imagining what Eman's reaction would be if he found out that instead of breaking down after he left, you partied, aren't you?"

"Is that petty? It's petty, isn't it?"

I lean in. "Honey, after being left at the fucking altar, you're allowed to be petty."

Remy stands. "Then instead of having a pity party, let's throw a *petty party*."

"Hells yes." I stand too. "And just know, you're not alone. I'll be with you every step of the way." I hold out my hand for him.

He stares at it for a beat before taking it. "You really never hated me? Eman was why you went distant?"

Sure, let's go with Eman being the reason I stopped hanging out with Remy. It definitely wasn't pure jealousy over seeing them together or the way Eman treated Remy like a prize or trophy. It was *all* Eman.

"I never hated you. Not even for a second. And in case it wasn't obvious already, I'm Team Remy all the way."

His confusion makes my chest ache because it's my fault he doesn't know I don't hate him.

We head for the door.

"You're not doing this so next time there's a fire in cross-jurisdiction, you can call dibs, are you?"

I snap my fingers. "Damn, you're onto me."

Remy manages a small laugh but then sucks in a deep breath.

"You ready?" I ask. "I can do this for you. Or be right by your side. Whatever you need."

"I ... I think I can do this."

But the closer we get to the ceremony ballroom, the shakier he becomes.

I pull him back before we head out there. "Just remember. Petty party of the year coming right up because being petty is awesome."

Three

REMY

Sanden not hating me is making my head spin. I mean, that *could* be the alcohol, possibly, maybe, but definitely mostly the him-not-hating-me thing. Odd. *So* odd. Redirecting my bitterness from him to Eman is taking some adjustment, but it's not as hard as I thought it would be.

Vodka helps with that.

So does being left at the fucking altar.

I haven't stopped to let myself feel much other than anger. Every time another emotion tries to kick in, I drink some more and dance the sadness away. Eman doesn't deserve that part of me. That lump of dread settling in my gut that keeps telling me this is *my* fault. I should have been a better fiancé, more attentive, more ... I don't even know.

So instead of thinking about it too hard, I strangle another bottle of vodka and kiss that bitch until I'm ass-up.

All around me, people are *drunk*. Some of Eman's side left after I announced that he's a douchey douche bag who's the scum of the earth—go figure—but most stayed for the free booze.

And there's a lot of it. Because Eman's card is down on the bar.

Hey, last I spoke to him, we agreed that I'd pay for the ceremony and the honeymoon, and he'd cover the reception. I'm still up for that money, so I figure he should be too.

"Another shot!" I cry, fist pumping the air like I'm Joan of Arc screaming about freedom ... or was that Braveheart? Elsa?

"Someone called for a shot?" Gabe asks, pushing his way through the crowd. The man is a giant. Even gianter than Sanden. A fucking mountain.

I take the itty-bitty shot glass from him and down it. "Mmm, Eman-eraser."

"Ah, what?"

Sanden, who's been planted by my side all night, says, "Just give the man whatever he asks for."

"Anything?" I launch at Gabe, face smooshing into his big man chest. I'm basically motor-boating his muscles he's so large, and I don't hate it.

"Need a minute?"

I roll my head to the side and find Gabe's famous hockey boyfriend watching us and trying not to lose his shit laughing.

Then I get an absolutely, posi-tootely *fabulous* idea. "Oh my Godddd," I say on a long gasp. "Photos. We need photos. All of the hockey photos."

Sanden's chuckle is warm in my ear as he pries me away from Gabe, and I'm not totally unaffected by his steady hands clamped tight over my hips. "What are you talking about?"

"Hockey! Eman loves hockey. And I have hockey players. Petty party!"

"Ah ..."

Gabe's face lights up. "I think he wants a photo with the famous hockey players."

I snap my fingers—well, *try to*— and point his way. "Bingo! Or ... touchdown?" I can't find the word through my alcohol-drenched thoughts.

"Score?" Sanden offers.

This time, I throw both hands up. "Score! Photos! Hockey players."

Aleks laughs. "On it." He disappears into the crowd, and I whirl on Sanden, struck by yet more genius. I'd forgotten his hands were still on me until suddenly, they're not.

"Maybe I can score *on* a hockey player."

"No."

"But Eman loves them and used me to get the NHL guys here. If I get jiggy with one, he'll *hate* it."

Sanden's forehead is sweetly crumpled, and I don't understand why *he* doesn't get it. "No way, Remy."

I yank away from him, but because he's not actually

holding on to me, I'm a bit too enthusiastic and almost face-plant.

"Steady there." Sanden chuckles, hands back on that glorious place on my hips.

"My hero," I swoon, cuddling into him.

Then the hockey players arrive.

They're not Gabe-huge, but these guys aren't messing around. All burly, muscular gods among men, filling out suits like a damn glove. I toss my phone in Sanden's direction as I launch myself into the fray. Aleks, Katz, and Bilson I know from a few group things I've been to, but the others I only recognize from watching the games on TV. I used to go to them live, but I can get a little, uh ... *enthusiastic*, which was downright embarrassing for Eman.

Watch me embarrass him now.

I'm in that wonderful state of warbly focus and soft edges, and even though we pose and crack faces, and someone lifts me up at some point, all I can concentrate on is the laughter choking me.

"You okay?" Sanden asks. His face won't stop swimming, but he's all smiley and pretty eyes and so, so close.

"How's this for petty?" Before I know what I'm doing, I lean in and smoosh my lips to his. It's fast and messy, and I grin my whole way through it. Sanden's hands are a vise grip on me now, and when I lift my phone to snap a photo, I get out, "Say cheese," before attaching my mouth to his again.

"Cheese," he mutters before tugging on my bottom lip with his teeth.

Oof, that's hot.

"Do it again," I whine.

Instead, he sweeps a soft, gut-swooping kiss over my lips before pulling away. "You're a mess."

"A horny mess. I was supposed to be having wedding sex tonight, damn it."

He chokes on his words. "Remy ..."

"You have to admit sleeping together would *really* stick it to Eman."

I swear he's teetering on the edge of saying yes when he swipes a hand over his conflicted expression. "I'm not sleeping with someone for revenge."

"But—"

"And neither are you."

I blow out a long, noisy breath. "Killjoy."

"Oh no," he deadpans. "Right in my feelings."

I stagger back toward the drunk sportsmen, taking more photos as I go.

"Petty party?" Gabe asks, reappearing and holding out another shot. The words echo from hockey players all around me as I take the shot with one hand and photo dump images of them to social media with the other.

That's right, Eman. I'm having the party you should have had.

And for having been left at the altar not too long ago, I'm ending my night on a high.

🔥 🔥 🔥

With every high comes a crash. Everything hurts. My gut riots. The pillow under my cheek that's soft as a cloud feels like a lump of cement against the pounding in my head. Each tortured throb in my temples makes me want to throw up.

I slip from the side of the bed onto all fours. Every movement is a struggle, but I crawl my way into the bathroom, take a long, *long* piss, and then drag myself back into bed.

Married. I'm fucking *married*.

I half flop toward the warm mass beside me—and almost scream.

At the sight of Sanden's amused expression, everything from yesterday comes crashing back. I'm *not* married.

The wedding didn't happen.

But the reception sure did.

"Oh, holy fuck."

"Morning," Sanden says. His tone is way too chipper for this time in the morning and way too ... present.

Sanden's here. In my bed.

"Tell me we didn't sleep together." My eyes fall closed. "You're very attractive, but we're colleagues, and you're practically best friends with Eman."

He laughs. "Nothing happened, and we're barely friends, let alone best friends."

A foggy memory of my lips pressed against his comes back to me. "We kissed though! Eman will hate you."

"Technically, you rubbed your lips against mine, and after what he did to you, the feeling's mutual."

I'm thrown off by the idea of Sanden actually *caring*

after how tumultuous our relationship has been. But it's a shitty thing for Eman to do to anyone, so it makes sense, and I have more important things to focus on. "How do you know that didn't lead to sex? You're hot, and we were drinking and—"

"We're still wearing our clothes, plus there's no mess."

"Of course there'd be no mess. I swallow!"

Sanden climbs out of the other side of the bed, like he needs to get away from the butthead with the hangover. He crosses to the minibar, pulls out a bottle of water, then fishes around in his bag for something. When he comes back, he drops some painkillers and the water on the bed right in front of me, then flops back down beside me.

"Take those and relax. Unlike you, I didn't drink my body weight in alcohol last night."

"That would be hard to do when you're enormous."

"Gabe is way bigger than me. Are you sure you're okay? You look like you're going to puke."

He's not wrong. I take the drugs. "I don't usually drink that much. I don't actually like it, considering Eman's always drinking enough for the both of us."

"Yeah ... I still ... I can't believe he left you like that. I feel guilty."

"So you should."

His gaze flies back to me.

"Kidding, obviously." Whether I'm still drunk or knowing Sanden doesn't hate me like I originally thought, I somehow have the guts to ask, "Now, come over here and rub my head. It hurts."

"You're an EMT. Surely you know that doesn't work."

"No, but it'll feel good." I wriggle closer to him and close my eyes. After what feels like forever, thick fingers slide through my hair. He's a little rough, but I can tell he's trying to be gentle.

Also, he was wrong. This actually does help. And it's not as weird as I thought it would be.

Sanden and I have had a weird friendship slash work relationship. We started out as friends, or what I thought was friends, but Eman came between that. I'm only now realizing that it was Eman influencing my opinion of Sanden. My memories might be fuzzy from last night, but one thing is crystal clear. Sanden didn't leave my side. He took care of me. He was kind. Nothing like the picture Eman has painted for the past three years.

I try to ignore my revolting stomach and the worry about what the hell I'm going to do now.

Eman lives with me—will all his stuff be gone when I go home? Nothing of him left but empty spaces where a life used to be. Even though I was having my doubts and know I shouldn't be upset, it doesn't change that I am. Upset for all that wasted time. For a day that was supposed to be special being robbed from me. For the embarrassment of having to tell people the wedding was off. And now ... where was he that night he disappeared? Why didn't he go through with it? Why did he act like I was his entire world, behave like a possessive child, and then disappear at the last minute?

How could he be so heartless?

Do I cancel my leave from work? There's no reason to keep it now. How do I face everyone's sympathy? Play it off like it was nothing, or call him all the names under the sun that he deserves?

I'm tired. Bone-tired. And not because of the hangover.

"Maybe I should call him," I whisper, not wanting to do that at all.

Sanden's fingers still. "Ah, probably not a great idea."

"Why?"

"You might have posted a whole bunch of photos to social media last night."

"Yeah?"

"With the caption 'pecky parto.'"

"Pecky parto?"

"Petty party."

"I fucked that up, didn't I? What did I post?" I glance around for my phone.

"You don't want to look. A few of them might have been of you with your mouth on mine."

I shoot upright. "I posted a photo of us kissing?"

"Let's not call it that."

"What else would you call it?"

"You drunkenly fish-mouthing me?"

I narrow a look at him. "This isn't a joke."

"I promise you I'm not joking."

"My *family* is on social media. What would they think?"

Sanden shrugs. "I think most of them saw it in person, actually. Your cousin was cheering you on, at least."

"Eman's going to see it."

"If he hasn't blocked you yet, sure."

If he's blocked me, it's going to take away my satisfaction at blocking him. "You don't care if he sees?" I check.

"He deserves whatever he gets."

I sigh, well and truly over it all. "Sorry."

"Don't be."

"I shouldn't have kissed you."

"Not a kiss, remember?"

My smile is weak, but it's something. "Why couldn't I have fallen for you instead?"

"Come again?"

I fall back against my pillow. "Don't worry, I'm not hitting on you. I was thinking of when I started at Station 21 and our firehouses crossed paths a lot. I ... I might have had a crush on you. But then I met Eman, and ... yeah. Clearly made a stupid decision there."

"There was only one stupid person in all of this, and I'm sorry I introduced you to him."

He's right that Eman was the stupid one, even if it's hard to admit. It's even harder to get the point across to the guilt hanging over me. Facing people after all this will be the hardest part. Now I'll forever be known as the guy who was left at the altar.

Not Remy, the EMT.

Not Remy, the overexcitable idiot.

Not Remy, who's there for people.

Remy, who was left at the altar and then kissed his colleague.

Fuck.

I want to run away.

And ... Actually, I can. A whole week on an island

sounds like an amazing break, with the added bonus of only approved places in the resort having reception. It's a place specifically made to unplug and be present. To spend time with people.

So screw it, I'm going to go.

"I'm going on my honeymoon," I say.

"You're what?"

"It's all paid for and past the refund period. So fuck him, I'm going. Sunny beaches, daily massages, a cabana right on the water. It's exactly what I need."

Sanden's smile catches me totally off guard, and it strikes me, for a quick second, how opposite he is to Eman. All crinkled lines around his eyes, dark, messy hair, and uneven tilt to his lips. It's ... real. Unstaged. "That sounds fucking perfect."

SANDEN

"You didn't have to drive me to the airport," Remy says.

He's in my passenger seat, wearing dark sunglasses, hair looking more orange than brown in the sun.

"Yeah, I did." Because he doesn't know it yet, but I'm going with him on this trip. He really doesn't need to be alone, and it just so happens I had a lot of favors saved up to cash in. Getting people to cover my shifts at the station for a week wasn't as hard as it normally would have been.

"It's because you know I'm starting to change my mind about going, isn't it?"

Sure, let's go with that. "I knew the second you decided

to go that you'd probably chicken out." It's why I offered to drive him. Why, as soon as I got home from the wedding yesterday morning, I made a few calls, packed my bag, and made sure I could change Eman's ticket to my name. Like the good groomsman I was determined to be—regardless of being bitter over their wedding or not—I knew their reservation details because I'd used my miles to spring for an upgrade on their flight to Hawaii and called the hotel to arrange champagne and rose petals in their suite on arrival.

Shit, I should've called to cancel that.

"Because going on my honeymoon by myself is too sad even for me?"

"Even for you? What's that supposed to mean?"

He shakes his head. "Nothing."

We arrive at the airport, and I head for the long-term parking.

"You don't have to park. You can pull up in the drop-off zone."

"No, I can't."

"Why not?"

"Because ... I'm going with you."

I pull up to the boom gate and get a ticket.

"What do you mean you're going with me?"

"I mean exactly that. You didn't think I was going to let you go by yourself, did you?" Besides, with Eman being MIA for the last day, I'm not convinced he isn't going to show up for the vacation anyway. If he knows what's good for him though, he'll keep his head down and disappear for a while after what he did.

"Well, yes. That was the point of it. I get to be alone in my thoughts. Have me time."

I park the car in the first space I find. "I can tell you now that the last thing you want after a breakup is to be alone with your thoughts."

"Why are you ..." He doesn't finish his sentence.

"Why am I what?"

"Why are you being all ... nice? A week ago, when I turned up on your doorstep looking for Eman, you looked like it physically hurt you to let me inside your house."

Yeah, that's because it did. Not to mention him telling me he used to have a crush on me. I try not to focus on regrets, because I have many, but the one I hold toward Remy is a big one.

I shouldn't have let Eman get remotely close to him.

Yesterday could've been my wedding if I'd played my cards smart. But I hadn't. And now Remy is paying for it with a broken heart, and it's all my fault. Actually, no. It's Eman's fault for being a jerk, but I can't help thinking if I'd had the guts to shoot my shot back then, maybe I could've saved Remy all the pain he's in now.

Or maybe we would've fucked around for a few months and he would've ended up dating Eman anyway, because God knows Eman doesn't know the meaning of bro-code. Which is fine by me because if he hadn't fucked my college boyfriend the same month we broke up, I'd feel more guilty about going on his honeymoon with the dude he left at the altar. And kissing him at their wedding.

Though, in my defense, I still maintain that wasn't a

kiss. Sure as fuck wasn't the type of kiss I'd imagined back when I met Remy.

"Sanden?" Remy asks. "You don't have an answer for me."

I do, but nothing that would be appropriate to say in this moment. "I wasn't mad that you came to me when Eman didn't come home. I was mad at him for fucking up what you two had. People everywhere pine for the type of love he had, and he fucked off because why?"

Remy glances out the window. "I've thought about it all week. Where he could've gone. Who he might've been with. You don't ... You don't happen to know, do you?"

I shake my head. "I asked him what happened, but all he'd tell me is he had cold feet, then assured me he was better."

"*So* much better. Waiting until the wedding day to call it off was a stellar move on his behalf."

"This is why I want to come with you. You can say no —I can stay in a separate room, I can do anything you want, but I need you to know that I'll be here for you no matter what."

His hazel eyes narrow. "Oh, jeez, this isn't some pity thing, is it? Worried I'll off myself in the ocean? I'm not that upset over him. In fact ... I'm worried I'm not as upset as I should be. I mean, yeah, fuck him and the horse he rode in on, and I'm so angry that he ended it in the way he did, but upset we're actually over?" He bites his lip. "I guess I should be thanking him more than hating him because if he hadn't done what he did, we'd be married, and it would've been a huge mistake. I just wish he'd done it in a more respectful way. At least to my face. The fact he put it on you—"

"I found the older Eman got, the more selfish he became. *Eman* was his number one priority, so getting someone else to call off his wedding is totally something he would do. I wasn't shocked. Disappointed and angry, but not shocked."

Remy lets out a sigh. "If you're telling me you want to come on my honeymoon as my friend and not because you feel sorry for me, then I'll let you."

"Oh, I'm only going on your honeymoon so I can get depressed breakup sex."

His eyes widen.

"Sure, you can drunkenly throw yourself at me at your wedding, but I make one joke and you freak out." I didn't know it was possible, but his eyes get even bigger.

"I ... I tried to have sex with you?"

"You offered. I declined. Because I am a gentleman." Even if it was one of the hardest things ever. Well, no, my dick was the hardest thing ever. Saying no was the right thing to do.

"Gentleman. Sure."

"Okay, fine. And because I knew you'd regret it."

Remy purses his lips. "Okay, then let's get our Hawaii on."

"I can't wait to get leid!"

He glares at me.

"You know, at the airport. Where you get leis. The flower wreath things."

"I'm regretting letting you be here already."

"But you're not thinking about Eman, are you?"

"True. Keep annoying me."

"Oh, I will. I'm going to annoy you until you love me."

"Mm. I've heard that's how you get people to like you. Keep bugging them until they give in."

"Exactly. Whoever said persistence is problematic behavior just isn't doing it right."

Remy laughs. "I really hope you're not being serious."

"I'm not. But I got you to laugh, so I'm taking it as a win. If I have to pretend to be creepy to cheer you up, I'll do it. I'll even walk ten feet behind you and jump into the bushes every time you turn around if you like."

"No, that's okay. Walking beside me is fine. Weirdly, the feeling of being stalked doesn't sound enjoyable to me."

"Fair enough."

And even though he's reluctant about me joining him on this trip, I'm happy I can be here. Remembering not to hit on him or make sex jokes will be difficult though. Hopefully, I can at least get another room when we get to the resort. I didn't book anything because I wasn't sure Remy would actually let me on the plane with him.

The plan is simple. We'll go to Hawaii, get separate rooms, have some drinks, swim in the ocean, and relax. All thoughts of Eman will be banned. It'll be fine.

🔥 🔥 🔥

"What do you mean you don't have any rooms available?" I ask at the reception desk. "You have to."

"I'm sorry, sir. The resort is hosting two different conventions this week and a wedding over the weekend."

And that simple plan goes out the window.

"You can stay in my room," Remy says. "I thought you'd be doing that anyway because I don't want you to be out of pocket on this thing."

I wave him off. "I have the money"—I don't actually, but hey, that's what credit cards are for—"and it was my choice to join you. I don't want to impose. I just want to be here for you."

"It's fine. We got a bungalow. They have more than one bed, don't they?" Remy looks at the receptionist with hopeful eyes.

She flattens her lips. "No, sorry. You've booked a king room. Ooh, but there is a couch." She lights up, but her expression feels forced, like she's telepathically asking us not to get angry at her.

"I'll take the couch," I say. Sharing a room isn't a big deal. Hell, on shift, we get as much sleep as we can in a dorm room with others from the team. That's not the issue.

The issue is that while I'm looking out for Remy, I really should've asked someone else to be here for him. His cousin Wren, maybe. Anyone but me. Because as much as I would jump at the chance to be in close quarters with Remy, to see him shirtless, to share his space, I worked out early in his and Eman's relationship that I can't be near him without thinking about doing inappropriate things to him.

And it's not that I'm worried I wouldn't be able to contain myself—I might joke about being a creep, but I'm not actually one—it's that the more time I spend with him, the more my chest aches.

It's why I kept him and Eman at arm's length. Why everyone at the station thinks I hate Remy, even though I've been nothing but professional toward him on the job. I might be here to make sure Remy's okay, but after this honeymoon, I'm not sure I will be.

Five

REMY

"What the fuck?" Sanden exclaims as he jogs up the steps to our private deck and ducks inside the bungalow.

In my head, I'm echoing him. On the outside, I'm trying to keep my rapidly fraying shit together. This place is incredible. I chose Hawaii, but Eman chose the hotel, and I trusted him enough not to look it up. I wanted to be surprised, and if I was here on my actual honeymoon with him, I wouldn't have thought twice about how lavish everything is. But now all I'm thinking about is the charge on my credit card. I'd known it was pricey, but I'd figured we paid a premium due to traveling in the summer. This is ... fuck me. As I look from the perfect ocean view to the cozy deck to the high ceilings, smallish living area, and enormous four-poster bed, all I can think is *he would have gotten some amazing photos out of this.*

I don't doubt that if he was here, we'd already be posing in front of that view, rings in plain sight, ready for him to upload the second he had a bar of service.

"Remy, come check out this tub!" Sanden yells from— I'm assuming—the bathroom.

I'm struggling to keep my head on straight with the rapid change in everything. I keep going to ask Eman what he wants to do first, or where we should go, or if I can unpack before we start to explore.

Then I remember he's not here, and I get the weirdest feeling of being off-balance. I don't miss him. I'm beyond pissed at what he did, but this whole thing gives me that prickling unease of an oncoming fight, and I can't make it go away.

I take a hesitant step inside, but my gaze catches on something that makes it impossible to keep going.

"*That's* the couch?" It's a two-seater. Tiny. Would struggle to hold me, let alone that massive firefighter ogling our bathtub. My head gives a stress throb, and I've reached the point where I can either laugh or cry, and I don't know which way to go yet. Apparently, forty-eight hours of sheer fuckery leads to a crash.

Sanden reappears from the bathroom, and his chuckle helps calm me. The tiniest amount.

"Hey, I've slept on worse."

"There's no way."

"I'll take the floor. Work's trained me my whole life for exactly this situation."

"You can't sleep on the floor for a week either. I'll take the couch. At least I'm smaller than—"

"No way."

"It's the most logical option."

"Actually ..." Then before I can stop him, Sanden ducks down, grabs me around the waist, and throws me over his shoulder. He carries me to the bed and tosses me onto it before falling onto the other side. "You have a *king*. This is plenty big enough for us both."

My gut flips, and there's that seedy heaviness of being in trouble again. "That won't be weird?"

"Nah, we already shared a bed the other night. If you're worried about me spooning you though, we can prop up some pillows."

"It's fine. Like you said, the bed's huge, and I'm not afraid of some accidental stray limbs."

He turns to me with that same unstaged grin that originally caught my attention all those years ago. "I wasn't exaggerating when I said spooning."

"Fine. You can have a cuddle pillow, but we're not building some enormous wall or whatever between us." I frown, finally noticing what we're lying on. "Are these ... petals?"

"I was hoping you wouldn't notice."

"Never took Eman for a romantic guy."

Sanden clears his throat, his cool blue gaze on the ceiling overhead. "Might have been me. Trying to make things special for you guys. I wanted to cancel it before we got on the plane, but you didn't leave my side."

"You did this? But ... you said you don't even like Eman all that much."

"I don't, but everyone deserves a little romance on their honeymoon, and I knew he wasn't going to do it for you."

So ... he did this ... for me? Some of those raging emotions inside me settle. "In that case, I'm glad you came. You get to enjoy your hard work."

"Now feels like the perfect time to mention the other thing I had set up for you, then." He jumps out of bed and strolls out onto the deck before returning with a bottle of champagne and two glasses. "Seems only right we celebrate dropping the dead weight from our lives."

I watch as he pours out the drinks, wondering if I can even stomach more alcohol. "You're really not staying friends with him, then? Simple as that?"

"I told you, things have been on the outs for a while, but ..." His jaw ticks, carefree expression slipping for a second. "This is the kind of low act you don't come back from in my books. He dropped a mess he caused in your lap, knowing you'd be freaking out, maybe upset, embarrassed, whatever. And he hasn't even checked that you're okay."

"How do you know that?"

"Because you would have told me."

He's got me there. I take the glass he offers, struck with an idea.

"This is super petty of me, but you know how Eman is with social media. I thought ... well, the first thing he would've wanted to do is let everyone know how fancy a place he was staying in. Could we get a picture in front of the ocean? With our drinks? Acting all happy and fun and like we don't give two shits about what that asshole is doing?"

Sanden sweeps into a bow, almost spilling his drink. "This week, your wish is my command."

"You're an idiot."

"I prefer loveable jester."

"Aren't jesters supposed to be funny?"

"Wow. I come on this trip to help you, and *that's* the response I get. I see how it is." He looks back over his shoulder. "For that, you're on the tiny couch tonight."

"But then who will you spoon?"

Sanden yanks the pillow out from under my head. "This is Paulie, and he'll be my spooning buddy for the trip."

"I'm sure you and Paulie will be very happy together."

"Whoa, whoa, whoa. Don't put that kind of pressure on our relationship. We're new."

I bite my lip to stop from laughing, but for one second, I'm reminded of how things used to be when Sanden and I first met. Him being a sweet, goofy idiot, and me being ... well, me. I don't feel as awkward and out of place with him.

His eyes soften, and he tosses Paulie on the bed, then holds out his hand. "Let's go get your photo."

My photo. Not his. Not Eman's. For some reason, that word choice hits me hard. When *was* the last time I got to pick *anything*? Sure, Hawaii was my idea, but Eman booked the whole thing. The wedding was all him. Fucking hell, even calling off the wedding was something he took from me too.

I go over it in my head, unsure of when I just *stopped*.

Sanden leads me outside onto the grass between our bungalow and the ocean, then holds up his phone. "Say, 'fuck you, Eman.'"

Gladly. We smile, and he takes the shot, then drags me to a few different areas to repeat the process all over again. By the time we get back to the bungalow, his phone is full of our selfies, some serious, some ridiculous, and that urge to cry from earlier has all but disappeared.

I flop onto the outdoor furniture and kick my feet up, picking from the welcome platter that's been left for us. If I take today at face value, I'm able to relax more, but the second Eman creeps in again, the darkness tries to take hold. Every time that melancholy kicks in, I reach out to Sanden to distract me. And he's good at it.

The man who showed us to our bungalow waves as he approaches. "When you're ready, I'll escort you both to your massage appointment."

"Massage?" Sanden asks.

I vaguely remember Eman mentioning something about that on arrival. "Sounds relaxing."

"Yeah, I'm in."

"Okay, then." Our attendant claps his hands together. "This way."

We lock up and follow. The whole way there, Sanden asks questions about the resort that range from "how annoying are tourists" to "can you explain the conservation you do here," and it's clear that while joining me might have been a spur-of-the-moment thing, he's done more research on this place than I have.

I'm still struck dumb by how incredible it is.

"Here you are," the man says when we reach a cabana on the water. It's surrounded by floaty curtains and greenery to shield us from the rest of the resort, and the breeze coming in off the ocean takes the edge off how hot it is.

"Welcome," a beautiful woman says. She's wearing the resort uniform and a welcoming expression. This savage little spike of relief hits me that Sanden's gay, and I'm not proud of it. But any female-attracted human would love to have her hands on them. "I love having honeymooners here," she says.

I'm about to deny it when Sanden's palm slides into mine. "I imagine you'd get a lot of us."

"We're a popular destination." She waves toward the bed. "Who would like to go first?"

Sanden squeezes my hand. "You go. The wedding was, ah, stressful for you."

That's putting it mildly.

"I'll duck out for a moment," she says. "Strip down to your briefs, then lie facedown on the bed."

I move to do as she's said, then glance over at Sanden. "Is there someone else for ... my husband, or does he stand there and watch or ..."

"No, no, this is a do-it-yourself couple's massage. I'll walk him through it once I'm back."

She leaves, and Sanden turns to me with wide eyes. "Does she mean what I think she means?"

"Oh, Lord."

He cracks his knuckles. "Prepare for the best massage of your life."

"You had to tell her we were newlyweds, didn't you?"

"Seemed better than telling the entire story."

I think about it for a second. "Yeah, you're right."

And even though stripping in front of him is awkward as fuck, I pull my shirt over my head and drop my shorts, then set them aside. I'm not big and beefy like he is, so I guess all I can hope for is that he's not completely repulsed by my body. My body that he's about to touch.

Fucking hell.

I'm hot around the ears as I lie down, and the massage therapist comes back. It's fine at first, once I let go of the sensation of his callused hands on me. She walks Sanden through how to work the muscles in my shoulders, their murmured voices blurring together as the breeze lulls me into this half-asleep, half-awake trance. It's exactly what I need.

Then they reach my lower back.

She encourages him to massage deeper, lower, his fingers grazing under the towel and my underwear. The trance disappears as I snap back to consciousness when Sanden starts on my legs. Strong fingers knead my feet, my calves, up and up to my thighs. My upper-*upper* thighs.

I swallow thickly at the sensation of his fingers so fucking close to my balls as my dick fills with blood.

It's completely silent now, so I'm overly aware of the blood pumping in my ears. His strong hands sweep down and creep back higher again. All the way to the crease of my ass. I swear Sanden's breathing has deepened, but it's impossible to tell over the sound of my own struggling breaths.

"And now roll over," the massage therapist says in a low, calming voice.

Like fuck I will.

My ears, which were hot earlier, are burning now, and I'm hoping I can get away with pretending I didn't hear her. Maybe I'm asleep? They don't know.

"Remy?" Sanden prompts. And fuck him very much.

"Ah, I only want my back done." Even I cringe at how my voice comes out.

"Seriously, it's fine," he says.

I squeeze my eyes closed. "Isn't it your turn yet?"

"Remy, what are you—"

But before he can finish the question, our massage therapist cuts in with her completely unhelpful and mortifying input. "It's a natural reaction to our loved ones making our bodies feel good. Nothing to be embarrassed about."

Easy for her to fucking say. I keep my eyes closed tight as I roll onto my back, skin suddenly feeling about a thousand degrees.

And even my humiliation isn't enough to get my cock to calm down because after a brief hesitation, Sanden starts on my shoulders again, and when his hands dip lower and brush my nipples ...

I think I'm going to die.

Six

SANDEN

For Remy's sake, I'm trying to keep the grin off my face, but it's really, really hard. Like his dick.

Well, it was hard. I think it's shriveled up from embarrassment, though from the brief glance I got, he has nothing to be embarrassed about.

"I can see your smirk," he rumbles in a raspy voice.

"Come on, babe. We're newlyweds. Perfectly normal to get turned on by your husband." I run my hands down his abs, and he whines when his cock twitches. The towel really doesn't hide anything.

"It's official. After this, I'm going to go drown myself."

"That doesn't sound like a fun honeymoon activity. We could go back to our room and put this massage to good use."

Remy closes his eyes. "I hate you."

I chuckle, but the massage therapist with us is glancing between the two of us like she doesn't understand our relationship. If I'm honest, neither do I at this point.

We went from being flirty acquaintances to him dating my friend, where I put a huge wall between us, to what we are now ... heartbroken man going through a breakup and the clown who's here to cheer him up? Fake husbands on a gorgeous island? Two friends who turn each other on with massages? Because not going to lie, knowing I'm turning him on from touching him is also making me horny as fuck.

Remy has his eyes closed but a smile on his face. "It's your turn next."

"I'm not ashamed of my body's way of showing love."

Remy covers his face with one hand.

"Sorry about my husband," I say to the attendant. "He thinks our love is shameful. Poor thing grew up in an orphanage and never knew what true love was until me. He still thinks he's undeserving, and I have to shake him and scream, 'You deserve all my love, my love!'"

Remy's trying not to laugh at my complete bullshit.

I almost dare the massage therapist to call me on my made-up story, but she's more professional than that.

She places a gentle hand on Remy's arm. "You do deserve love. I want to do an exercise with you. Breathe in for three seconds, hold all those negative thoughts for another three, and then let it all out as you release your breath."

Oh great. I accidentally made Remy do airy-fairy meditation crap. Though, he doesn't seem to mind.

He does as she says, and they breathe together while she points for me to start working on Remy's feet.

All I can say is he's lucky he was left at the altar because I'd normally draw the line at feet. Yet, when I start massaging near his heel and work my way up to the arch that never hits the ground, the moan that leaves him is anything but whiney. I'd totally give him a foot massage every day if it makes that noise come out of him.

Before I know it, the massage therapist says Remy's done, and when he sits up, he looks drunk. Relaxed. Happy.

"Ready for your turn?"

I wish I could say I hate the challenge in his tone and the glint in his eye, but I don't. I reach back and pull off my shirt. "Born ready, baby."

I strip down in front of the massage therapist because I still have my underwear on, so it's not a big deal to me, but she says, "I can leave if you need to—"

"As you can see," Remy says, "my husband is completely shameless."

"With a body like mine, it should be shared." I throw myself on the massage table and put my face in the hole, all the while telling myself to think of dead puppies or kittens or anything else that will keep me somewhat calm.

Remy stays in only his underwear, which surprises me, but not as much as when he walks around me, trailing his fingers up my back, and then leans in close to my ear and whispers, "So you know, payback's a bitch." And that's when I know I fucked up.

He starts by standing near my head, but instead of

massaging my temples or running his hands through my hair, he leans over me and kneads above my ass. He's practically lying on top of me, his dick and balls right there *on* my head.

I laugh, but fuck, his cock hardens at the friction.

He's right. Payback is a bitch.

And no matter how much I think unsexy thoughts, his hands on my skin are more powerful. It's tempting to give in to it, but I don't want him to think I'm coming on to him or trying to cross lines.

He's silent as he works knots from my back and slowly moves around the table, but he keeps that close contact the whole time. When he stands by my feet, I think it's time for the foot massage, but no. He pulls my underwear under my ass and starts massaging my ass cheeks—something I wasn't even instructed to do to him. Oh, he's playing to win. This isn't just revenge. He's going all in. He leans in so fucking close I can feel his fucking breath on my ass crack, which makes me imagine what it would be like for him to rim me and finger fuck me, and shit. Fuck, fuck, shit, my hips practically lift off the massage table, encouraging him.

No, bad body. Stop. I force my hips as low as I can get, squashing my cock to almost the point of pain.

Then, as if knowing I'm right on the edge of losing not only my control but my load, he slaps my ass and says, "Okay, rolling-over time."

Fucker.

There's no way I can hide how fucking turned on I am, so I feign confidence, roll over, and then almost die when I glance down and notice the head of my dick is actually sticking out of the top of my briefs. With some fucking precum leaking out the tip. The massage therapist covers me with a towel, which I'm thankful for, but if the word "gloating" had a picture next to it in the dictionary, it would be Remy's face right now.

Okay, he wins.

🔥 🔥 🔥

Remy's still laughing as we head back to the room. "Are you sure you don't need to change your underwear?"

"You might have magic hands but not that magic. I didn't come." I *nearly* did. Those magic, healing hands didn't even need to touch my cock to get me teetering on the edge.

Fuck, I'm getting hard again reliving it.

"Surely we'll make some top five list of weirdest couples that massage therapist has ever worked with," Remy says.

"I reckon we wouldn't even crack the top ten."

He snickers. "You should have seen how fast she spun around when I got your ass out."

"Yeah, that was fun for me."

"I think I was practically dry humping your head at one point."

"I bet she's had people have sex in front of her."

"Man, I went into the wrong profession. I should be a couple's massage therapist."

"You can't quit being an EMT. You're amazing at it."

"Thanks, and I was actually joking. She deserves a big tip after the awkwardness we put her through."

Okay, it was a little awkward, but only because Remy and I aren't actually together, and I don't think she would've noticed that.

"She probably thinks you're a repressed gay guy with abandonment issues and that I'm the awesome one in the relationship. It's fine. But yes, I did tip her well when I signed the room charge."

"I can't believe you made me an orphan."

"I had to come up with something, and I figured being raised by wolves was too far-fetched."

Besides, I couldn't make *me* the orphan. That's too close for comfort. Even if I'm not an orphan, my parents are dead to me. The feeling is mutual.

Remy shakes his head. "Thank you for ... well, everything, but more, thank you for making that very awkward moment less awkward by pretending to be Eman so I didn't have to explain what I'm doing here alone."

I throw my arm around him. "Aww, hubby, you're not alone. Your stand-in husband is here whenever you need it."

"Just don't start acting like actual Eman, and we'll be fine." He glances up at me, his hazel eyes shining, and being this close to him—

I drop my hand from his shoulders and take a step back. "It's too soon. Way too soon to be touching you after—" I wave back in the direction of the massage hut.

Remy bursts out laughing, and it's the most amazing sound I've ever heard. How Eman could walk out on him,

I'll never know, but this right here is why I had to distance myself once they were together.

Because Remy is amazing, and he deserves so much more than he was given.

But it's not too late.

I'm going to give him the best fake honeymoon ever.

Seven

REMY

Sharing a bed was a terrible, horrible idea. Every night, once it's dark, all our happy, playful chatter instantly disappears. Sanden wishes me good night, rolls over, and spoons Paulie, and I lie there staring at his broad back, jealous of a fucking pillow.

I should have thought that suggestion through. I wouldn't have minded being spooned in his big arms.

Instead, I'm reminded that I have no boyfriend, no fiancé, no husband, and every day that passes gets me closer to heading home and having to deal with it all again.

Maybe I can convince Sanden to run away with me forever.

He was right. Being alone with my thoughts sucks. Thankfully, we're so busy during the day that I'm able to forget about it all and have fun. We get up at dawn to do yoga, go on hikes, and I even challenged myself, going cave diving with sharks while Sanden kept his ass resolutely on the boat.

It was kinda cute. Both how scared he was of the sharks and how relieved he was when I climbed back on board with all my limbs intact.

I roll onto my side and walk my fingers up his spine. "Sanden ..."

He snuffles in his sleep. "Fine. But you're doing all the work," he murmurs into the pillow, then flops onto his back, long arms stretched over the bed, still sound asleep.

I laugh and let my gaze trace his shadowy features. His normally cheeky expression is relaxed with sleep, dark hair all mussed up, and stubble longer and thicker than he usually keeps it. What would have happened if I never met Eman? If we'd kept flirting and joking around? Would it have always stayed how easy it is now, or would we have crossed lines that made us drift apart anyway?

I roll onto my stomach, cradling my head on my crossed arms. We're not touching, but his arm is resting above my head, and I'm close enough that every time I breathe in, I inhale his scent. It's comforting. Almost makes me forget I'm alone.

When I wake up, I have a split second of disappointment that he isn't spooning me.

It's for the best. Obviously. He's making this week easier, and I don't want to do anything that would turn it weird.

Except when I watch Sanden move around the room, getting ready, I'm worried I kinda do.

He's so fucking hot. And while I know that sleeping with my almost-husband's friend is crossing a million and one lines, especially so close to being left at the altar, I also know it'd help.

I don't think I could find a better rebound than Sanden.

His phone vibrates on the table beside the bed.

"I think you have a call," I say, stretching out.

He crosses to check the display, and like a few times yesterday, instead of answering, he rejects the call instead.

"Still don't want to talk to anyone?"

"It's nobody's business why I'm here with you."

"I still can't believe I posted that photo of us."

"Which one? The fish kiss at the wedding or the one that shows I came on your honeymoon with you?" He grins at me. "Actually, it doesn't matter. Both are top-tier petty. Highly approve."

I climb out of bed. "What do you want to do today?"

"I thought we could have a pool day."

"Sounds good to me."

"Cool, just let me get changed." Sanden grabs his swim shorts and heads for the bathroom, then, at the last second, backtracks to grab his phone before disappearing.

I stare at the door for a second, an unsettled feeling creeping along my spine.

Since posting the photo of us on the day we got here, I haven't bothered to turn my phone back on, and now I'm very, very worried people are reacting badly toward it. Is that why people are trying to call him?

Or am I being super paranoid and projecting?

Eman would never leave the room without his phone, and they used to be friends. Maybe it's a habit they picked up ... and feeling uneasy about it is a habit I picked up.

Maybe getting home and dealing with this thing head-on will be for the best.

We have a few more days left here, so fuck it. I'm going to block it all out, enjoy every moment, and face whatever's waiting for me when I'm home.

I pull out my swimsuit, then drop my briefs at the exact moment the bathroom door clicks back open.

"Shit, ah, sorry, I—"

I look back over my shoulder to where Sanden is stammering in the doorway. "Never seen an ass before?"

His stare immediately drops to it, and then the bastard's lips hitch up on one side. "Not one that looks like that."

Smelly socks, gasoline, suffocating smoke ...

My cheeks are hot as I yank my trunks on. "Okay. Good. Yes. Let's go."

I make for the doors out onto the deck when Sanden grabs my forearm and reels me back in. He holds up a tube of sunscreen and shakes it in front of my face. "Not so fast."

I glare at the tube, both hating and loving the sight of it. "Who would have thought you were so sun conscious?"

"You can never be too careful."

With a groan, I turn my back on him and try not to flinch at the click of the cap opening. In his defense, he's fast and impersonal, but it adds to the mixed-up "want him

to spoon me in my sleep" urges going on. His hands on me
... rubbing against my skin ...

"This is like the massage all over again."

Sanden's hands freeze and—

"I said that out loud, didn't I?"

"Sure did."

"Any chance we can forget it?"

"Sure can't."

I hang my head forward, and when Sanden starts to move again, it's different this time. His thumbs rub steady circles against a knot by my spine as he leans in by my ear.

"It's a natural bodily reaction, Remy." The laughter in his tone snaps me out of it, and I shove him away.

When it's my turn, I keep it quick and light, but Sanden doesn't let me get away with it that easily.

He lets out a filthy moan. "Oh, Remy, *so* good."

I pour a generous amount into my palm, then reach around and swipe it down his face.

"*Urg*, that got in my mouth!"

"Serves you right for teasing me."

"Hey, you're the one who brought up the massage."

"By *accident*."

"That makes it even worse!"

I'm about to ask him *how* the hell that makes it worse when he lunges for me. His arms close around my waist, and he lifts me off my feet as he rubs his face from my cheek to my neck to my chest.

"Okay, you're big and strong and can manhandle me, I get it."

Sanden drops me back to my feet, looking way too pleased with himself. He still has sunscreen everywhere.

"You're lucky you're fun," I grumble, reaching up to rub in the white smear above his eye and another by his jaw.

He does the same with my neck, and for a second, his thumb passes to the other side, like he's holding my throat. A wave of heat rushes through me, and I jerk back out of his hold.

"Race you!" I don't wait for him to agree, just take off. The resort has a private infinity pool for the people who've booked the bungalows, and I run straight there. Sanden's hot on my heels, but I'm fast, and as I reach the pool edge, I turn, nail my backflip, and flip him the bird as I go under.

Sanden's grinning when I come up for air. "Wow, I never knew you were a show-off."

"There's a lot you don't know about me."

"I got one for you." Then he jumps, pulls up his knees, and shouts, "Cannonball!"

A tidal wave splashes over me as he hits the water.

He pops up a few feet away in all his perma-grin, scruffy-jawed glory. "Impressive, right?"

"I'm surprised there's any water left in the pool."

"It's a skill. Seriously though. Where'd the backflip come from?"

"I was a gymnast right to the end of high school. Trampolining."

"Were you good?"

"There were talks about me qualifying for the Olympics, but I just missed out. I did well in competition but never took out the top spot. Seemed to always be good but not good enough, so that's when I decided to put that dream on hold and grow up."

"So you became an EMT instead."

"Yep."

"What made you go down that path?"

Now, there's a question. I swim to the side of the pool, where I cross my arms over the edge and look out at the water. Sanden joins me, waiting for the answer. "You want the truth or the *I wanted to help people* version?"

"Truth, duh."

"There was a small fire in the gym at school one day, and we were evacuated. One of the firefighters who showed up was a fucking dreamboat, and I swear I fell in love then and there. It prompted an entire summer of jerking off to firemen porn, and I guess it stuck. I was going to become a firefighter, but then I found out a firefighter EMT gets paid more, and I've always been really good at biology and science, so it was a no-brainer." I pretend to sigh. "I never did see the love of my life again."

"Firemen porn, huh?"

"Oh, yeah. Thankfully, the guys I work with are all great but repulsive, so I'm not constantly walking around boned up at work."

He pumps his eyebrows at me. "You know ... *I'm* a fireman."

I let my gaze run over his round shoulders and glistening chest. His huge biceps. The faint tan line from the tank tops he's been wearing all week. "I noticed." It's supposed to come out teasing, but I sound stupidly breathless instead. "Aaand I'm going to go drown myself now."

I duck under the water, but Sanden grabs me by the arm and pulls me back up again.

His eyes are creased as he laughs. "Don't be embarrassed. I get it. I'm hot."

"Now I'm not embarrassed, but *you* should be. Did you really call yourself hot?"

"Of course. I'm the total package." He winks. "Have my firefighter uniform at home and everything."

A flash of him in his uniform, fucking me from behind, simmers in my gut. I whimper. "Don't think sexy thoughts. Don't think sexy thoughts."

"Aww, but they're so fun."

"Hey, remember how I told you I was glad you came with me on this trip? Yeah, I take it all back."

"You're cute when you're pouty."

"Don't call me cute."

"Why? Giving you sexy thoughts again?"

I turn things around on him. "Wanna know what I think's cute?"

"What?"

"The reason *you're* a firefighter."

"Oh, yeah? What's that?"

"Because you're a hero."

Sanden blinks his dark, wet eyelashes at me. "What?"

"Mmhmm. Some people get into the job for the adrenaline; Gabe said he loves how every day's different. Some guys want the uniform and the perks that go with it. Some genuinely want to help. But you? You're a hero type."

"Bullshit."

"Everyone knows. You know how our stations have that

silly rivalry thing going on? They can find something to pick at about every single person at your station except you. They hate how much they respect you. I hated it too when I thought you were jealous of me being with Eman."

His jaw flexes. "I'm not a hero type. I just like to help."

"Yeah, not buying that. The helpful ones are the ones who'll do whatever is asked of them. You don't need to be asked." I hold out my arms. "Case in point."

"You don't know what you're talking about," he mumbles.

"You're selfless. It's kind of amazing."

He snorts and turns his back on me, looking out over the water.

Huh. Apparently, his Captain America heart is the one thing that makes him uncomfortable to talk about.

So I let it go and creep up close behind him, as silently as I can. When I'm by his ear, I drop my tone and say, "*Duh-dun.*"

"Remy ..."

"*Duh-dun ... duh-dun ... duh-dun, duh-dun, duh-dun ...*"

I bite down into his shoulder.

"You little shit."

Then before I can stop it, he spins around, picks me up, and throws me across the pool.

I'm getting dangerously addicted to how easily he throws me around.

Eight

SANDEN

Ah, this is the life. I'm on our deck, listening to the waves crash, my eyes closed, shirt off, soaking in the heat, with a cocktail in my hand. I hate that it's our last day, that we've been here for a full week already, and we're going home tomorrow. If I could keep us here another week, I would, but we both need to be getting back. I just wish Remy didn't have to go home and face everything alone.

He doesn't have the same energy that he used to, but I'm putting that down to the rough week he's had. There are moments he shines through though, where he'll get flirty or joke around, and it fills me with this deep yearning for how easy things could've been between us if I'd told him how I felt three years ago instead of standing by and watching Eman charm his way into Remy's life.

If I could reverse time, I'd make sure Eman didn't get anywhere near him.

Remy's had his phone off for the week, so he doesn't know what he's going back to, but I've kept mine on. As recently appointed lieutenant for my station, I've had it on in case any of my team calls. Which they haven't. Because of course. They have Cap there with them. But ... I dunno. It feels unnatural to be unreachable, and maybe that's part of why Remy thinks I have some hero complex.

He's in the shower at the moment, washing the day's beach activities off him, but I can't help dwelling over the hero comment that he said a few days ago in the pool.

I'm not sure how I feel about Remy thinking that I have some kind of hero ego where I want all the attention and glory, but at the same time, it's not like I can dispute it. From the outside. I do play that part at work because in those high-intensity situations, there needs to be someone in control at all times. I like control. I like delegating. But most of all, I like knowing everyone gets out safely. Because focusing on the control stops me from focusing on what happens when they don't.

I didn't get into firefighting because I wanted the recognition and to be the big hero everyone looks up to, but I don't want to share with Remy the truth. I don't tell anyone the truth because it's too painful. Eman's the only person who knows, and that's because he was there for the whole thing.

My phone vibrates on the coffee table beside the

outdoor couch I'm spread out on, but when I lift it, it's not anyone from Station 40. It's Eman. Again.

He's called at least every day, sometimes two or three times, but I've ignored each attempt. I have nothing to say to him, but more than that, I haven't wanted Remy to know. With Remy in the shower, I have a few minutes to tell Eman to fuck off and leave us alone.

I reach for it, take a deep breath, and hit the Answer button. "What do you want?"

"Really? That's how you answer the fucking phone after stealing my fiancé?"

I scoff. "Stealing the guy you left at the altar, you mean? Can't really steal something when you threw it away." I don't even mention we're not together, because fuck him. Plus, we're still being petty.

"I didn't throw him away. I ... I ..."

"You didn't even have the balls to end it yourself." I lower my voice and hiss, "You didn't even send me to do it. You were going to leave him to worry for fuck knows how long."

"I didn't know if I was flaking because I was nervous. I might have come back. But you had to get in there as soon as you could to go after him, didn't you? Trying to pay me back for college? He certainly didn't waste any fucking time getting over me. Where's my fiancé? I've been trying to call both of you all week."

"To yell at him? Fuck you, Eman. What you did was pathetic, even for you. You hurt Remy. Embarrassed him. Probably cheated on him that night you didn't come home, and yet, he was willing to work on it all with you. He's kind and deserves to be fucking cherished, not treated like dog shit."

"Cheating, that's rich—"

I cut him off. "Don't call either of us ever again."

I hit the big, red, angry End icon, but it's nowhere near as satisfying as I want it to be. I'm tempted to throw my phone, but Eman's not worth it.

"He was going to leave the wedding and not even tell me?" Remy's voice is so small behind me, and in all the yelling, I hadn't even realized he was out of the bathroom.

"Fuck," I say under my breath.

"You think he cheated on me?" he asks.

I turn to him, and he's only wearing a towel. Fuck me, I love his body, and it's really difficult to have this conversation when his everything is within reach. "I can't say for sure, but I personally wouldn't trust a partner who disappears all night."

"You said everything would be fine. That he probably crashed at a friend's place."

"I wasn't going to tell you to leave him. I didn't want to be responsible for your relationship breaking down. I ... it wasn't my place to say that."

"Did you mean what you said to him on the phone?" His voice is even smaller now.

"For him to never call either of us again? Yes."

"Not that. The part where I deserve to be cherished."

I stalk toward him, closing the gap between us, and I cup his cheek as I look him in the eyes and say, "Every. Fucking. Day."

His eyes become shiny, and they flutter closed for a brief

second. I hate seeing the pain, the broken heart. I grip his hair and run my thumb over his cheek.

"I wish you could see you the way I do."

He lifts his gaze, his big hazel eyes shining up at me. "How's that?"

"Precious. Rare. We might not have always gotten along, and while the blame could be put squarely on my shoulders for that, I told myself I was doing the right thing. That you were happy with Eman, and even if I did confess my immature thoughts that I saw you first, you'd still choose him because he's so much more put together than I am."

"You saw me first?" he rasps.

"There's not a day goes by that I don't kick myself for not asking you out before he did." I don't mean to say it, but it's out there now, and it's as close to the truth as I can get with him.

We breathe each other in, and what was supposed to be comforting him shifts. It goes from telling him he deserves better to asking myself what it'd be like to kiss him for real.

I don't have to wonder for long. He surges forward, his mouth landing on mine. It's sudden and hard, and I stumble back a step, but Remy comes with me. Then his lips become soft, pliant, like he's giving up control and urging me to take over.

I'm still frozen in shock, but when his tongue parts my lips, the ifs, whys, and all the other questions I have disappear.

I grip the back of his head tightly and hold him to me,

opening my mouth for him and letting him dive in deep. He's too intoxicating, too irresistible.

Remy's arms wrap around my back, gripping my ass through my board shorts and pulling me against him. His hard cock through the towel makes my mouth water.

I want more of him. All of him.

But when he pulls back, severing that connection with our mouths, our tiny kissing bubble bursts, and reality sets in.

Remy has been my dream guy since I met him, but I can't be with him. Not like this. Not here.

"Now, that's what I call a kiss." He smiles, and a little voice inside my head says I could keep kissing him. I could forget the real-life shit going on and give myself this, but …

I shake my head. "I can't."

"You can't tell me that was a better kiss than the one I barely remember and you called it the smashing of lips together?" He steps back again, breaking the connection between us even more. He looks confused, and I don't like having made him feel that way.

"Not like this," I whisper. "I can't take advantage of you. You know I want you—it's been obvious since our couple's massage. You turn me on something fierce. Hell, my dick is screaming at me. But you're in a vulnerable place, and you need a friend—"

"I need a fuck, if I'm really honest."

"No, you don't. You need support, and—"

He moves in closer again and glances up at me. Even fucking bats his eyes, for fuck's sake. He's testing my restraint and my strength. I always prided myself on being strong-willed, but even I have my limits.

Remy Porter is a big fucking limit.

"Please take advantage of me. This whole week, you've been there for me. You've made me laugh and have fun, which is something I never would've had on my honeymoon otherwise."

"If you'd gotten married, it would've been fun."

"See, even that I'm not so sure of. I think I would've spent my week asking Eman to stop trying to find cell service and pay attention to me instead of all the likes and shares he was getting online. Which would have led to him getting pissy with me, like always. You came here with me to make me forget, and it's our last night. Please help me forget about going home tomorrow. I want this trip to last. To have good memories instead of tarnished ones. I want to remember you."

Aww, fucking hell.

"Give me more of that dose of fun. It's the best medicine for embarrassment and shame."

"Fucking, fuck, shit, shit, fuckery."

Remy chuckles. "Is that a yes?"

I grip him under his thighs and hike him up so his legs wrap around my waist. "It's a get on the fucking bed now."

He has his arms around my neck and his breath right in my ear as he says, "It's not a fucking bed yet, but it will be. As soon as you get inside me."

I drop Remy on the mattress.

He flicks off his towel, revealing his naked body and every inch of skin I want to taste. I crash on top of him, chest to chest, skin to skin, and we join together like magnets, touching everywhere. Our legs, our hips, our cocks line up perfectly. I am regretting not getting rid of my board shorts before climbing on him though.

I want to get them off, but Remy's glancing up at me with hooded eyes and parted lips, want and need written all over his face, and there's no way I can move away now.

Instead, I lean in and touch my lips to his. If this is the only time I get to have Remy, I'm going to show him his worth. I'm going to prove that I meant every word, and I'm going to cherish him, worship his goddamn body, and then make him come so hard that he'll forget everything back home. Just like he asked.

I kiss his cheek, his neck, and move further down, running my tongue over his nipple and teasing the other by pinching it.

He whimpers, and his abs contract under my fingers as I trail them over his skin. I keep making my way down, licking his skin, tasting his clean scent, and wanting nothing more than to mark him so he doesn't taste freshly washed but tastes of me instead.

He moans, long and loud. "Please don't tease me. Prep my hole already."

I glance up at him through my lashes, and he throws his head back.

"Fuck, I need it. I need it now."

For someone who's so calm and collected on the job, I never pictured him as this desperate, needy, and impatient guy in the bedroom. Could he be any hotter? I don't think so.

His skin flushes red, and he shifts beneath me like he can't get comfortable or wants me to hurry up and touch his dick. I can feel his hardness against my chest as I lower myself down and keep teasing the fuck out of him with my tongue. Lower, lower, over his hip, down his slim V ... the join between his pelvis and his leg ...

"Fuck. You," he breathes.

"I thought you wanted me to fuck you?"

"I do, and you're teasing me instead. Here, I'll make it easier for you." He shuffles out from under me and flips over onto his knees, exposing his delectable ass and the tight hole he wants me to stick my dick in.

Fuck, I might come before we even get to that point though.

The couple's massage, the touching, everything this past week has practically brought me to my knees in desperation for a release. I've been a good boy, not even touching myself or jerking off in the bathroom because I didn't want to be that creep.

"Sanden," Remy whines as I undo my shorts and kick them to the other side of the room. "You better not be having second thoughts, or I'm going to be pissed."

I sink to the floor behind him, run my hands up the back of his thighs, and then squeeze his ass. "Not changing my mind. I'm trying to get myself under control before I ruin this."

"I hope you're talking about my ass."

I laugh. "Fuck, I wish. No, you turn me on so fucking much I'm worried about not lasting long for you."

Remy grunts. "I don't care how long you last, what you

do to me, or how you do it. I just need you inside me. Any part of you."

Well, if that wasn't an invitation ... I lean forward and seal my mouth over his hole.

I'm rewarded with one of the sounds he gave me when I massaged him. My dick is aching, and I'm sure it's leaking again. This man drives me so wild, and I can't get enough.

I know I'll have to because once we're back home, Remy will heal and move on, and me being Eman's friend, I'll probably be the last person he wants to start something real with, but I have the here and now, and that's enough for me.

Remy's hips rock backward while I eat him out, my tongue working inside him. When he tries to take it deeper, I replace my tongue with my finger. Just one. The second I push through his tight ring of muscle, his breathing quickens.

I love how desperate he is for me. How his body is doing most of the work instinctually. I slide my finger inside him, finding that spot that will make him lose his mind.

As soon as I do, he lets out a harsh "Holy mother of fuck," and I'm too turned on to even snark about "Fuck" being a weird kind of god.

"I need more. Another finger. Oh fuck, I'm close."

I add another. "Suddenly, I'm not so okay with fucking you." Before he can freak out, I continue. "I want you to come like this. You look so fucking hot."

"What about you?" He pushes back on my fingers, his whole body shaking and trembling.

"You have no idea how close I am from watching you."

With my free hand, I reach between my legs and stroke my aching cock.

We only have this one night, and I was going to try to savor it, but I fucking can't. I can't hold out.

"Remy ... I ..."

His ass clamps down on my fingers, his body pulses, and I know without a doubt that he's spilling over onto the mattress.

I keep jerking myself off while he trembles and curses under his breath. I'm so close. So fucking close.

And when he pulls himself off my fingers and lies flat on the bed, he turns to look over his shoulder at me. "Come on me. Please. Fuck."

I quickly stand, knowing I don't have much time, and when he reaches back and spreads his cheeks for me, giving me sight of that used hole, my orgasm slams into me. Hard, fast.

My release hits his back, his ass cheek, and drips down into his crack.

And as satisfying as it was, the disappointment that it's already over slams into me. I fucked up. Didn't savor it. Because tomorrow, we're back on that long flight home.

Back to reality.

Man, real life sucks.

Nine

REMY

The whirring of the jet engines vibrates around us. I lean toward Sanden and drop my voice into what I'm hoping is a sultry whisper. "I need to use the bathroom."

"Oh. Yeah. Let me just—" Sanden goes to stand, and I quickly pull him back into his cramped plane seat. He could spring for an upgrade for us on the way there, but apparently, he ran out of miles for the flight home. But that's okay because this works for what I want to do. I stand, and with my hands gripping the headrest on either side of him, I *slooowly* step over his long legs.

Sanden stares up at me with a smirk, and when I'm finally in the aisle, I send him a wink and add a sway to my step as I head for the bathroom at the back of the plane.

If Sanden doesn't get *that* hint, there's no hope for him. After spooning with him all night, we'd slept through his alarm this morning, and instead of my glorious dreams of lazy morning sex, we'd scrambled around packing and barely made it to the airport on time.

Is it *my* fault I'm hard up and desperate? I didn't even get a good view of his dick yesterday.

I'm in that tiny echoey bathroom for five minutes, and no telltale knock comes. I head back to my chair frustrated, ears burning, and glare at Sanden's obvious amusement.

I check to make sure the woman next to me still has her headphones on before I round on him. "Really?"

"What?"

I aim my pointer and middle fingers toward my eyes. "I gave you the *come-hither* eyes."

"Okay, Dolly Parton."

I snarl. "I can't believe you slept through your alarm."

"I can't believe *you* slept through my alarm."

"But you were so snuggly."

Sanden pumps his eyebrows. "I warned you. Grade A spooner."

And as much as I can't deny that, I wish we'd blown off sleep and fooled around all night. "You could have at least let me suck your dick."

Sanden makes a sound in his throat and glances around. "This is a side of you I've never seen before."

"Funny what being left at the altar, taking off on your honeymoon with your ex-fiancé's groomsman, and then sleeping with said groomsman will do to a guy."

The woman next to me chokes on a laugh and pulls off

her headphones. "Yeah, these things aren't on. And while you're more entertaining than the telenovelas I watch with my abuela, I think I'll give you a minute to sort this out." She shuffles past us, pausing by Sanden to say, "Don't worry, I'll keep my *come-hither* eyes to myself."

I face-palm and sink into my seat. "And that settles it. Officially not horny anymore."

I split the parking costs with Sanden, and all too soon, he's dropping me back home. He offers to come up to the apartment with me, but I wave him off. A chance for round two? Definitely interested in that, but now I'm home, the whole situation is too raw.

I don't think walking in to find my apartment stripped half-bare is going to get me in the mood, and Sanden really doesn't want to see me freaking out over some other guy.

I need to face this and a potential quarter-life crisis on my own.

My sigh is heavy as I unlock the front door to my apartment and walk inside.

And come to an immediate stop.

Nothing's changed.

I take a moment to look around, but everything from the cushions to his artwork to the damn book he was reading and left on the coffee table are all in the exact same place.

Is it possible he hasn't been back here?

Nope, his clothes are gone from the wardrobe, so I guess that answers that question, but as I kick my shoes off and walk back out into the living area, I'm clueless about the rest.

The string lights over the TV for "aesthetics," the whatever-rug he found for a discount online and loves to mention to people because, apparently, it's super hard to find, the large potted trees and wall hangings—all still here.

He really tried to bring the SoCal vibe to Seattle, so ... why did he leave it all? That's *so* not Eman. He's money-oriented, and throwing away expensive things doesn't sit right. He used to joke that I was his sugar daddy because my family are comfortable, and while I'm probably going to inherit a good amount, and I know they'll always be there to help if I need it, their money is their money, and I fund my own life.

So why would he—

Oh, holy shit.

He did this on purpose.

Instead of running away to live in a hole where we never have to encounter each other again, he purposely left his stuff so we'd have to talk. But *why*? He left *me*. Why the hell would he want to see me again after that?

I pick up my phone and turn it on for the first time since I posted that photo of Sanden and me in Hawaii so I can fire off a quick message to Sanden.

Me:

He left his fucking stuff. Everything.

It's not until after I close out of our messages that it hits me that out of everyone I could have messaged, it was him. I mean, we spent the last week together, so it kinda makes sense, but pre-wedding, Sanden would have been the last person I turned to for advice.

It's hard to make sense of how much has changed. I wish I could say *fuck Eman* and never think about him again, but now I'm here, in our home, the memories hit hard. I'm waiting, braced, expecting him to walk through the door at any second. Waiting to see what kind of mood he's in. How would he react to seeing me after he did something so epically fucked-up?

If the conversation I overheard with Sanden is any indication, he's not about to apologize.

He's probably doubly angry after how Sanden spoke to him. Even remembering the phone call, I'm filled with warring emotions of betrayal and disappointment because of Eman and sheer fucking elation at the way Sanden stuck up for me. Every word he said was validating, and knowing he was on my side ... I sigh happily, replaying every day of the last week, and my anger at Eman fizzles away.

He can play his game. He can come for his stuff and say whatever it is he wants to say, but at the end of the day, it's over. Sanden said I deserve better, and I believe it.

But he also said he thinks Eman cheated on me.

Eman, who I've been sleeping with bare for ... a while.

I'd like to say that there's no way he'd put me at risk like that, but after the wedding, I'm not sure I know him well enough to make that call. My gut twists, and all I can hope for is that *if* he was unfaithful, he was safe about it.

If it turns out that bastard gave me something, I'll kill him.

I know how to save a life, so I know how easy it is to reverse-alive someone.

Before I can get panicky, I pick up my phone and open Sanden's messages again. I should probably be texting my friends about this, but Tig's with his family, and the only other person that comes to mind is Wren, and aside from the wedding, I can't remember the last time we actually spoke.

Me:

> I know you're probably still driving, but hey, fun thought! If Eman was cheating, I now need to go and get tested. Probably a good thing we didn't swap bodily fluids. You're welcome xx

Almost immediately, my phone rings, and I have to hold back the little squee at Sanden's name.

We separated maybe fifteen minutes ago, Remy, be cool.

I clear my throat and answer. "Hey. Look, I know I was a sensational fuck, but it's been fifteen minutes. You're smothering me."

Instead of a smart-ass comment from Sanden, laughter fills the line. Deep laughter. Laughter that is *not* Sanden's.

"Ah, you're on speaker. With me and Gabe." At least *he's* trying to hold back from laughing at me.

"Of course I am."

"I agree with you though," Gabe says. "Sanden's

smothering me too. He stole me away from Aleks for *coffee*. I could also be getting a sensational fuck right now, myself."

"This constant ridicule is going to be a fun time for me."

"To be fair," Sanden adds, "you did it to yourself."

"You didn't tell me I was on speaker!"

"If you'd given me more than point oh oh two seconds, I would have."

Fair call. "Right. Umm ... so ..."

"I won't tell anyone," Gabe says. "I thought you hated each other, so I'm struggling with whiplash. I'll block my ears, you guys carry on."

"Since Gabe's ears are blocked, I just want to say, that thing you did with your tongue—"

"Not blocked enough!" Gabe says. "Remy, you're great, but you'll have to continue this another time."

"Hey, wait," Sanden says. "I called him. Don't hang up, you jerk."

"Fine, but I'm holding your phone ransom in case the sex talk starts again."

"Who knew you were so sensitive," I say.

"My old roommates had no boundaries. I'd like to maintain a few in my life."

"In that case, Remy, that thing you texted me about. Are you okay?" Sanden's softened his voice, and it does all kinds of things to me.

I know I'm immediately supposed to say yes, but how the hell do I be okay with something like that? "I ... I don't know."

"I'm sorry. If it helps, that was only a thought. I'm probably being overly critical of him."

I wish I could have that kind of confidence in Eman. Unfortunately, now that my trust has been broken, I'm looking at the red flags for everything I should have seen them as. Opportunities to get out. That I ignored.

Maybe he didn't cheat, but what man needs to be out all night with zero contact? He didn't even bother to let me know he was okay. "Either way, it needs to be done."

"Yeah. Probably."

"Thank you. I know I've said it before, but I don't think this week would have been half as fun without you."

"Hey, I got a free vacation out of it. I'm not complaining."

"And an orgasm, apparently," Gabe mutters.

"Butt out, you." Sanden clears his throat. "Have you, umm, checked that photo?"

"Nope, why?"

"Prepare yourself. There are a handful of not-nice comments on there from some of Eman's friends."

"I don't really give a shit."

He chuckles. "Good. Your pettiness won."

It did. And it feels great to know that I hit the mark. After being humiliated like that, I sure as fuck hope that Eman feels a fraction of it himself. He didn't break me, and I'm not a sobbing mess over him. Whether he wanted those things or not, it doesn't matter, because Sanden helped me through.

Sanden's a thousand times more of a man than Eman will ever be. It hurts to think that I can't climb out of bed and join Sanden on the deck to talk smack or share silence. He's a great guy to be around.

"So, question."

"Yeah?"

Well aware Gabe is still listening, I say, "After this week, does that mean we're friends? We are, right? No more snarling at me and getting snappy at work and things?"

"I never snapped at you. I was professional."

"Professionally cold," Gabe says.

"Thank you, Gabe!"

"I'm not friends with either of you anymore."

I latch onto the word. "Ohh, you said anymore, so therefore I was a friend, and you can't take it back."

Sanden's tone morphs into seriousness. "We're definitely friends now. You don't need to worry about that other stuff."

And while he's given me the answer I was after, it hasn't hit the way I hoped it would. I don't just want to be colleagues; I want to be the type of friends who hang out together. Sanden's a lot of fun, and I think I need someone like that in my life right now.

I force some pep into my voice. "In that case, if you ever want to get together, you know, to be petty. It worked the first time, so ... yeah. That'd be cool. Maybe post another photo or—"

"Yeah. Maybe."

His short answer throws me into silence. Did I push too far?

"I don't mean for sex or anything like that," I ramble.

"Yeah, I got you." He gives a short cough. "We're pulling up, so I've gotta go. But we'll talk."

"Okay."

"See you, Remy."

He's already hung up before I can say goodbye back.

Ten

SANDEN

My work husband glances over his cup of coffee as he takes a sip, his eyes crinkling at the edges. I've heard of smiling with your eyes, but I've never seen it in person before.

Gabe and I quickly bonded when he was assigned to our station because we're both gay, but while we joke about being work husbands and are close friends, we're not the type of close friends who go deeper than surface level. Hockey games, hanging out, going for drinks, yes. Talk about the real stuff? I don't do that with anyone.

But when Remy and I arrived back in Seattle, I realized I had no one else to talk to about this because a lot of our friends are mutuals with Eman, and because of Remy's petty photos online, a lot of them are taking Eman's side. Accusing us of cheating.

They've assumed Eman found out and that's why he left Remy at the altar.

So that's why I drove straight to Gabe's place and convinced him to grab coffee with me.

"I thought you hated Remy," Gabe says.

"I've never hated Remy."

He frowns, but it doesn't last long. Then it's like he gets hit with the truth. "Oh. Oooh. You *Love Actually*'d him."

"I'm sorry, I did what now?"

"Keira Knightly marries this dude, right, but his best friend hates her. It turns out he's been a dick to her the whole time because he's actually in love with her and kinda creepily obsessed with her, and he does this whole 'You're perfect' cue card thing behind his best friend's back, which is actually a bit of a dick move, and then she kisses him. Also a dick move."

I cock a brow at him.

"My point was the whole being a jerk because you can't have what you want thing. Not the creepy stalkery thing and the cheating." Gabe puts down his coffee. "Wait, is that why Eman left him? Were you doing the cheaty thing?"

"Fuck no," I growl. "And I'm not in love with Remy. He's just ..." My ideal guy, perfect in every way, and—I drop my head to the table and sigh. "He should've been with me that whole time," I mumble into the glossy wood.

"Ouch. You've got it bad for him. And you slept with him. Question? Do you always fuck yourself over, or is this a new trait?"

"New. Definitely new." I finally lift my head again. "I went on his honeymoon with him because I was genuinely concerned about him after Eman left him like that—"

"It was brutal."

"I didn't think we'd fool around, and when he suggested it on our last night, I said no. And then ..."

"Then you fell on his dick? Or did he fall on yours? So clumsy."

"We didn't have sex sex. Just messed around." Though, if I hadn't gotten so worked up, so close to the edge so fast, we would've fucked. He probably didn't have supplies with him—I sure as fuck didn't—so maybe it is a good thing we didn't go there because I'm not sure no condom would've stopped me. Eman cheating on Remy wasn't even a thought I had while I was kissing him, grinding on him, rimming him ...

"What do I do now?" I ask.

"You think just because I'm in a relationship, I know stuff? Fuck, if I was you, I'd run away."

"He offered to be petty some more, meaning he still wants to taunt Eman to show him how he fucked up, and I might not be strong enough to resist having a repeat."

"So, you're going to let him use you? That doesn't sound healthy."

It really, really doesn't. "I don't think he sees it that way. He doesn't know the extent of my feelings for him, just that I had a crush on him years ago and thinks he deserves better than Eman."

"I think you know what you have to do," Gabe says, and as much as I hate to admit it, he's right.

"I need to either tell him how I feel and ask for something real, even though he literally almost married another dude last week or ..." I can't say the other option.

"You have to cool it off with him."

"I don't want to pressure him into anything he's not ready for, so I'm going to have to end it now before I do become like that weird stalker person in a movie I've never seen."

"You could tell him that I think you need to remain professional? Our stations cross paths a lot, and it could be super awkward if you kept going, it blew up in your faces, and then you had to see each other at work. I mean, awkward for you. I'd make popcorn in whatever fire we're putting out."

"You are so supportive. So, so supportive."

Gabe grins. "I am, aren't I?"

"You also don't understand sarcasm."

"Oh, I do. I'm just ignoring you. Because I'm a supportive partner and the best work husband you've ever had."

"Sure. Let's go with that."

Even if he's right. I do need to step back from Remy. I do need to distance myself from him and his shitty situation. But ... we just agreed to be friends, and I don't want to cut him out of my life. It has been difficult to do since he's been with Eman, and I don't want to go back to that.

I want to be there for him. I want to help.

Maybe this is one of those times where I can't save everybody, and since I've chosen myself before, I refuse to do it again.

🔥 🔥 🔥

After the week off in Hawaii, it's easy to put distance between Remy and me because we both have to get straight back into work. And for my first two twenty-four-hour shifts, our station doesn't cross paths with his.

I tell myself that he might be on early starts and I'm on lates, so we shouldn't bump into each other anyway, but every time we get a call out, my nerves kick in, and I think this is the night it'll happen.

But when we get an alert that there's been a massive car pileup right in between our two stations and it's an all-hands-on-deck situation because people need to be cut out of cars, it's raining cats and dogs, and it's a huge mess, I know tonight's the night.

I'm going to see Remy again, and I need to act like I haven't had my tongue in his ass. While also being professional and nice. But not too professional because apparently keeping him at arm's length like that makes me a dick.

I've got this. I've so got this.

I don't really, but I'm very thankful for my recent promotion because after becoming lieutenant, we got a new DE behind the wheel. I don't think I could drive with all the adrenaline and nerves coursing through me.

A car pileup doesn't hit me the same way a fire does, but every time there's the potential for casualties, this deep darkness tries to take over. I stamp it down the way I've taught myself to do over the years because it's a distraction I can't afford, but it's a struggle not to be thrown back to that point in the past.

Our siren blares, and our bright red and white lights flash while Loren weaves in and out of traffic, which is already building up thanks to the wreckage.

My leg bounces, and I'm ready to get my rescue on. From the sounds of it, I'll be too busy saving lives to even worry about Remy. Captain is with us, so I'm not in charge. I'll go where I'm told, I'll do what I have to, and then I'll go home feeling like I've accomplished something worthwhile like I always do after a big shift.

We arrive on scene, and it's worse than I thought. The rain has at least slowed to a light drizzle, but it's still a pain in the ass to deal with, even if we're used to it living in Seattle.

Our captain talks with Station 21's cap, and then we're put to work.

Usually, I'd be controlling the jaws of life to get some of these people out of the rubble that used to be individual cars, but that's Loren's job now. Gabe and I set off to prioritize victims and work out who's in the most need of medical treatment.

Station 21 is already cutting into cars on the northern side of the crash, so we need to get a move on. Can't have them showing us up.

The accident wasn't just a pileup; one car after the other rear-ended the car in front. It's literally a crumpled mess that crossed two lanes of traffic.

I bypass the closest cars to us and head for the one that's flipped on its roof first. If the people in that car are hanging upside down, they're going to have a whole world of health problems.

Kneeling, I pop my head in the passenger-side window. It's smashed all over the ground, and there are two vics inside. One conscious, one I'm not so sure about.

"Hi," I say, and the conscious man behind the wheel on the other side moves his head toward me. "Don't turn. You could have spinal damage. Just keep your head nice and straight for me, okay?"

"My wife," he croaks. "Help my wife."

"I'm going to help both of you," I say while reaching through the window to check his wife's pulse. It's faint, but it's there. "We're going to get you out of here." I stand again and wave over Gabe. "We need to start here."

He rushes over to me. "Dude back there has a fucking pipe through his chest."

Shit. Okay. We've got this. We can do it.

"We could probably get this door open." I try the handle, but it doesn't budge, even though it's unlocked. "We need to get these two out." I lower my voice. "She doesn't have long. But we can't get them out on our own. We need a stretcher, we need hands to keep them steady in case they have spinal injuries. We need ..."

Fuck.

"We need Remy," Gabe says.

Yup.

Eleven

REMY

The adrenaline is rushing so loudly in my ears it helps block everything else out. I'm sweaty, and mixed with the mist of rain, I'm drenched from my hair to my shoes. This accident is one of the worst I've seen, with flashing lights of the police cars blocking the road on either side and redirecting traffic while all teams from Stations 40 and 21 scour the area. It looks like pandemonium, but we're a well-oiled machine by this point. Unfortunately.

With something like this, my partnership with Tig is the most important thing. Everyone else is assistance. A blur of familiar faces who do as I tell them to. My role is on the ground, and Tig's is to coordinate the trucks and communicate with the hospital trauma team so they know what's coming at them. And there's a lot coming at them. We load up the first ambulance and then the second, seeing everything from shock to lacerations to potential brain injuries.

I compartmentalize. It's what I do best. Calm voice, steady hands. It's on me to set the tone, and the only tone I've been trained to set is that *everything's fine*. I'm like that fucking meme. I go from car to car, following procedure. Safety, triage, ABC ...

A fourth ambulance pulls in beside mine as my name is called. "Remy!"

Sanden's waving at me from a car, and I set a brisk pace over there.

"Two adults, both restrained. One conscious. The other has a faint pulse."

I jump into it.

The airbags have deployed, which is awesome for keeping them safe but a pain in the ass for extraction. The passenger's door is jammed, but thankfully, the three of us are able to wrench it open. The driver's movement seems slow but unimpeded; it's the woman who's my priority.

She's unresponsive and already blue around the mouth. Suspected spinal injury be damned—she needs oxygen and a hospital now.

Even with the roof banged in and the front end of the car bent out of shape, it seems to be mainly the seat belt keeping her in place.

I call through to Tig for assistance, and between the two medics, Gabe, and Sanden, we immobilize her as best we can, then get her the hell out of the car.

My heart is in my throat the whole time. The last thing

we want to do is make her injuries worse, but time is against us, and in a decision between injured or dead, injured is the easy choice to make.

I barely catch my breath until she's on the stretcher, and then Sanden and I turn our attention to the driver while the medics rush to the ambulance and Gabe moves on to another car.

It's a long night.

After what feels like a million years, I'm left with a mom and her daughter in the back of my ambulance. They're both shaken and were in the car at the very front of the pileup, but other than some scratches and bruises, they're doing okay. I've checked all their vitals and ruled out shock, thankfully.

I've got them both wrapped in blankets as I clean up the cut on the mom's head. Her cheeks are sticky with tears, but the little girl just watches me.

"Do you have a lollipop?" she asks after a while. "When I see the doctor, I always get a lollipop."

I chuckle and reach into my bag. "What does Mom think?"

The woman nods slowly. "Ah, yeah ... it's fine."

I pull a lollipop from my bag and hand it over.

Despite the amount of blood, her wound is long but surface level, so I'm able to seal it with glue. "How's your neck feeling?" I ask her.

"Stiff."

"The ambulance is on its way back to get you both. My tests are looking good, but they'll give you a more detailed assessment when you're there."

"Thank you."

"Me next," the girl demands.

I strip off my bloody gloves and grab a new pair. "Let's see that knee."

She pulls back her dress a little, and I clean up the small cuts she got from the broken glass. Her car seat was wrecked, but she's otherwise completely unharmed.

I stick a few kitten Band-Aids over the area.

"All done."

"Thank you."

Tig appears in the open door with a man beside him.

"Daddy!" the girl cries and immediately bursts into tears as she launches at him.

Her mom stands slowly, looking on the verge of tears herself.

"Make sure you talk to somebody," I tell her. "Your daughter too. Even if you got out of this mostly uninjured, an accident can affect people in different ways."

Her mouth tightens.

"But kids are resilient. She'll be okay."

"Thank you."

I help her climb out of the truck and then go over instructions with her husband before the ambulance arrives to take them to the hospital.

And now, with the site clear, my tunnel vision eases up, and I'm able to take in details again. The smell of gas and smoke. The ache in my muscles from being coiled tight all night. The clusters of emergency medical responders assessing the scene.

I grab a wet wipe from my bag and lean against the truck as I wipe the grittiness from my face and neck.

Tig offers me a bottle of water that I gratefully accept.

Our shift technically ended an hour ago, so while I need to get back and clock out, I take a moment to come back down from the job.

Gabe pulls off his heavy helmet as he approaches. "We're going for breakfast after this. Unofficial debrief. You in?"

"Sure."

"I'll text you the place." He clasps my shoulder. "You did good."

I know what he's saying; I know that we all did exactly what we could do in the situation, but nights like tonight hang around in my mind for a while. The smell of fear, the screams, the begging to be okay, and—even worse—the silence. I have blood down the front of my uniform that isn't mine and next to no hope that everyone will make it through.

Tig and I pack it up and head back to the station, give our reports, change, and then head to the cafe Gabe mentioned. He and Sanden are already there, and even though I just saw him, it didn't register during that kind of scenario. Sanden was just another colleague doing his job. Now though?

Even exhausted as I am, that lopsided attempt at a smile makes a tickle of butterflies creep across my gut. His presence is like pure warmth, and after a lonely, frustrating few days alone, all I can remember is how he looked after me.

Tig and I slide into the booth opposite them. Gabe's

sitting with his head back, eyes closed, and Sanden's soft eyes watch mine for a moment before dropping to the table. We all sit there in a tired silence.

"Something to drink?" the waitress asks. I opt for a tea with the hope that I'll be able to pass out as soon as I'm home. Which isn't likely, but hey, I can pretend.

She walks away as Gabe's phone starts going off. He snatches it up and climbs from the booth, but I catch the "Hey, babe" as he walks away.

I watch him for a moment, missing Eman for the first time since ... a while.

Though, it's not him so much. It's that. The phone call. The person who I can be vulnerable with after a night like I've just had. Having someone to go home to who can hold me and keep me together. Who checks up on me and actually cares. Even when things were rough toward the end, after a bad night, Eman always called and made sure I went straight home to him.

I haven't had this type of after-work catch-up in a long time. Most of the guys from the station will do it now and then, but for me, it was always straight home. But ... for what? Comfort, initially. The more I think about it though, the more I turn memories over, inspecting them in a different light. Eman opening the front door and pulling me into his arms. Making me tea. Tucking me into bed. Those things used to help, but then ... when did it stop? When did it go from wanting to go home and see him to needing to get home because of obligation? It was what was expected. What he expected of me. Eman always needed to be my priority, and going out to decompress after a stressful shift made him think I was putting my coworkers and colleagues before him.

The last major incident we had before the wedding was the same day we had plans to meet up with his friends. I was tired and drained, but I didn't want to let him down. So I'd cried in the shower, then got ready and went out, only to end up in a fight later over me being surly all night. After so long on the job, I should have been used to bad accidents.

Maybe he was right.

"Need to hit the head," Tig says, getting up and breaking me out of my thoughts.

I slump over the table as he walks away, wishing I'd just gone home to bed.

Sanden kicks my shoe. "You okay?"

"As good as I can be," I say into the table, then lift my head. "You?"

A shadow of a smile. "As good as I can be."

I sit upright completely. "Question."

"Yeah?"

"How do I go home after that?"

Sanden's forehead creases. "What do you mean?"

"For the last few years, I've had someone there waiting. Eman might have had his faults, but after a tough job, just having someone helped. Now ..." I redirect my gaze to the next booth, not able to look at him anymore. "I dunno. I think the silence at home is what I'm dreading the most."

"Yeah." He clears his throat. "It's a real killer."

I'm struck by an awesome idea. "Come over."

"What?"

"I have a spare room. Come over, we'll both sleep, then we'll get up and hang out and talk about it and—"

"Remy ..."

"Or I can come to your place. Whichever."

His finger taps out a fast beat on the tabletop. "I don't have a spare room."

"Then mine. Please?" I clasp my hands under my chin and give him my best puppy dog eyes. I'm not even sorry about trying to guilt him into it because ... I need this. And it'll be good for him too. "We can help each other."

Gabe gets back before he can answer, and unlike before, he's smiling. Not much, but it's something.

"How's Aleks?" I ask.

"Good. He tried to get out of training camp by telling his coach I had an emergency at work. The unlucky thing about dating a fireman is that emergencies at work are kinda in our job description. Coach said he gets a maximum of three emergencies a year, otherwise he'd never be there."

"Wow, harsh."

Gabe laughs. "Nah, his coach is cool. And those hockey people take it very seriously. For a player, it's not an emergency unless someone's unconscious. And even then, it only counts if the body isn't blocking the goal."

"Or being used as a rebound for the puck," Sanden adds.

"While I'm loving the morbid humor, I'm suddenly starving."

Tig gets back, and we order. While we don't talk about the accident much, it helps just to be around people. It's like a gentle slide back into real life, where the smell of blood isn't clogging everything up. Where I don't focus on the fact that all those injuries could have been avoided if the accident didn't happen in the first place.

Not that thinking about that helps.

Once we're finished eating and the last of my tea has gone cold, I can't delay it anymore. Tig leaves first, going home to his family. Gabe makes his move next.

I stare across the table at Sanden, waiting to see what his plans are, almost desperate for him to stay with me. I know I'll have to get used to being alone at some point, but I'm a social guy. Maybe not when it comes to having a lot of friends and going out all the time because I don't really do that anymore, but having company is good for me.

Sanden slides out of the booth, and I scramble to do the same. We walk out with Gabe, and I'm on edge the whole time, hoping that Sanden isn't planning to just leave me.

"See you next shift," Gabe says, climbing into Sanden's passenger seat, almost as if he's giving us privacy.

Sanden grasps his door handle but doesn't open it yet.

"Come on ..." I all but beg.

"You're a pest, Remy."

"Is that a yes?"

His smile is fast and warm. "Like I'm gonna say no."

Then he climbs into his car, and I have to resist the urge to fist pump the air. He's just making sure I'm okay. I know that. I'm *fine* with that.

I'm so desperate to spend time with him I'm long past caring how it happens.

Twelve

SANDEN

After dropping Gabe off at his new mansion he shares with his NHL superstar boyfriend, I head for the apartment Remy used to share with Eman.

I've been there many times, mostly when Remy wasn't there, and for some fucked-up reason, I'm nervous to show up, even though Remy's the one who asked. He practically begged for company. If I'd had any willpower toward him, I would've said no, but I'm not going to lie, after nights like the one we've had, I could do with some company too.

Some of the people we helped last night were in a really bad way, and as much as I want to call the hospital to find out how they're doing, I'm not sure I want the answer. That, and HIPAA laws. But mainly, I don't want to make myself feel like a failure. Sometimes, with crashes really big like the one last night, the news will cover it, and I get a body count then, but I try to steer clear of getting answers. In my mind, I helped them all, gave them the best outcome, and they're all happy and healthy when they come through the other side of recovery.

It's the only way I can live with myself.

Yes, I don't want to be alone, and out of everyone, Remy understands what it's like, but after hooking up on his honeymoon, distance would be smarter. At work last night, it wasn't as bad as I was expecting. We were both professional, we got the job done, and there was no awkwardness. Then at breakfast, we were back to how we were in Hawaii. Things were easy between us.

If I go into his apartment, who are we going to be? Will we be in firefighter and EMT mode or fake honeymooners mode that turned into sex?

I didn't get nearly enough of him to be able to ignore my attraction though. For years, I dreamed of what it would be like to kiss him, to taste his skin, and the second I do, I basically blow my load before I had the chance to really savor it.

Then on the plane, when he was trying his best to get me to join the mile-high club—I really don't think he thought my size through on that one because I can barely fit in those small cubicle things, let alone both of us—my six-two frame wasn't the only thing holding me back. One time we could've chalked it up to a rebound. A friend helping another friend through a hard time.

A mistake.

If we do it again, there's the real danger of it becoming a habit, and Remy is not in the right place to have something real or serious again. Not so soon after Eman. I would be a prolonged rebound, someone to use to get over the asshole that left him at the altar, and I want to be so much more than that for Remy.

I always have, but because of some fucked-up sense of loyalty toward a friend who I grew apart from years ago, I never went for it. Never told Remy how I felt.

I complain about the timing, but I guess it could've been worse. While he was dating my friend, while he was engaged to my friend, or maybe even twenty minutes before they were set to marry.

I shake my thoughts free. I'll go in there, lend a supportive ear or shoulder, whichever he needs, and I will keep it platonic. Totally friendly. All I have to do is keep my tongue in my mouth and my dick in my pants.

Easy.

I have a lot of friends whose asshole I haven't licked, so this will be a piece of cake. An actual piece of cake. Not his ass.

After finally gathering the courage to go to his front door, he opens up before I get the chance to knock.

"When I invited you over, I did mean you were allowed to come inside. I was worried I'd have to come get you out of the parking lot."

I force nonchalance. "I was just ... thinking."

"Ah, can't do that and walk at the same time, huh?" Remy steps aside to let me in, then closes the door and slides the dead bolt across.

"Well—" When I turn back, he's already right there, standing in front of me, our chests almost touching.

He shoves me. "Can't walk and talk at the same time either?"

"No."

"Okay, let's go to bed."

"Uh ..." My gaze darts around the apartment, the one that still looks like Eman lives here with all his crappy taste in art and decor.

"In separate beds," Remy says. "If we *have* to." When he smiles up at me, I falter in my resolve, but I won't let myself crack. "Though, I wouldn't say no to some of your grade A spooning again. If anything's going to help with the adrenaline crash from last night, that will be it."

I have to admit, holding someone after an event that makes you realize life is fragile would make me feel better. Recover quicker. And while that rational thinking is one hundred percent fact, it helps me hide from the truth. I really, really want to.

"Only spooning," I say. "And not in your bed that you shared with *him*."

"Imagine how petty that photo would be." Remy steps forward and runs his hands over my chest. "You could be shirtless, and we'd mess up your hair and take pics under his sheets." His eyes twinkle, and while the image of us in bed together like that is mouthwatering, the fakeness of it for the sake of revenge cuts me deeper than I want to allow it to.

"I'd rather not."

"Ah. Scared I might jump your bones again?" He waggles his eyebrows. "Spare bed and no photos, it is."

Just friends.

Nothing more.

Tongue in mouth and dick in pants.

I can do this.

🔥 🔥 🔥

I can't do this.

Remy's hair smells fucking divine, and his ass is pushed back against my raging hard-on, yet he's talking to me like I'm not two seconds away from dry humping him.

"Unless they die en route to the hospital, I'd rather not know the outcome."

I snap back to reality and realize he's talking about serious shit, and I should stop thinking with my cock. "I'm the same," I mumble, trying really, really hard not to inhale again. Who needs to breathe?

"Hell, even when we're still doing chest compressions until the doctors take over and I've been at it for twenty minutes already, in my head, the doctors bring them back. I don't want to know how many lives have slipped through my fingers."

I don't have an answer for that. Well, I do, but I don't want to say it. Because I know exactly how it feels to have a life slip through my fingers, and it's the exact reason why I hate getting follow-ups to those I am able to help.

I hold on to him tighter. "As much as I like it when people we've saved come by the station to thank us, I hate it the minute they leave. Because it makes me think of others who I've rescued out of burning buildings or cut out of cars, and then I spend the day wondering if they're alive too and just didn't thank us—which is fine. They don't have to—or if they didn't make it."

"I never thought about it that way before. I always try to tell myself everyone makes it when I know for a fact they don't."

"I do that too. And it works for a while. Until it doesn't anymore, and then I dwell on statistics and try to average out how many people I've lost. How many lives were cut short because I didn't get there in time."

Remy puts his hand on top of the one I have resting on his stomach. "If you hadn't been there at all, they would've had less of a chance of making it."

"Logically, I know that," I say softly. "But when I'm spiraling, I can't stop the memory of being helpless and frozen."

"Memory?" Remy turns in my arms, rolling over to face me.

I really wish he'd stayed facing the other way because anytime I get like this—anytime I think about what happened that night all those years ago ...

"Hey," Remy soothes and reaches to wipe a tear that's rolling down my face.

Fuck, it's already happening.

"Remember in Hawaii when you said you knew I became a firefighter for the glory? Because I have some kind of hero complex?"

He nods.

"I let people think that of me because the truth is ... the truth ..." I choke on the words I've never been able to speak about. No one in the fire department knows. They asked me in my interview what made me want to become a firefighter, and I couldn't bring myself to say the truth.

But right here and now, with Remy this close, the adrenaline seeping from my system from last night's events, I find myself saying, "My sister died in a house fire when I was sixteen. She was eleven."

"Fuck, Sanden, I'm so sorry."

"It was my fault." I wrap my arms around him tighter. I sob while I hold him close, too tired to care about losing my shit on him when my biggest worry before I came up here was keeping my hands to myself.

"Did you set the fire?" he asks.

"No. It was old electrical wiring, but—"

"Then it's not your fault."

He doesn't get it. "I was babysitting her." I pull back and look into his sympathetic hazel eyes. "Mom and Dad went out, and because I was old enough to take care of Billie, they didn't bother hiring someone. Everything was fine. I made her go to bed, I stayed up playing video games, and then ... I must've passed out on the couch because I woke up downstairs, the whole place was ablaze, and ... and ..."

"It's okay," Remy whispers.

"It wasn't okay. It's still not okay. Instead of ... Instead of going upstairs to get Billie, I only thought about myself. I ran out the front door and watched as she ..." I can't get the words out. "I have never forgiven myself for it, and neither have my parents."

"You were sixteen," Remy says. "You were still a child."

"I should've ... I *could've*—"

"What? Ran upstairs, and then you'd both be dead? You've seen on the job what can happen when someone who doesn't know what the fuck they're doing goes inside to save a loved one."

"Sometimes I wish I'd died alongside her. Because the guilt ... the fucking guilt eats at me."

"So you became a firefighter to punish yourself?" Remy's hand weaves into my hair and strokes my head gently. His fingers are soft and warm, and the more I focus on his touch, the faster my tears dry up. He pulls me back into the present.

I sniff. "I became a firefighter because of Billie. Because I couldn't save her. So I save others to make up for being that selfish teen who ran away and didn't even think of her until first responders were already there."

"You. Were. Sixteen," he says again.

"My parents blamed me. Have always blamed me. Their souls died with Billie. They used to be fun, but after losing her, they became shells. Hateful. They moved away from Seattle when I turned eighteen—said it was too hard to be around so many memories of *her*—and gave me the choice to go with them or stay, but I got the very distinct impression they didn't want me to follow them. They left, and other than the yearly phone call for my birthday, we don't have contact. They never ask me about my life when we do speak. I died the same day Billie did. At least to them. They don't even know I'm gay. The only person who knew back then was …"

"Eman. Fuck." Remy leans up on his elbow. "That's why you held on to your friendship for so long and how you became so different."

"I have to admit, he was there for me when all of that happened, but being on my own from eighteen—sixteen, really, if you think about it—I grew up fast. I still don't think he's grown up, but I couldn't go after his man, no matter how much I wanted to. I couldn't do that to him."

Remy runs a finger up my arm, sending shivers down my spine. When he gets to my shoulder, he pauses. "But you could now?"

"I kinda already did back in Hawaii. And even though you're not ready for anything more than a rebound, I can't resist you."

"Then don't."

Thirteen

I'm out of words. All out of words, which is fucking useless when Sanden just poured all the darkness in his soul out to me. I wish I could make him see that there was absolutely nothing he could have done. As much as it kills me to say, she was probably already gone before he even woke up. If he was using his work logic, he'd see that too, but pain has a way of blinding us to everything else.

Another tear leaks onto his cheek, and this time, instead of brushing it away, I lean in and kiss it.

Sanden inhales sharply, breath rushing past my jaw, but he doesn't pull away.

I never would have guessed that Sanden's been carrying around something so heavy. He's always sweet and sometimes goofy, and he's everything I've needed since Eman pulled his shit. Now, now it's my turn.

I'll support him and hold him together if he needs me to. I kiss him again, lower this time, a brush of lips over skin, followed by another, closer to his mouth. Sanden's deep moan eases a little of the pain in my chest, and I fucking hope I'm doing the same for him.

"He's not the only person you have anymore," I say against his jaw. "Let me be here for you."

"Remy ..."

I kiss the corner of his lips. "You can cry, or I can cuddle you. We can sleep, or we can take things further. You've been here for me through everything, so let me return the favor."

"How are you so goddamn perfect?" he mutters before crushing his lips to mine.

My gut flips so hard I feel dizzy, out of control. Sanden's mouth on mine is excitement like I've never felt before, but there's something else there too. Something warm and comforting, something I want to grab tight and cling to. His body presses to mine as I slide my fingers into his hair.

It's been a really, really, *really* long time since I made out with someone like this. Since I felt starved of them, like I'd never get my fill, like I could never touch him enough to satisfy me.

Sanden's large hand splays over the small of my back, and I arch into him, bringing our hard cocks together through our briefs with friction that makes my limbs tingly.

I want to see him. Want to touch and taste and get my chance to explore his body, to make him feel good, but then Sanden rolls on top of me, pinning me to the bed.

"You know what?" I ramble as he makes his way along my jaw. "Maybe we should decompress together more often. I'm feeling much, much better about the direction the day is headed in ..."

He laughs, stubble scraping the sensitive skin on my neck. "Definitely less stress on my end."

"Perfect."

"Not yet." He goes back to kissing my neck as he runs his rough hands down my sides until they snag on my briefs. He shoves them under my ass, then wriggles down to drag them off the rest of the way before shucking off his own. When he lowers his hips to mine again, there's nothing between us.

The feel of his heated skin against mine is heaven.

Sanden bucks against me a few times before letting out a grunt of frustration. He pushes up onto his knees, eyes dark, and spits directly onto my cock. My dick twitches off my abs at the sight, and Sanden unleashes a breathtaking grin.

"Spread those pretty legs for me, sweetheart."

I've never opened them faster. With one hand, Sanden grabs my wrists and pins them above my head, and with the other, he lightly drags his fingertips through the mess on my dick.

"You look so sexy and desperate."

"That's because I *am* desperate." Hell, if he expected me to play it cool, he probably shouldn't be torturing me like this. The tingles racing along my dick and into my balls make my hips rock forward, seeking out more from him.

But if he thinks *I* look sexy, it's nothing on him. All those muscles towering over me, holding me down, stopping me from getting to the most beautiful cock I've ever seen. Because damn, I've spent the last few days imagining what it looks like, and I never pictured anywhere close to that. I'd seen a glimpse while massaging him, knew the tip flushed red, but it's thick, veiny, long enough to wreck me with.

I've always been a sucker for a pretty dick, and I think I might have just fallen in love.

I squeeze my eyes closed, fighting the way I want to plant my feet onto the mattress and thrust up against his hand.

"Sanden ..." I whine. "This is torture."

"I sure hope so."

"I need to come."

"That's the plan."

"My poor balls."

A wicked glint catches in his eye. "These balls?" Then he spits into his fingers and rubs them across my sac.

My head tosses back. "What did I ever do to you?"

He chuckles and steals my mouth again, strong lips, tongue surging forward. I can barely breathe through his assault, and I don't care because he finally, finally brings our cocks back together and wraps his hand around us both.

I'm already dangerously close to coming. The slick slide of our shafts together, the way I'm dying to touch him but can't; he's controlling everything, and I've never felt this deliriously good before. If you'd told me a month ago that I'd be having sex with my fiancé's friend in our spare bedroom, I would have brushed it off, but I can't think of a single thing I'd rather be doing.

If Eman had shown up, we'd be *married*, and then I never would have had this chance to know Sanden better. To follow through on everything I'd felt back when we first met, before he turned into a total dick and I pretended he didn't exist. Because *this* Sanden? This is the Sanden I'd always known was there. And now I get to experience it all to myself.

He's swept me up in a goddamn hurricane, and I never want him to set me down again.

His thumb swipes over my tip on every upstroke, palm squeezing tight, balls brushing against mine.

I'm panting, sweat building between our chests. Sanden picks up the pace, and I can't stop myself.

I scramble for a grip on the pillow above my head as my toes curl into the blankets.

"Sanden," I gasp before unleashing all over us both.

His grip on my wrists loosens.

"Don't let go."

"Yeah?"

"Feed me your cum."

Sanden's eyes blaze, and his grip tightens again. Then he pushes up to straddle my chest, his cock right in my face.

"Open up for me."

I part my lips, tongue out, and Sanden slides the round mushroom head inside. As soon as he's in my mouth, I hum around him, loving the taste of his precum. He jerks off, slowly at first, keeping eye contact the whole time, but the more I suck and lick, the closer to the edge he gets. His hold on my wrists is so tight I wouldn't be shocked to find bruises there tomorrow. His red lips are parted, breath ragged, eyes hooded and unfocused.

Then he gives a strangled cry, and my mouth floods with his taste. I swallow around him, greedy for everything he has to give me, and when he's done, I don't immediately release him. I swipe my tongue back and forth over his slit until he hisses.

His gorgeous eyes crease at the edges as he pulls back. "Getting sensitive."

"That was the plan."

With a long, sated groan, he drops down beside me. "Past Sanden would be fucking thrilled to know that just finally happened."

A bubble of happiness fills me as I smile back. "Yeah, Past Remy would be too."

He sighs. "Now, we can sleep."

"Orgasms and sleep. Could we be any smarter?"

The words are barely out of my mouth when someone starts to pound on my front door.

Sanden and I frown at each other for a split second before Eman's voice follows. "Open this door, Remy."

All the happiness from a second ago drains from my body. "Think I can pretend to be sleeping?"

"I know you're in there, Sanden. I saw your fucking car!"

"Not unless you want your whole building to hear this."

Fuck.

I scramble out of bed and pull up my briefs before hurrying into the bedroom for a pair of sweats and a T-shirt. By the time I get to the front door, I'm basically panting, so I force a deep breath, thank fuck I fastened the dead bolt and Eman didn't walk in to find us in bed together, then pull the door open.

Eman's wearing a suit, which means he's on his way to work, but as I look into his handsome face, the clear eyes and slicked-back hair does nothing for me anymore.

My glare comes easily. "What the hell do you want?"

"I want to know what the *fuck* my best friend is doing sleeping with my *goddamn fiancé*."

"Fiancé? You lost the right to that title when you left me standing at the fucking altar. What the hell were you thinking?"

"Maybe if you'd bothered to talk to me at all, I could have explained."

"*How* do you explain something like that?"

Realizing I'm pissed and not sad like he probably expected me to be, he changes tactic. The fight drains out of him, and he grabs my hand before I know he's even going for it.

"I got scared, Remington. Marriage is a big thing, and I was already starting to doubt you even loved me anymore, and so I went for a walk to clear my head, and when I came back—"

"You came back?" My gut jumps into my throat because I'd never, ever considered that could have been a possibility.

He blinks back tears. "You were having a party. That I left you. I ... Do you have any idea how much that hurt?"

"Eman, I—" I don't even know what to say because my gut twists like I might be sick. I hurt him?

Eman's expression hardens, and his eyes go from on the brink of tears to filled with ire. "Then I saw *that asshole* with his mouth on yours."

I flinch at the sudden shout and brace myself for the floodgates, but Eman's gaze snaps to the side. I follow it, dying when I see Sanden standing in the doorway to the spare bedroom, briefs on and arms crossed over his impressive bare chest. How can I go from being so excited to see him one moment to being full of dread now?

"How could you?" Eman asks him.

"I think you need to go," Sanden says.

"From my own house? You don't make the calls around here."

"No, but Remy does."

"*Remy* is my fiancé. Or did you forget that detail when you were sticking your dick in him?"

"Who says he's not sticking it in me?"

Holy shit, I really might be sick.

Eman glowers. "Because I know everything there is to know about Remy. I've made him come in ways you'd never even dream about."

"Well—"

My face is blazing. "*Shut up*," explodes from me. My heart is pounding, and the pressure at the backs of my eyes makes me worried I'm going to start crying any second now.

"Not that it's any of your business," I say to Eman, "but Sanden's here because we had a terrible night at work last night, and I didn't want to be alone. I don't care what you're doing here or what your plan is, but this isn't the time. You *left me* at the *altar*. Do you not even get how fucked-up that is?"

His eyes go cold. "Rich, coming from you. How long have you wanted to sleep with him, huh?" Eman leans in. "How long have you *been* sleeping with him?"

"Fuck you."

"You've done that, and now you've moved on to my friend. I always knew you were naive and stupid, but I never took you for a slut." Eman's voice drops low enough that Sanden won't hear. "If you really think he's interested in *you*, I feel sorry for you. He's played this game before."

Then Eman glares at us both, spins on his heel, and leaves.

"You okay?" Sanden asks as I nudge the door and stare at it as it clicks closed.

I don't answer. I can't. I'm ... confused. So goddamn confused. *Did* he come back? Did I get this entire thing really, really fucking wrong?

"Come on," I say, taking Sanden's hand and pulling him back into the bedroom. No matter how much my head is spinning, I haven't forgotten what Sanden shared with me earlier. After everything that's happened, neither of us should be alone.

I want to give him the kind of comfort he gives me, even when I have no goddamn clue what's going on in my head. Even if I want nothing more than to be alone to process.

This time, I stay dressed. This time, I curl around his back and hold him, keeping my dick firmly away from his body.

I savor how he feels against me because I don't know if it'll happen again.

Fourteen

SANDEN

Fucking Eman. I expected him to show up in our lives at some point, especially Remy's, but he's gone and ruined one of the most perfect moments of my life.

The burdens of my past sit lighter on my chest after letting Remy in, and then the intimate moment we shared was the most intense sexual experience of my life because it wasn't about the orgasm. It was about drowning ourselves in each other and getting lost in a bonding moment. And then that *fucker* had to come and ruin it.

Remy falls asleep after some tossing and turning, and we end up facing away from each other, but I can't switch off. Not after Eman barged in and accused both of us of being shady when he's the shadiest person I know.

I couldn't hear everything he said to Remy, just bits and pieces, but I saw what his words did to him, saw the way Remy shrank in on himself. When Remy turned back toward me, there was doubt in his eyes. Doubt that hadn't been there before now.

Sure, when I started acting friendly toward him, he was skeptical, but that's not what this looked like.

I want to ask him what Eman said, but I also don't want to wake him up after the night we had. The feeling of being unwelcome begins to creep over me, and I contemplate sneaking out and heading home, but I don't want Remy to wake up and find me gone. Even if he doesn't want me here, he can tell me that. I'm not going to make him feel abandoned again.

It's also tempting to text Eman to fuck the hell off and don't come back here, but it's not my place, and I know that's crossing a line. If anything, I should be telling Remy to chase whatever unfinished business he and Eman have so that maybe, just maybe, we'd have a real shot together. But I know how Eman operates. I know from experience how he gaslights and manipulates people because I've seen it happen right before my eyes.

Eman is the type of guy who gets what he wants because everyone believes his lies. For a long while, I did too. And then I grew up.

Please. Best friend? He hasn't called me that since we were kids, but he brings it out when he wants to punish Remy for sleeping with me.

Before I know it, Remy's alarm is going off, and when I

look at the time, I realize I've been overanalyzing everything for two hours. Without a wink of sleep.

Remy rolls over and reaches for his phone, which is on the nightstand next to me. His warmth at my back, the smell of his cologne mixed with sex and sweat … I want to hold him and breathe him in.

But then he's gone, his phone is silenced, and he slumps against the pillow with a soft thump.

I turn to face him, but he doesn't look at me—just keeps staring at the ceiling.

"You should keep sleeping," I say.

"Nah, if I nap for any more than two hours, it throws off my whole sleep pattern." He still refuses to look at me.

"Are you ready to talk about it?"

"No. I'm still angry. At him. At the situation. At you."

"You're mad at me?"

Slowly, his head turns toward me. "Did you know Eman came back to the wedding?"

I want to call bullshit, but I don't. "Literally the last thing he said was 'I need to get out of here. I can't do this,' and he left."

"So, he might have changed his mind again and come back."

I grit my teeth and swallow my pride because the truth is I can't have known what Eman did or didn't do, and bottom line is Remy and Eman were together for years. You can't throw away that much history just because you're having sex with someone else. Rebound sex, emotional trauma sex … Remy and I aren't dating. We're not … together.

It hurts to admit it, but maybe I need to feed myself some hard truths.

"If you have unfinished business with Eman, you should talk to him. Get everything out in the open."

"I don't want to believe him, and there's something in the back of my mind telling me he's lying, but ... what if he's not?" Remy's voice cracks. "I had doubts before the wedding too, and if I'd chickened out and then saw him with you ... Maybe I am in the wrong here."

I lean up on my elbow so I can look him in the eyes when I say, "You are not in the wrong. The second he walked out of that hotel without telling you, you were over. You had every right to do whatever you wanted after that. And I also want to remind you that the photo of us kissing wasn't even a real kiss. Nothing happened between us that night or any night after that until the last night of your honeymoon, where you just wanted to forget he ever left you. You're the wronged party in all of this, and even though I knew you had baggage when we started ..." I wave a finger between us. "Whatever this is, I've never wanted to come between you and happiness. If you think you could be happy with Eman, then go chase that life. But I want you to go into your decision with clear eyes. If your gut was telling you to not go through with the wedding, maybe you should've listened to it. If your gut is telling you that he's lying, it's probably right."

Remy's eyes are filled with so much pain. "Everything is so skewed it's impossible to know what to believe anymore."

"I'm going to head out."

His gaze flicks to mine. "What? Why?"

"Because you need to work out what and who you want. I want to be your friend. Though, if I'm putting it all out there, ideally, I'd want more than that. But I'm not going to pressure you into anything you're not ready for. You're going through a lot, and I don't want to be a complication or added stress. So, I'll give you space and just hope that you're able to work out everything that's going on up here." I tap his temple. "I'll be here for you no matter what, but this is something you need to do on your own."

I go to slip out of bed when he grabs my wrist.

"I don't want you to go."

Damn him. "I don't either, but I'm trying to be the bigger person here. I don't want you to think you have to do anything for me, that you have to be with me, that you should uproot the last three years of your life because we made each other come a couple of times, but I'll be here if and when you're ready."

Remy drops my wrist. "In other words, you're telling me to sort my shit before calling you?"

"Hey, I don't mind messy Remy too, but we should probably cool it on the sex front until you work out what it is that you want."

Remy averts his gaze. "I want to be happy."

"That's something you're going to have to find on your own. If you can't be happy alone, I don't think you'll ever be happy in a relationship."

"That's deep."

"That's what she said."

"Okay, now you can officially get out of my house. No bad jokes allowed."

"Well, then you need to tell your face to leave."

Remy laughs. "I can't with you. Hurry up and leave before I beg you to stay. I don't want to screw you around either, and I have a lot of confusion going on right now."

I lean over and kiss the top of his head. "I'm still here as your friend. Whenever you need me."

Even if it tastes bitter rolling off my tongue, I do truly mean it. I've only ever wanted Remy to be happy because he deserves it.

I'm not so sure I'm as deserving.

🔥 🔥 🔥

Remy:

I need you. It's an emergency.

Sanden:

I'm at work.

Remy:

That's the emergency. It's that there are no emergencies, and I'm bored.

Sanden:

You did not just say that, you fucker.
Now we're going to get all the calls.

Remy:

That's better than sitting on my bunk while everyone snores around me, leaving me alone with my thoughts. And also questions. Tig could enter a contest of animal sound imitations. He sounds like a grizzly tearing apart dead bodies.

Sanden:

And now we're going to get a call about a bear attack. Why do you hate me?

My phone rings a minute later with Remy's name lighting up the screen. I'm alone in the kitchen while most of the others get some shut-eye. Gabe is the only other one awake, but he's in the rec room watching TV.

I haven't heard from Remy this past week, but I haven't expected to. Eman hasn't reached out either, and I've stayed off socials because his posts were starting to piss me off. I don't want to take our drama public. I have no idea what's going on with their situation or mine and Remy's, but I wasn't lying when I said I'd be there for him if he needed me.

Boredom doesn't really count as a need, but I'm not going to deny him.

I hit Answer. "Please don't tell me you're the asshole teammate who uses his phone in the sleeping quarters."

"Like they could hear me over their fucking snoring. I came outside. I don't think I'll be getting to sleep anytime soon. I need something to do. I need action."

"Look, I'm flattered, but I thought I told you we had to slow down on that." I said we couldn't have sex. I didn't say we couldn't flirt. Even if it means slicing myself open every time.

"Funny. But seriously, is it bad karma to wish for a horrific accident or fire that will occupy my brain other than snoring and stupid Eman? I don't wish harm on anyone, but I dunno, maybe an abandoned building?"

"This is why so many firefighters turn out to be pyromaniacs, isn't it?"

"I didn't say I'm going to set one. Just that ... I maybe want one to happen."

"Definite pyro." I grin, even though he can't see me.

"You got me."

I hold my breath and ask the question that's been killing me. "How are things with stupid Eman?" If he says they're back together, I swear I'm going to scream, but I did say for him to make his choice. To lead his life. If his life is Eman, I'm going to have to deal with that. Or make Eman have an accident. Off a cliff. Remy did say he wanted action.

"I haven't seen him again," he says softly. "He called and asked if we could talk without you there, and I said I have to think about it."

"What's your head saying?"

"That he's an asshole."

"I always knew you were smart."

"But ..."

"Oh no. You went and said 'but,' and that makes you not smart."

"Ergh. You're right. Why am I even contemplating meeting up with him? What could he possibly say that will make me feel better or want him back when what he did to me was so positively douchey ... But then—"

"Oops, there's that word again."

"I'm serious. I don't know what to do." He hesitates. "I feel like I have to."

As much as I hate it, I really do think he needs to have a conversation with Eman. "Call him. Arrange a time to meet. On neutral territory."

"We were in a relationship, not rival street gangs."

"No, trust me. You can't be impartial and unemotional at home. You need to see Eman through new eyes. Not Eman from years ago, not the Eman you fell in love with. Who is he now, and is he someone you can see yourself with? Until you answer that, I don't think you're going to get what you're looking for."

Remy's silent for a moment. "You know what I hate?"

"How good-looking and irresistible I am?"

"Obviously, but aside from that, I actually hate that you're right. Because I don't want to talk to him. I just want to get over what happened. But to do that, I have to talk to him. Get closure or whatever."

I hope to fuck he finds closure. My fear is he'll rediscover all the things he loved about Eman to begin with. And then I'll lose him. Because there's no way Eman will let us be friends anymore if they get back together.

I wouldn't even blame him for it.

I have to hope that Remy sees the truth and gets what he needs to move on.

Fifteen

REMY

Sanden's been messaging me nonstop all day, and whether it's because he's nervous or he senses I am about to meet with Eman, for the billionth time in the last month, he's there for me when I need it.

Talking to Eman's going to be hard. It was painful enough to message him that I wanted to meet up, where I was faced with a long history of all the things we'd said to each other back when we were together. Seeing the message history, the "I love yous," the "I can't wait to see you today" that he sent the morning of the wedding, made me ache to go back there. I might not have been happy, but things were simple.

Then Sanden's name lit up my phone, and my smile almost broke my face, and the brief moment was gone.

I know three years is a long time, but somehow, it feels like that was barely a blip in between Sanden.

The thing is, he feels the most right of anyone I've ever met. Maybe I'm being as naive as Eman called me, but if Eman had never shown up the other morning, I don't think I would have hit the brakes. I would have jumped in, sex or no sex, to see where this thing with Sanden could have gone.

I miss the peace I feel with him around.

It's soon, I can acknowledge that. Which also puts a lot of pressure on a new relationship, but if Sanden was willing to give it a chance, I could have done the same.

And now ...

Eman had to go and fuck it all up. The happy bubble I was living in has been popped by a heavy dose of reality. Eman's angry words as he stood on my doorstep. *He's played this game before.*

What does that even mean?

Eman's in my head again. His voice had gotten quiet since the end of our relationship, but he's back, and he's loud.

And I'm ... drained. Sick of being on the edge and anxious.

"I didn't think you'd come."

I jump at the deep voice, dread sweeping over me before disappearing again. My shoulders have pulled tight like I'm bracing for a fight, but I promised myself we wouldn't go there.

This isn't a resolution. This isn't a couple's spat. It's a

relationship postmortem, and reminding myself of that helps loosen my nerves.

"We need to talk."

Eman takes the seat across from me and signals for service. "Couldn't agree more."

"That should make things easy, then."

He spares me a tight smile as the server arrives, and then Eman places an order for our usual. This is the restaurant where we always used to have date nights. It has photo-ready lighting and palm trees indoors. Because of the waitlist for a table, Eman's booked us a spot here one night every month.

I considered fighting him on coming here, but he'd just get his way. He always does.

"Baby—"

"Don't."

"You're being unfair," Eman whines.

"You know what's unfair? Having to tell all our wedding guests—who you insisted on inviting—that the wedding was off."

"I told you—"

"That you were coming back. Yes. I heard that."

He presses his lips together and looks at me through sad eyes. "I was worried this would happen."

"What?"

"Sanden's already poisoned you against me. He worked fast this time."

Uneasiness passes through me, but I don't answer him.

"Let me guess," Eman says dryly. "He told you about Billie?"

My gaping must give me away.

Eman chuckles. "Oh, Remy. That story always got him laid back in the day. I can't believe you fell for it. I've told you what he's like—how did you fall for it so easily?"

"I didn't fall for anything."

"What happened ..." He shudders. "It was a horrible tragedy. I was there for him through the whole thing, supported him. Was his only friend. But just because you've been through a bad thing, it doesn't give you the right to use it to your advantage and screw over the one person who's always been there for you."

"Let me guess, that person's you?"

Eman takes a sip from his water glass. "I never told you about Kent, did I?"

"Who?"

"My college boyfriend. I was in love, even though we were only together six months. Then one night, at a party, I found him and Sanden in a room together." He waves a hand. "I don't need to relive the whole thing. I think you can put it together for yourself."

Something hot and heavy presses on my stomach. "Sanden? Really?"

"I know. He had me fooled too. Almost made me believe it was *my* fault." Eman reaches for my hand resting on the table. "I've told you, Rem. You can't trust him."

I curl my hand into a fist under his. Eman *has* told me. About Sanden's jealousy. About how Sanden's corrupted Eman's friendships so that Sanden's the only one he has.

Trying to fit everything he's told me over the person I've seen ... I can't make it work. Sanden's the one who encouraged me to talk. He's the one who said we couldn't make more of whatever's happening between us until I was sure. Until I was ready.

Was he just trying to make me have a clean break from Eman?

"You're *my* fiancé." Eman squeezes my hand. "Don't throw it all away, baby."

"Sanden or no Sanden, we ended when you walked away."

A smug look crosses his face. "Who's the one who told you I left?"

I eye him.

Eman fixes me with a look. "I was gone for twenty minutes tops. I have to give it to him. He's got screwing me over down to an art form. You lasted longer than most guys. I usually only get a couple of months with them before Sanden turns them against me." Eman lets go of my hand. "I thought I finally had it."

"Had what?"

"An actual shot at happiness." When Eman's pale brown eyes flick back my way, they're shiny with tears. "I miss you so much."

I ... have nothing. What do I say to that? Do I miss him? No. But the only defense I had for everything I've done is that Eman left me at the altar. If he didn't ... If he's telling the truth ... Would Sanden actually be capable of doing something like that? Sanden said he couldn't do it and he left ...

"What did you tell them?" I ask, and my voice actually

shakes. "Your groomsmen? When you left? What did you say?"

He scrubs a hand through his meticulous hair, messing it up just slightly in the way I used to love. "I told them I needed some air." His voice breaks, and *holy shit*. I think he's telling the truth.

But if he's telling the truth, that means ...

The entire month crashes down around me as I'm hit with the solid knowledge that *I'm* the bad guy.

I called off our wedding.

I posted photos with another man on our wedding night.

I went on our honeymoon with someone else, without even trying to contact him.

I slept with another man.

The server comes back with our food and sets it on the table, but he's barely walked away before I push the food as far from me as I can. "I think I'm going to be sick," I mutter.

Eman shoots up from the table and comes around to kneel in front of me. Exactly like he did when he proposed.

Dear fucking God, this is even the same table.

"It's okay," he says, cupping my face. "I'm here. I'll forgive you. I just want everything to be okay between us again. I've tried so hard to be mad, but he deceived you. I get it. I want you back."

I sniff, well and truly on the verge of tears.

And still, my brain is blank. I have nothing to say to defend myself because there's no defense.

I fucked up.

"No. I can't ..." I breathe out.

The passion in Eman's eyes shutters. He stands stiffly and drops back into his chair, running his fingers over the side of his phone. "I ..." He cuts off.

"What?"

Eman glances my way, pity written all over his features. "No. I can't show you."

"Show me what?"

"Do you remember back when we first got together ... I ... I told you what Sanden said about you?"

It takes me a minute for the memory to click into place. Our first date. I'd only said yes to get him to stop asking, but within minutes of sitting down, I'd coughed up the reason I wasn't that excited. I had feelings for Sanden. I'd told Eman, up front, that dating him didn't feel right. And then he'd dropped the bomb. Sanden had tried to warn Eman away from me ... by telling him that I fucked anyone with a dick and then moved on to the next guy.

Eman nudges his phone across the table. "You still know my passcode."

"What are you ..."

"Check my messages."

I'm wary as I pick up his phone and key in my birth-date, then navigate to his message app. There are a few from his dumbass friends, his mom, his sister, and then ... Sanden.

I open the messages and find the most recent one was sent an hour ago.

Sanden:

Enjoy your date knowing I had Remy's
cock in my mouth an hour ago.

I drop the phone.

Eman clears his throat and slides it closer again. "There
are more."

Hey Eman, just fucked Remy on those
Egyptian cotton sheets you love so
much. Thought you'd like to know. x

Hey, did you know Remy squeals when
he comes?

Hey Eman, remember when I told you
Remy was a whore? He moaned like one
on my cock tonight.

Oh, holy fuck.

I stare from the phone to Eman and back to the
messages again. They're so ... so ...

My jaw tenses as Eman lifts his hands.

"I'm so sorry. I told you I didn't want to show you."

I'm barely in control as I shove away from the table and
toss his phone back onto it.

"I didn't write back to any of them," he says. "I
couldn't. I won't give him the satisfaction of letting you be
degraded by him because I still love you. Even after everything you've done."

I'm *shaking*.

And then Sanden's words come back to me.

If your gut is telling you he's lying, it's probably right.

Was that more manipulation by him though? More words to turn me against Eman?

Whether it was or it wasn't, it's sound advice.

Trust my gut.

And what's my gut telling me?

It's saying it's impossible to know who to trust. Eman, Sanden … Neither? The only thing it's screaming at me is that Eman's not the man for me.

"Thank you," I tell him.

Eman's face relaxes. "Yeah, of course. You know I'm always here for you, baby. Always. I've got your back."

I shake my head. "I'm not thanking you for that. I'm thanking you for walking away when I couldn't. Otherwise, we'd be married, and honestly … we're not right for each other. I'd rather read that Sanden's sent a hundred of those messages than have to spend the rest of my life with the wrong person."

He shoves out of his chair. "And what? You're going to tell me *Sanden's* the right person? Gonna marry him too?"

"No. Fuck. I doubt I'll ever attempt to get married again after what I've been through."

"What *you've* been through? You fucking cheated on me!"

"Sirs." The server gives us a stern look. "I'll need to ask you to take your seats or take this conversation outside. You're being disruptive."

"Sorry," Eman says, struggling to get control of himself. "My fiancé is being silly again."

"No I'm not. I'm leaving."

"Remy! Don't be a fucking child."

I step around him, headed for the door, but he grabs my upper arm and yanks me back. "Go be his little slut, then. You'll see. In a few weeks, he'll toss you aside like every other guy I've ever dated, and then you'll be left, stupid and alone, and you'll realize how good you had it with me." He lowers his voice. "You were nothing before me. This is your last chance to fix things because I won't be embarrassed by your pathetic desperation again."

"Fuck you," I spit and yank my arm away.

"Wait," he snarls, coming after me. "I'm sorry, I shouldn't have said that."

I'm walking as fast as I can without breaking into an all-out run.

"Remy! Come back. Let me explain."

Tears prick my eyes as my shoulders get all tight again, braced for his words. It's basically a script at this point.

I didn't mean it. You're blowing it out of context. I've only ever been good to you. No one will believe you. That didn't happen.

Eman follows me all the way out to my car, and I rush to get in and lock the doors before he can get in here with me.

"Oh, come on!" he shouts, slapping the window and making me jump. "You're just gonna run away?"

Damn fucking right, I am. I'm shaking as I switch on the car and throw it into reverse. Eman goes for the door handle again, and before he can even think to block my way, I throw the car into drive and get the hell out of there. My heart hammers wildly, and I have no idea what just happened, but dear fucking God, I'm glad it's over.

As painful as it was, this was the closure I needed. The affirmation that I'm doing the right thing by not going back to him.

As for Sanden ... For the last three years, he barely acknowledged me. He's been standoffish, cold, and distant. Eman said it was because Sanden wanted him. Sanden says it's because he wanted me. Did he send those bullshit texts to Eman to make Eman want to give up on me? So he'd win me by default?

If that's the case, they're both playing head games and are as fucked-up as each other. Maybe they should date.

I separate the Sanden from the last three years from the Sanden in Hawaii and look at his actions from the past month. How we turned each other on while on that massage table, yet he didn't make a move. How he pretended to be my husband so I wouldn't be embarrassed about having to tell everyone there that there was no wedding. How he suggested I put on a brave face at my petty party and stayed relatively sober to look after me. He treated me with kindness and respect, so to turn around and spread lies and call me a whore ... there has to be a reason behind it.

Is there a reason for something like that? Or am I as desperate as Eman said I was and looking for any excuse to hold on to my one anchor through this whole thing?

Either way, Sanden owes me an explanation.

Whether he'll give me one or not will show me who's really the asshole in this fucked-up love triangle I've fallen into.

Sixteen

SANDEN

There's loud banging on my door, and I jump up to answer. I'm supposed to pick Gabe up to go to his boyfriend's hockey game tonight, but maybe he got a rideshare here.

Only, it's not Gabe at the door.

It's a very pissed-off Remy, but not the type of pissed off where he's irate and ready to scream. He looks like a serial killer who's about to snap and go into a killing frenzy.

"Soooo, dinner with Eman went well, then?" I step aside to let him in, and he charges past me.

"Where's your phone?"

"What?"

"Ah. Here." He takes my phone off the armrest of the

couch, brings it over to me, and holds it up to my face so it unlocks.

I don't stop him because I don't really care, and I'm still super confused.

Whatever he's looking for, it makes him sag. "Have you deleted them?"

"Deleted what?"

"The text messages between you and Eman?"

I cock my head. "What are you talking about?"

Remy slumps down on the couch. "I don't know what's going on."

"That makes two of us. What did Eman say?"

"He showed me his phone. In his texts, there was a whole thread from you gloating about how we'd slept together and how I was a whore for you and—"

Anger erupts from my chest. "He fucking said what?"

Remy's brow scrunches. "He didn't say it. You said it. I saw the texts with my own eyes."

"I haven't texted Eman since before the wedding." I take my phone and scroll up to the last messages Eman sent me while we were in Hawaii. "He sent me all these accusing me of trying to steal you like I did to Kent when he was in college and all this other bullshit that made me think he's as delusional now as he was back then—"

"Wait. What did happen with Kent? He said he saw you two hooking up."

Playing the martyr. How new for him. "Of course he'd say anything to make himself look like the victim." I sit on the armchair across from Remy. "Kent was upset. He and Eman were fighting because Eman was nonstop flirting with all these other guys at a party. When Kent called him on it, he got upset and yelled that he can flirt with whoever the fuck he wants, and just because he had a boyfriend, that didn't mean he wasn't allowed to have fun."

Remy sucks in a sharp breath, something like recognition or maybe relatability flashing in his eyes.

"I was consoling Kent because, once again, Eman was creating drama that he knew I'd clean up for him. Then when he caught us talking in one of the bedrooms, he erupted in accusations of us hooking up behind his back."

"Sounds familiar," Remy murmurs. "Only in our case, it was true."

"It *became* true," I point out. "He was accusing us of cheating together as soon as that drunken kiss photo was online."

"But the texts ..."

"They weren't from my phone. There's no way to prove that other than— Hold up. When we were back in high school, my parents had to take Billie to some dance competition out of town and told me to sleep over at Eman's house, but we wanted to have a party. So we changed my phone number in his phone to my mom's name and then showed his mom the text saying Eman was allowed to sleep over at our house that night if it was okay with his mom. It worked ... until we made a mess that wasn't cleaned up by the time my parents got home the next day, but my point is—"

"That fucking asshole," Remy growls. But then the fight leaves him, and he lowers his head into his hands.

"He's manipulative," I say.

Remy huffs. "He says the same thing about you."

"I'm sure he does."

Remy lifts his head. "How am I supposed to know who or what to believe anymore?"

This is the thing about Eman that I've been trying to put my finger on all these years. Our mutual friends could never understand what I meant when I said he was making me uncomfortable. When I said I wasn't sure about him anymore. That he changed. Or was getting worse. To them, he's always been this amazing and charismatic guy, so I couldn't tell if he was the one changing or if I was.

The more I think about it now, the more I realize it might go deeper than simply me growing up and he didn't or the two of us taking separate paths.

Lying to Remy and me about each other is a new level of fuckery. Preplanning horrible texts in his phone is psychotic. The short temper, the way Remy always seemed so reserved and standoffish around him. It was the same way Kent became too.

I'm beginning to think Eman's not just an asshole. He's controlling and abusive. And he's doing it on purpose.

It makes me look at Remy and everything he's going through with fresh eyes. "Eman has an effect on people. He's charming and so damn convincing that he could prob-ably tell you the sky is green and make you wonder if you're crazy for thinking it's blue. And short of calling Kent so you can talk to him yourself, there's no way to prove what I'm saying is any truer than what he is. I don't have the best track record when it comes to you. Being friendly when we first met to shutting you out to basically inviting myself on your honeymoon and into your bed ... I can see why you wouldn't immediately realize Eman's full of shit. Hell, if I was in your position, I'm not sure I'd believe me either."

Remy blinks at me, thinking it over so slowly I can practically see the cogs of his mind turning over. "I could trust my gut."

"What's your gut telling you?" I hold my breath.

"That you're telling the truth."

I let out a relieved breath.

He stands and stalks over to me, looking down into my eyes as he whispers, "Please don't let me be wrong about you."

I grip his waist and pull him down on my lap. "I'll try to prove to you every day how much I genuinely care for you. If you'll let me."

"My trust is shot, not going to lie."

I hate what Eman has done to him. "I might not have messages to Eman about you, but want to see the ones I sent to Gabe?"

"Your work husband?"

"Yup." I show him the last few messages I sent to Gabe a couple of hours ago when I knew Remy was meeting up with Eman.

Sanden:

I hope Remy doesn't get sucked into Eman's world again. He deserves better.

Gabe:

You, you mean?

Sanden:

I'd like to be that guy, but it's messy right now. Maybe our timing isn't right. Maybe it will never be because of Eman. I should've asked him out three years ago when I had the chance.

Remy smiles, but it drops quickly. "Uh ..."

He turns the phone in my direction when I read: *Dude, where the fuck are you?*

I stand, knocking Remy off my lap. "Oh, fuck. Sorry. I didn't mean to ... Gabe and I were going to the hockey game, and I was supposed to pick him up."

"Oh. Umm, okay."

"Hold up a sec." I hit Dial on my phone to call Gabe and put it on speaker.

"You forgot, didn't you?"

"Forgot about going to see the love of my life play hockey?" I wink at Remy, who appears amused but also like he's missed the joke.

"Stop calling my boyfriend that, asshole."

"We tell you all the time, what Aleks and I have is special. If you loved hockey, maybe he would love you like he loves me."

"Are you coming to the game, or am I going to have to call a rideshare?"

"None of your ex-roommates taking the third ticket tonight?" The best thing about Gabe dating Aleks is the season tickets he buys Gabe and me. Last season, we only got two, but this season, he bought three for if I wanted to ever bring someone who, quote, "Actually likes hockey." Unlike Gabe.

"No. They apparently all have lives that don't revolve around sports ball. I was tempted to join them, but did you know that as a partner of a hockey player, I'm supposed to show support and what the fuck ever? And if I go by myself, I have to deal with WAGs. Please don't make me deal with WAGs. It's an abomination I even know what WAGs are."

"Umm, so I have Remy with me. Is it okay if he takes that third ticket? He just had dinner with Eman, so to say he needs cheering up is an understatement."

"And ... he thinks watching boring hockey is the way to be cheered up? There's something wrong with that man. You should stop fawning all over him."

My eyes widen, and I wince as I glance at Remy, but Remy laughs.

"Hi, Gabe."

"Oh, fuck. Umm, fawning as in, you know, being friends with you and making sure you're okay. Not sleeping with you. Which he isn't. That I know of. He didn't tell me anything."

"I want a work divorce."

"Okay, moving on. Why would you want to come watch hockey, Remy? I have to be there. You don't. Run now while you've still got the chance!"

Remy chuckles. "Actually, I had no idea about the hockey game before now, but I would like to come if there's an extra ticket. Every time the players get into a fight, I can imagine it's Eman they're beating up."

"Ooh, in that case, I'll message Aleks and tell him to get in lots of fights tonight. Just for you. I'm a great friend like that. Terrible boyfriend but great friend."

"We'll see you soon." I end the call.

We're on an uphill battle. Eman's telling him complete bullshit and lies and pulling the sympathy card that people eat up. He's so charismatic it takes a long time to see through his charms. Hell, apparently it took me this long to understand the full extent of it. I always felt something was off but kept him in my life because of some fucked-up bond that grew when I was at my worst.

My parents turned their backs on me, but Eman didn't.

Then I grew up, wanting to be better. He's always had this narcissistic *I'm always right* attitude, and for a long time, I told myself that was just him. It was his quirk. His personality trait. I shouldn't hate him for it.

Yet, right here and now, I couldn't hate him more. Because he not only hurt Remy, but he's twisting Remy's whole perspective on reality and making Remy feel guilty for being left at the altar.

"Let's go have some fun, and we'll forget all about Eman, okay?"

We have some work to do, I know that, but with Eman out of the picture, maybe we'll be able to start something new. Something fresh. And if he ends up only wanting friendship, then I'm going to have to be okay with that.

I want—no, I *need*—him to know that Eman's the one playing him, not me.

And I'll do anything to prove it.

Seventeen

REMY

"Let's go hockey!" I shout, pounding on the Perspex glass as the teams take to the ice. It's still early in the season, so the arena isn't overly busy yet, not that it matters how many people are here because Gabe's "usual" seats are ice side.

When I compare these usual seats to mine and Eman's usual seats in that restaurant—

No. No thinking. Hockey only.

It's been forever since I've been to a game. I might not be a fan, but I love the atmosphere, whether it's hockey or football or basketball. I love the speed and the intensity. Eman and I used to go on dates to—

Goddamn it.

I slap the glass again with both hands as Aleks skates past. "Go for blood!"

He shoots me a confused look but joins his team. Then the puck drops, and it's on. I barely take my seat the whole game. Every time Seattle scores, I cheer, and every time there's a big hit or a fight breaks out, I cheer harder.

My gaze catches on a player from Montreal called Grant as he takes to the bench. He pulls off his helmet, squeezes a drink bottle of water over his head, and when he drags a hand back through his hair, it's slicked back, like Eman wears his.

The second Grant's back on the ice, I want blood.

"Him, Aleks, go for him! Smash him! Give him a shin kick! Gloves off! Gloves *off*!"

Gabe's amused snort behind me is just loud enough for me to hear over the rest of the crowd. "Think he knows Aleks can't hear him?"

"I don't think he cares," Sanden replies.

With that reminder of them behind me, I sink back into my chair, ears burning. They're on either side, but I refuse to look their way.

"Ah, sorry," I say.

"What for?"

I can't stop from glancing quickly at Sanden. "Causing a scene."

"A scene?" He exchanges a look with Gabe. "We're at a hockey game. Isn't that the whole point?"

I shrug because I don't see anyone else yelling and jumping around like an idiot. I never have had much self-control at sporting events; I pick a team to cheer for, and it makes me competitive as fuck. This bloodlust is new, but with all the shit I've been through tonight, I need the outlet. I don't know what to think or who to believe because Eman's story *is* plausible. And if he never actually left me, that takes all the innocence out of what happened.

I don't want to regret the time I've had with Sanden. There's this deep need to *want* to trust him, to want him to be the incredible man he's been since the wedding. The same guy he was before Eman. I couldn't handle it if that was all an act like Eman says it is, and even though there were no messages in his phone, he was quick to come up with the changed number explanation. How do I know Eman didn't give him the heads-up and Sanden deleted the evidence, just in case? Though, that wouldn't make sense if Eman's trying to cover his own ass.

Urg, I need to scream at someone again because everything is so ... jumbled.

Unsure.

It's hard to keep in my seat, but I force my ass to stay put. The entire time, I'm buzzing with agitation.

"Yes." Gabe jumps to his feet, both fists high, as the lights flash with a Seattle goal. "Great assist, babe. Keep it up!"

I mutter, "He knows Aleks can't hear him, right?"

"It's cute he pretends he doesn't know hockey." Sanden's eyes shine with amusement at the sight of his best friend cheering.

Aleks skates over to us, and he and Gabe both high-five the glass.

And I stare.

Struck with the overwhelming urge to cry.

Why a stupid high five does it, I'm not sure, but something about Aleks and Gabe being so publicly dorky makes me ache for that.

I don't want to be the couple who barely holds hands in public, who goes to fancy restaurants to take our photos there, whose only time to be affectionate is locked away in our own apartment.

"Hey." Sanden's elbow bumps mine, and when I look over, he holds out his soda cup.

"What's that for?"

"Sugar. You've gone quiet, and there are still some guys out there not bleeding yet. You've got work to do. You can't burn out on me now."

Even though I'm not thirsty, I take his drink. I'm not going to go back to screaming again now they've made me self-conscious about it, but the offer warms me anyway.

So Sanden takes matters into his own hands.

"Smash him into the boards! Take out his skates!" He turns to me, eyebrows raised.

When all I do is stare pointedly at him, he turns his sights on Gabe.

"You gonna make me do this alone?"

Gabe sighs. "You just want Remy to stand up again so you can check out his ass."

I snort into the drink.

Gabe reluctantly stands and yells, "Hit him with the chair!"

Sanden shoves him. "Dude, wrong sport. You're a disgrace to the Crosby name."

"Ah ... knock out his teeth?"

"Now you're getting it."

Then Gabe and Sanden spend the rest of the game shouting obscenities at any Montreal player who skates past. The best part is no one throws them shitty looks, no one tells them to shut up or that they're causing a scene.

And so I take Gabe's advice and enjoy the view instead. Not the view on the ice. The view of Sanden's juicy, round ass.

I might not know what the hell I'm doing after tonight, but for now, I let myself be in the moment. Checking out a hot man, while he's being a dork with his equally dorky friend.

It's worlds apart from what I'm used to. I love it.

"Last chance," Sanden says, holding his hand out to me. It's close to the end of the game, and if I want to scream myself stupid, this is my last moment.

Fuck it.

I jump up, and the three of us spend the last few minutes yelling ... I don't even know what. I'm not even angry anymore, just grinning like an idiot as I try to turn off that voice telling me to stop.

I've missed this.

By the time we pull up back out the front of Sanden's place and he parks his car, the warmth dims as the nightmare tries to creep back in.

"So that was a side of you I haven't seen before," Sanden says, turning to look at me over the center console.

"Yeah, I ... sorry."

"Stop saying sorry. I liked it."

"You did?"

"Yeah." He rubs his stubble. "Not as much as I like naked Remy, and funny Remy, and showing off Remy, but verbally abusive hockey fan Remy was an experience."

I unclip my seat belt but don't make a move to get out of the car. I shift around in my seat to see him better, and Sanden mirrors me.

"I know you said not to say it anymore, but I am. Sorry. I wish I could believe you and move on from everything—"

"We've been over this. Take your time. Don't rush it. I'm not going to earn your trust by ordering you to do it."

Obviously, he's right, but it doesn't make me any less frustrated with myself. It's getting to a point where the more I think back over my relationship with Eman, I can't tell what was real and what wasn't. What was the truth, and what did I blow out of proportion?

"I just wish I wasn't so stupid, you know?"

"What?" Sanden scowls. "How the hell are you stupid?"

"I keep being sucked into it. Whatever game Eman's playing. My brain feels like a mess, and honestly? If it came out that you were fucking with me ..." I suck in a determined breath. "I think it would mess me up worse than what Eman did."

"Why?"

"Because I so badly want to trust you."

His smile lights up his eyes. "We can work with that."

"We can?"

"Yep. Starting with one thing. I don't care if you believe

anything I've ever told you before this moment, but this one is a nonnegotiable."

"What is it?" I ask, not sure I want to know.

"You're not stupid. You're an amazing EMT. You save lives. You have a big heart. You've been through some things, sure, but it's not going to beat you because you're incredible, Remy. You're so many things, but stupid isn't one of them, sweetheart."

I'm already feeling high from the compliments, but then he hits me with that one word, and a flush sweeps through me.

I make a weird *meep* sound, and Sanden's eyes sharpen.

"What was that?"

"What was what?"

"Your chipmunk impression."

I cover my face with both hands. "That word."

"What word? What are you talking about?"

"Sweetheart. You said it when ... and just now ..."

"Ohh ..."

He moves, and when I peel my fingers back from my eyes, Sanden is leaning over the center console, smug face close to mine. "You like that word, huh?"

"It's never occurred to me until this moment. Then you said it. And I—"

"Got turned on?"

"Shut up."

"You liked it, then?" His voice drops. "When I told you to spread your pretty legs, sweetheart?"

Another wave of heat hits me, and my dick thickens. I

slap my hands over his mouth. "No. You're not allowed to use it against me."

"Mhut it's so fun."

I let him go.

"Come on!" he says. "How am I supposed to have that knowledge and not use it?"

"Because you're a good boy."

"When it comes to you, I'm beginning to think I'm really, really not."

"Stop it."

A short, breathy laugh. "Stop what? You're moving toward me."

And now he's pointed it out, I am, in fact, arching his way.

"Argh." I pull away and throw open my door, knowing if I don't put distance between us, I won't be listening to my gut anymore. I'll be listening to my cock.

I hear the other door close, but I don't turn around as I charge toward my own car I left here before the game.

"Sleep well, sweetheart."

I turn to face him as I walk backward. "For the record? I've officially never hated you more."

Eighteen

SANDEN

I don't hear from Remy after the game, and I can't blame him. Am I hurt that he doesn't completely trust me? Maybe a little. But there's the bigger part of me that knows what Eman's done. He's pulling the sympathy card and turning everything back around on Remy, making Remy think everything that went wrong with them was his own fault.

He's done it since we were kids, and Remy's had three years of Eman manipulating his way of thinking. It's a real form of emotional abuse, and I wish I'd picked up on it earlier so I could've warned Remy, but even if I had said something, Remy would've assumed I was trying to ruin their relationship to get to Eman because, as it turns out, Eman thinks the sun shines out his ass. I never wanted him.

It's only ever been Remy.

And I know if I want to keep him, I have to let him work all this out on his own. I don't want to be part of the problem, but I can't be his solution either. That would make me as manipulative as Eman.

Remy needs to get there in his own time, and I'm not going to push him to do anything he doesn't want to.

I am, however, going to use every moment we have together to my advantage by showing him he's worthy, he's not stupid, and if he wants to yell and scream at some hockey players, I'm going to yell and scream at some hockey players alongside him because he should get to do what he wants. Live his life the way he chooses.

I'll use all of my power to make him see how amazing he is. But more than that, I want him to remember what it's like to have fun without being self-conscious.

Eman is all about image. It's why he was excited to learn that I have NHL friends through Gabe and why he invited them to his wedding. He wants to be the best of the best, and something as embarrassing as Remy's yelling at the hockey game would've brought the wrong kind of attention.

Life is too fucking serious to live like that.

Which is why, when both of our stations are asked to have sign-ups to the fall festival next week, I put down for Gabe and me to attend. Remy does it every year, and I used to before he started dating Eman. It's a whole lot of fun, and I plan to make it extra fun this year. We have a rivalry to uphold and a Remy to get out of his head.

As the festival approaches, I get more and more excited

about spending the day messing around, teaching people about fire safety, especially going into the fall, where they'll be firing up their old space heaters and electric blankets from last year. That might not sound as fun as the games and stuff we'll be playing, but it's important. The number of houses we've seen go up because of faulty old equipment is by far the most callouts we get in the colder months.

I jump in our second truck like an excitable puppy while Gabe glares at me.

"I can't believe you put my name down too. It's our day off, man."

"Eh, think of the overtime. Plus, all the single moms can't resist your dimples, and the more attention we get, the better." I reach over and poke him in the cheek. "And I need your muscles. We have games to win and rivalries to uphold."

"To impress your booooooyfriend?" Gabe taunts.

I grunt. "Definitely not my boyfriend."

"Still haven't heard from him?"

"Nope, but I respect and understand that it's not our time. Forcing something now simply because we acknowledge our attraction to each other isn't going to work, so I need to be patient."

Gabe laughs and slaps me on my shoulder as I pull out of the station and onto the road. "How's patience working out for you?"

"Hey, I went three years without Remy sleeping with me. A few more months won't kill me. Might kill my right hand though." I pretend to shake it out.

It is hard, but I'm willing to be patient for him. Wait for

him. If there ever comes a time where he says he can't trust me enough to be with me, I'll find a way to accept it.

"How does it feel to be back behind the wheel?" Gabe asks.

"Like coming home." I miss driving, but I was happy to give it up when I became lieutenant. Better pay, more recognition. One of the other shifts' DEs is in the back, but I told him I was taking over today. He was happy to let me have it.

When we get closer to Seattle Center, I turn on the siren as we reach Memorial Stadium to gain everyone's attention, and we're let through the crowd to get to our post on the field where Station 21 is already set up.

"Tell me it would be wrong to reverse this rig right into their table and knock it over." I'm joking. Mostly.

As if reading my mind or having the hearing of a bat, Remy appears in front of us, shaking his head but trying to suppress a smile. Damn, he's so gorgeous.

"Well, now you can't do it and make it look like an accident," Gabe points out.

"Fine." I park the truck expertly next to theirs, and we all jump out.

Part of the games is showing the public what our training regime is like, so there's a structure in the middle where we'll have ladder races to the top, and at the end, we'll burn it down in a controlled fire and then put it out.

Remy approaches me. "I didn't realize you'd be here this year."

"I don't have a reason to stay away this year." I wink at him and head over to his lieutenant to shake his hand and go through the plan for today.

Gabe and Remy are talking in my line of sight, so I barely take in the plan for today. Remy's too distracting. He looks happy. Relaxed. Maybe the most I've seen him in years.

It's one of those things I didn't notice completely until the whole wedding drama—just how much Remy had lost or hidden himself while he was with Eman.

Maybe if I'd spent more time with him over the last three years, I would've seen this side of him, but of the times I did hang out with Eman and Remy, this laid-back energy was missing.

"Did you hear me, Sanden?"

I snap out of it. "Yes? I definitely heard that thing. That you said. I am all for it."

"Good. Thanks for volunteering yourself and Gabe Crosby to drum up the crowds throughout the festival by wearing nothing under your jacket and flashing some skin. Show up them calendar boys from Australia."

"Umm, what?"

"I knew you weren't listening, but seriously, do anything that will bring the attention."

"I'll go, but my shirt stays on. And I'm taking one of yours with me." I glance back at Remy, who's still talking animatedly with Gabe. "Remy."

"All right, take him. But don't think for one second you can steal him for tug-of-war later. He's ours. He might look small, but he has this unnatural upper-body strength."

"Damn. You foiled my plan," I deadpan. "I'll make sure to get him back to you in one piece. You guys are gonna need the help."

"Them's fighting words."

"Bring it on." I take a bunch of brochures to hand out to people, a basic pamphlet on fire safety in the home, and then head for Remy. "You're stuck with me."

Remy doesn't look at me though. He glances at Gabe.

"I'm always stuck with you," Gabe complains.

"Not you. Remy. Your lieutenant ordered it." Definitely wasn't orchestrated by me.

"What did I do to piss him off?" Remy asks.

I laugh. "Ouch. I'm a punishment now?"

"You're the enemy today, my friend. We're going to kick your ass."

"Mmhmm. Sure. Keep thinking that, little one." I pat his head.

"Want to get a head start on our wagers for this year?"

"What'd you have in mind?"

He steps closer to me. "Person who gets the most civilians for their tug-of-war team wins." His eyes glimmer, and I can't help but smile at how fucking happy he looks.

Gabe clears his throat. "This just entered some weird kind of foreplay, and it's making me uncomfortable that I find it hot, so I'm gonna—" He backs away, but Remy and I don't take our eyes off each other.

"You're on," I say. "What will I win?"

"Other than bragging rights?"

I nod.

"If you win, I'll ..." He taps his chin.

I want to say, "*Go on a date with me,*" but I also don't want to get him to date me by trickery.

"Do a song and dance in front of everyone saying your station is the best."

"I will never, ever do that."

"That's okay. If *I* win, you ... have to wash Station 21's entire fleet. From ladder to tire."

"I'd rather do the song and dance." Actually, no, I wouldn't. I hate washing the trucks, but I would never say they're the better station. Even if theirs is newer than ours. Shinier. Their lieutenant and captain get their own sleeping quarters. No, I'm too stubborn to admit defeat. "You're on." I glance back at their rig. "Yours could do with a good wash. Whoever's doing it now is terrible at it."

Remy shoves past me, his shoulder bumping mine. "You're an asshole."

"An asshole who's gonna win," I say under my breath.

Nineteen

REMY

We walk through the crowd, handing out flyers and trying to rope—heh—people into our team tug-of-war. While I go for the biggest people I can find, Sanden breaks away from me and approaches a group of kids who are around ten or so.

He looks them over. "Any of you strong enough for a game of tug-of-war?"

Hands immediately shoot into the air.

"Yeah, I can do it," one of the kids says.

Sanden narrows his eyes the kid's way. "Oh, yeah? Prove it."

The kid pushes his sleeve up to his shoulder and flexes his scrawny arm.

"Impressive. Tell you what: you beat me in an arm wrestle, and you're on Station 40's team."

"Deal."

Sanden lowers himself onto the ground and then props his elbow up on the grass. "Scared?" he taunts.

"No way."

The kid mirrors him and clasps hands, and my brochure distribution is long forgotten as I walk over. Sanden's long body stretched out like that is a tempting sight, but I'm determined to keep things professional today.

Mostly.

Okay, that's a total lie. All I've wanted to do since seeing him is take him home and ride him, but until I work out the issues in my head, it's not fair to drag him into my drama. I have to sort myself out and separate everything Eman's ever told me about Sanden from what I've experienced myself.

And what I'm experiencing right now ... ooops, there goes my heart. Sanden's smack-talking the kids, challenging them to best of three, where he kicks their asses in the first round, then pretends his arm is tired. By the time he stands up again, shaking out his arm and calling the kids cheaters, they all have the biggest grins on their faces.

"That tent over there in twenty minutes," Sanden says. "Let your parents know you have a very important rivalry to uphold."

They race off, and Sanden turns to me, looking smug as hell.

"Kids. How do you expect to win with kids?"

"Two-pronged attack. First, we agreed that whoever had

the *most* civilians wins our bet—not whoever wins the tug-of-war. Second, get the kids there, and we can teach them all about fire safety."

"It's kind of adorable how excited you are about that."

Sanden's bouncing on his feet as we start walking again. "Obviously. You've gotta get them young. Teach them the steps for protecting their properties and looking out for hazards. You'd be surprised how much those little brains absorb. Plus, letting them use the hose and sit in the trucks is always a hit. I love our open days. Kids are pure, you know."

"Tell that to their parents." From everything the guys at the station have said, kids are Satan's army. Adorable, sure. But you've got to watch them. "You like kids?"

"Yup."

I glance at him from the corner of my eye. "I wouldn't have picked that."

"Really?"

"You seem ... independent. Is that the right word? Like someone who ... I don't know what I'm trying to say."

He pulls me to a stop and turns to me, massive grin in place. "What are you trying to say?"

I laugh and squeeze my eyes closed so I don't have to see his reaction as I say, "You're always fun and happy and go with the flow. You go on a honeymoon just because. I see parents as stressy and high-strung, and that's not ... *you*."

When I finally peel my eyes open again, I'm blown away by the softness that stares back at me.

"First, there was nothing 'just because' about me going to Hawaii. Maybe it was selfish, but I *wanted* to be there for you. I never thought it would lead to the things it did, but I don't regret it. Second, parents are only stressy and high-strung because they know they're constantly being judged. I don't care if people judge me. Sure, I have fun in life, but the way I see it, having kids gives you more people to have fun with."

I chuckle and pull him back into the crowd. "It doesn't work like that."

"You don't want kids?"

"No, I do, but I'm realistic about it." I throw him a smirk. "Yours are going to eat you alive."

"Eh. Maybe I'll be the pushover parent." He throws me a wink. "You can be the one fighting over homework and handing out the groundings."

It's such a stupid thing to joke about, but I push down my smile and force a serious expression. "You'd never survive them without me."

We finish our lap of the festival, and after seeing how outgoing and friendly Sanden is with everyone, guilt creeps over me for being the reason he stayed away from this event for the past few years. He obviously enjoys this, thrives on it apparently, and holding himself back because of me?

Either Eman was right in that Sanden hated me because he was jealous or ... Sanden was telling the truth, and his feelings for me are bigger than he's letting on. More than the simple crush he told me about.

The little *ouch* that pains my chest makes me want to pull him into a hug, but I hold off. First, it'd be wildly inappropriate when we're both here working, but second, if my hunch is right and Sanden really has felt something deeper for me all these years, I owe it to him to be sure.

We separate when we get to our station tents, but I can't help glancing back over his way to where he's talking to his chief, big hands gesturing and that crooked smile taking over his face.

When I think of Sanden, I think of happiness.

When I think of Eman, my shoulders immediately tense.

The two reactions are a clear sign of which direction my gut is leaning, but the doubts and voice in my head are loud.

Be his little slut.

He'll be done with you in a few weeks.

It never occurred to me over the years the number of sly comments Eman let slip about Sanden.

Great guy, but not the type you'd tell your secrets to.

Be careful with Sanden—he's got a temper.

He likes to drink and gets handsy. I don't trust him around you.

Memory after memory hits me. If Eman thought Sanden was into him, why would he have cared if Sanden was around *me*? I mean, Eman knew how I originally felt about Sanden, so I'd always assumed it was me he didn't trust and worked harder to separate myself from Sanden to prove I was trustworthy ... Which I shouldn't have to do with a partner in the first place. I shouldn't have to prove I'm trustworthy when I've done nothing to make him think otherwise.

But did Eman know how *Sanden* felt?

Despite everything Sanden has said about Eman since we broke up, I can't think of a single time he talked down about him before that. I'd always viewed Sanden as being a dick when he blew me off. He'd be short and professional, but never anything more than that, and maybe I'd felt the change in him more because of how flirty he used to be before Eman.

He was never rude.

He was never a jerk.

He just wasn't *him* around me.

Because he had feelings for me that must have gone deep if he had to avoid me for three years.

And *I'm* the one who completely misinterpreted why.

Oh, look. Once again, Remy's the asshole.

I leave my tent to cross over to his. He's turned away from his chief, so without a word, I grab his arm and drag him around behind one of the trucks.

"Not that I don't love seeing this forceful side of you, but is there a reason you're manhandling me?"

"Yes." I plant my hands on my hips. "I was the reason you stayed away from these things."

"Well, I mean—"

"And you were never *actually* an asshole to me, were you?"

Sanden frowns. "I wasn't exactly friendly, but I sure hope I wasn't an *asshole.*"

I lick my lips and step closer. "You had a crush on me when we first met."

"Yeah ..."

"And you want something between us now ..."

"I've made that clear, but—"

"It didn't stop, did it?"

Sanden's jaw tightens. "What are you—"

"Have you had feelings for me this *whole time*?"

He doesn't even need to answer. His eyes fill with ... regret? Panic? I don't want to know exactly what's going through his head because mine is already full.

"I'm such an idiot."

Sanden swears and closes the distance between us, both hands cupping my neck. "What have I told you about saying that?"

"Yeah, but how do I not when I keep being *this* stupid? Did Eman know?"

"I ..." Sanden sighs. "Yeah. Pretty sure."

Fury races through me. The last three years, he's been feeding me shit about Sanden and using the way Sanden brushed me off to support his words when really, all Sanden was doing was trying to protect himself and respect our relationship.

Was the entire last three years of my life a complete fucking lie?

"I'm going to kill him."

"Or—and I could be completely out of line here—you cut him out completely. He wants to control you, and he tried at the dinner, so it must be killing him that he failed. I'm not saying to pick me or anything like that, just don't pick him. Pick *yourself*."

"Myself?" I manage a shaky smile. "Kinda forget what that's like."

"Then I'll help you relearn it. No ulterior motives. I

want you to be happy, and you were this morning. Right up until now, until he got in your head again."

I reluctantly agree. "Actually, it was right up until I realized that you'd been hurting. Because of me."

"Oh, don't make me out to be some pathetic pining loser—wait. Yeah, that sums me up. But you know what else?"

"What?"

"It's not *your* fault. I didn't tell you how I felt, and Eman's gotten good at what he does. Stop trying to blame yourself for everything."

"But that's something I actually *am* good at."

Sanden laughs. "You know what I'm good at? Tug-of-war." He lifts his arm and kisses his bicep. "So why don't we start with me kicking your ass and go from there?"

I'm not sure I'm ready to let go of villainizing him for three whole years when Sanden might be the best person I know, but I go with him. This is a step in the right direction, and maybe I don't need to be sure of everything all at once. Maybe I can just be sure that in this moment, I want to have fun with Sanden.

So I will.

Even with the yucky feelings struggling to hold on to me, I force myself to ignore them.

When we reach the tents again, ours is already full of the adults I recruited, but Sanden's side looks suspiciously empty. There are three kids out of the ten he recruited, and when a perplexed look crosses his face, it takes everything in me not to cackle.

"*This* is your idea of a team?" his chief asks, shaking his head.

"There were more ..." Sanden sounds adorably confused.

"Maybe their parents weren't so eager to let them follow the stranger."

He huffs. "I'm in uniform! Who would have thought that kids could be this flakey?"

"Devils, I told you. Have fun cleaning those trucks." I slap him on the ass as I pass him. "Lucky you're good at tug-of-war."

Twenty

SANDEN

As much as I hate—no, *loathe*—cleaning the rigs, coming to Station 21 during a day shift when I have an overnighter tonight is still better than admitting Remy's firehouse is better than ours.

Of course, with Remy having switched out for morning starts, I'm sure he only has a tiny bit to do with why I'm happy I lost. I couldn't ask for a date in the bet, but at least this way, I get to spend time with him.

He and his work buddies are watching me, arms folded, with amusement on their faces.

"Why do I feel like you all want me to strip off while I do this? You're looking at me with this look of lust in your eyes, and I'm sorry to tell you, none of you are my type."

Remy's face falls but slowly, like he thinks that's subtle.

"Actually, I take that back. Nearly all of you aren't my type." I wink at Remy. "Finnigan is superhot."

Finnigan gives me the finger and walks away while Remy laughs.

The small group disperses, but Remy steps toward me. "I can't believe how long it's taking you to wash one truck. You've still got another one to go, plus my ambulance."

"I'm not slow. I'm thorough. Can't be tearing down the street in a rig that's covered in dirt and grime. How unprofessional would that be?"

"Mmhmm."

"It has nothing to do with getting to hang out with you, so I'm dragging it out. Not at all."

Remy picks up one of the spare cloths. "If you wanted to spend time with me, you could've asked. Now you're guilting me into helping you, and this all could've been avoided if you had asked me out. You're making me do my job, Sanden, and I'm not happy."

I've been dying to ask him out for years, but he's the one who's going to have to do it. "You know what I love about being gay?"

"Aside from all the dicks?"

"Aside from that. It's that there are no set roles. No who should ask out who. There's the whole societal thing of it being emasculating to have a woman do the asking and all that other heteronormative bullshit that makes me shake my head." I stop wiping down the truck and cross to where he's working on the opposite corner. "If I knew you were ready for me to ask you out, I'd do it in a heartbeat, but as far as I know, you're still conflicted. Don't know who or what to trust. So I'm afraid the asking is going to be on you. And I will wait forever if I have to because the main thing you need is no pressure from me."

"Go out with me," Remy blurts. "Please, fuck, I need to go out with you."

"Ah. That was my other tactic. Make you want me until you're so desperate to go out with me. I have you right where I want you." I try for a deep, wicked laugh, but it comes out more like the Count from Sesame Street. "Insert better-sounding evil laugh here."

He turns toward me. "I'm serious. The more I think about what Eman has told me about you, the more I realize you're not that guy, and if you are, you're most likely a sociopath who can fake being this carefree, amazing person. The only way I'm going to work out who to believe is to see where dating you can lead. And I want to. Date you."

"Good. Because I want to date you too. When can we make this date happen? We're on opposite shifts at the moment."

"The next day off we have together?"

"So not until next week? You've made me wait three years for our first official date, and now that's happening, I have to wait another seven days?" I stomp my foot like a tantruming toddler.

"Already the worst date ever."

"We should call it all off now. Not waste our time."

"Agreed. Maybe I should call off helping you too." Remy drops the cloth and turns on his heel, walking away with a whistle.

"I'm getting that date!" I call after him.

"Correction. You were getting that date. Now, I'm not so sure."

In reality, not being able to rush into anything is a blessing, not a curse, but even so, I'm impatient as fuck.

🔥 🔥 🔥

Our first day off together isn't for another five days, and I've spent the last two planning down to the minute of where I'm going to take Remy and what we're going to do. Gabe suggested I rent out the entire revolving restaurant on top of the Space Needle because his boyfriend did that for him once, and he said it was the best date he ever had. But then when I googled how to do that, he burst out laughing because he was merely showing off how much money Aleks has.

So that was out. Though, we could still have dinner there without the showboating of having no one else in the room. I want to plan more than dinner though. I want so many activities and places to go that we spend all night with each other, having fun and letting go.

Gabe said it sounds like I want to hold the man captive, and he's not wrong. In the totally consensual, if he wants to be held captive way, that is.

I have so many plans I don't think I'll be able to fit them all into one date, but that's okay because if I get my way, Remy and I will have many dates to do everything I want. From a day trip to Victoria's Butchart Gardens to hiking Snoqualmie Falls, I have all the best dates ready to pull out of my pocket and knock Remy Porter off his feet.

And just as I think that, the fucker shows me up.

I'm in the dining room at the station, which overlooks the truck bays, and in walks Remy, looking amazing in his civilian clothes and styled hair. He has a picnic basket in his hand.

I stand, leaning over the railing as I look down at him.

"I couldn't wait until next week." He holds up the basket.

Gabe and the others wolf whistle behind me, but I ignore them.

"If you all need me, I'll be on the roof."

More catcalls echo around the space.

I'll never live this down with them, but I also don't want to.

I nod for Remy to join me upstairs before leading him to the roof access.

"I guess this is one good thing about having the older building. When you don't have pointy architecture to admire, you get lawn chairs and a view of ..." He walks to the edge of the building. "The gas station across the street. I'm so jealous."

"Hey, if I organized a picnic at your station, we'd have to sit at the dining table and share. Don't be dissing our chance for a private date."

Remy turns to me and smiles. It still takes my fucking breath away. For a long time there, he'd stopped smiling, even before the wedding fiasco. I'm so happy to see it back on his pretty face.

"Maybe I wanted everyone to join us? I've been in a relationship for three years, and group sex sounds fun."

The growl rumbling in my chest is involuntary, I swear. "Who are you wanting to bang? Cap?"

"Hell yes. He's sexy."

I shudder because he so is not.

"You're picturing us having sex, aren't you?"

"Why are you being so mean on our date?" I pout.

Remy steps closer to me, glancing up through his thick lashes. "Because you're so fun to mess with."

"Is that what we're calling making me want to bleach my brain?"

Remy laughs. "Eh, that won't affect your intellect much."

"Ooh, you're asking for it." But honestly, I love this side of him. Playful. Happy.

"I hope so. I have plans for us."

"As much as I'd love to get my dick out right here, I'm on shift, and that tone in your voice is making me hard, so you should stop that."

That only makes him smile wider.

I sigh. "You're going to torture me this whole date, aren't you?"

"What? Firefighters can still put out fires with a hard-on."

"I officially don't like you anymore."

He pats my chest. "Wow. How could I question your intentions when you're such a bad liar?"

"Fine. I still like you. A lot. So much so I'm regretting

not thinking of this sooner." I wave to the picnic basket. "What's on the menu?"

Remy pulls out a picnic blanket and lays it down. "We have a very expensive meal for tonight, so I hope you have a sophisticated palate to savor the amazing flavors of ..."

"The suspense is killing me."

Remy pulls out the food.

"Dick's!"

"You might not want to yell that too loudly."

"How'd you know I love this disgusting food?"

"Only people with horrible taste hate Dick's."

"Agreed. Dick's are the best." I unwrap a burger and shove it in my mouth.

"Are we still talking about the food or actual dicks now?"

"Why can't it be both?"

He holds up his burger for me to cheers with him.

We eat in silence for a few minutes, and a calming energy passes through me. It's nice out here. It's not fucking raining for once, and the sound of traffic, the smell of gas, and the cool air are ... perfect.

I think about all the dates I'd been planning—extravagant dinners, pretty gardens, and waterfalls—and I realize I don't need any of that. Because whether we're wearing suits to expensive restaurants or eating cheap burgers and fries on a noisy rooftop, the main thing is we're together.

When Remy's done with his burger, he throws the wrapper back in the picnic basket. "I know I shouldn't bring him up on our date, and I need to stop talking about him completely—"

"You can stop talking about him when you're ready to stop talking about him."

"That's not really fair to you, but what I actually wanted to say is how great you are. If I'd turned up to his work with a picnic basket, he really would've expected champagne and caviar and all this other showy bullshit. Then he would've spent an hour taking photos to post online. How did it take me so long to see that he wasn't the right guy for me?"

"Because he knows how to be charming."

Remy's hazel eyes meet mine. "You're charming, but you're not an elitist snob."

"Ah, but you see, I'm one of a kind. The most amazing human there ever was. Selfless, heroic."

"Humble?"

"That too. Basically, I'm the perfect specimen of a man, and you're in so much trouble when it comes to me."

I expect him to laugh at my ridiculous, over-the-top claims because fuck knows there are so many more men out there who could make Remy happy, but he reaches over and squeezes my hand with the most genuine look on his face.

And when he murmurs, "I'm actually beginning to think that's the truest statement to ever statement," my heart damn near explodes. "I really am in trouble with you."

REMY

I hate my job. It's probably the first and only time I've had that thought and meant it, but every day I work is keeping me from Sanden. We're on opposite shifts, barely seeing each other, and if we don't get time together in this dating period, is a relationship really on the cards for us?

Like always, I shake away thoughts about the future. I promised myself here and now is what I'll focus on until I'm comfortable with my decision-making again, and right now, I'm *finally* getting ready for a date with Sanden.

Sure, the rooftop picnic was a date, and it was amazing, but it was a stolen pocket of time. Tonight's the kind of date that could lead places. I don't know if it will, but I'm prepared if it does. I've eaten right, manscaped, and cleaned every inch of me that I can reach. All it takes is a flash of Sanden eating me out to get my entire body on board with the sex plan, but my brain is still a twisted mess. So I'm not putting pressure on myself. I'm just going to see how the night goes.

It takes me approximately seventy-billion years to fix my hair and shave, and I can't remember the last time I was this fucking nervous. It's not helping with my "take it as it comes" approach where Sanden's involved, but I can't switch off. I'm going to hate myself if Eman turns out to be right about him, and as much as I want things to work out to prove Eman wrong, the louder, stronger side is more concerned with how I'd survive another betrayal.

It's soon. It's happening quickly. Where my relationship with Eman started out slow and reluctantly, he grew on me.

With Sanden, I feel like I'm clawing out of my skin to see him again. I don't feel like myself unless he's around.

He sends a text that he's in the parking lot like I told him to. This nervous excitement is so new and addictive I have to take a moment to check that I've got everything. Then I race to the door, throw it open, and—

"Shit." I stumble back before I crash headlong into Sanden.

He chuckles. "Now, I *could* be wrong, but someone seems excited to see me."

"And someone else couldn't wait in his car."

"I didn't want to prolong the moment you were in my presence again."

I have to bite my lip against my ridiculous smile and

remind myself that no, it's not appropriate to launch myself at him and kiss him. Maybe the next date? Still, I move closer as I step out into the hall and lock my door behind him.

"Such a gentleman," I tease. "Meeting me at my door like this."

"It was my insurance policy. To stop a million other men jumping out and sweeping you off your feet."

"Yes, people really are lining up for a man who was left at the altar."

"I'd believe it. It was your main selling point for me."

And even though I *know* he's joking, Eman's voice taunts that Sanden's playing with me. Using me. Confirming it.

But I've already decided to ignore that voice and hope it isn't true, so I shove it right back out again.

I push up onto my toes and brush a soft, lingering kiss on Sanden's cheek. "Play your cards right and maybe one day you can leave me at the altar too."

"Wow. You sure know the way to a man's heart."

I pull back, but as Sanden heads for the elevator at the end of the hall, the urge to be near him and touching him is too strong. I suck down a breath and link my arm through his.

"I like how cuddly you are," he says like he doesn't mean to.

Instead of answering, I squeeze his arm tighter. "Where are you taking me?"

"Well, I had grand plans for a romantic dinner, maybe a movie, hiring a hot tub boat, or making the trip out to

Victoria's Butchart Gardens, but then I realized something."

"What?"

"You're a cheap date."

That pulls a laugh from me, and I nudge him with my hip. "Mean."

"No, but seriously. Everything you've said makes me think you don't *want* to do things like that."

I think about that for a moment. "It's not that I don't like those kinds of things because I do. It's more that I don't want to do them for show. I'm not interested in broadcasting that I go on the best dates; I want to *experience* the best dates. If that's in a restaurant or the gardens, great. If it's on a smelly rooftop"—Sanden gasps—"that works too. I think ... for me, it's all about time. Having it and giving it. It's finite, you know? You can't buy more. If someone gives you theirs, that's important."

We step into the elevator, and Sanden pulls me around to stand in front of him. He leans against the wall, me between his legs, and runs a thumb over my cheek. "Not just a gorgeous face."

"I literally save lives, and you're only figuring that out now?"

He leans in, face brushing mine and lips by my ear. "Remember everything you said tonight."

"Should I be scared?"

"Not with me." He kisses my ear, and my gut lightens.

The elevator dings, and Sanden's large hand closes over mine as he leads me out into the foyer. The sky is dreary and gray, warning us that rain is coming later.

"Prepare to have your socks knocked off."

We climb into Sanden's car, and he drives down the block.

Then parks.

"What are you ..."

"Fancy restaurants aren't good enough for my Remy, so tonight, I'm going to take you on a tour of the very best—and possibly worst—takeout places downtown. We're going to order something off every menu and try it and then make a list of our favorites."

"*Every* place?"

"Every food truck, every cafe, every questionable-looking hole-in-the-wall establishment. Well, the ones rated over two stars."

.I watch him, unsure if I'm amused or concerned. "We're either going to spend tonight having sex or with salmonella poisoning. I've gotta say, I didn't think those were my options when I left home."

"Damn, if I'd known sex was a possibility, I would have lifted my standards to three stars."

"Not too late."

"Of course it is. We're committed now, Remy.

"Are we?"

"Yep. And then afterward, we're going to go back to my place, where I've got Netflix cued up with some '90s rom-coms."

"Really pulling out all the stops."

"Only the best for you."

And while I'm still skeptical about playing roulette

with our food—the last way I want to spend the date is locked in his bathroom—I go along.

We hold hands as we walk down the street, stopping at every place he has marked on his map and buying everything from tacos to Indian to some suspicious-looking pizza. He thinks it's hilarious to read shitty reviews after every place we go to, which only gives me two reasons to be careful about what I'm eating.

He eyes me as I nibble on some dry rice.

"I would have taken you for a bigger eater than this," he says.

I give him a *look.*

"What?"

"Think about it." I try not to laugh at his oblivious topness.

Sanden looks from the food to me to the food again. Then a smile breaks across his face. "You dirty boy. You want my dick."

My face heats as I try to shrug it off. "If you don't want to fuck me, say so."

"I didn't think it was on the table."

"Hey, if you keep feeding me all this, it won't be."

Sanden turns, picks up the trash can sitting by us, and swoops everything off the table and into it. "Suddenly, I'm not hungry anymore."

"Damn, now if only you could have done that, then picked me up and fucked me on the table."

Sanden groans. "You're killing me here."

"*Me?* You're the one who pulled that power move."

"Liked that, huh?"

"Literally everything you do turns me on at this point."

Sanden's grin softens at the edges. "You sure?"

I totally get why he's asking, and the fact he's hitting pause and checking in, that *makes* me sure. Because what I'm starting to learn about Sanden is that he puts me first. Always.

"Never been more sure of anything."

"I guess we're cutting this date short, then." He grabs my hand and tugs me up with him, just as the clouds overhead finally break and a raindrop hits me.

"Actually ... I think this date still has hours to go."

The look Sanden gives me almost knocks me off my feet. I'd swoon if it wouldn't hold us up from getting to his house because in the spirit of being sure, I can say with complete certainty no one has ever looked at me like that before.

Sanden takes off at a jog as the rain comes faster, but right as we reach his car, I tug him back to me. His rain-drenched shirt meets mine, and the heat coming off his torso warms me to my core. Rain drips from his hair, follows a path down his cheek. Those sweet blue eyes study my face, and everything about him is so. Damn. Happy.

Sincere.

"Speaking of '90s rom-coms," I say. "I've always wanted to do this."

"Do what?"

I press up onto my toes and kiss him.

Sanden's arms immediately circle my waist, crushing our bodies together as my tongue sweeps into his hot mouth. And the strangest moment passes over me as we make out on a street corner, rain coming down around us.

I feel *safe*.

His hold on me is protective and careful. Full of barely restrained want. I'm not as put together. My hands tangle in his wet hair, brain disconnected with reality as I let myself get lost in the moment where it's only me and Sanden and no one else exists.

He breaks away, panting, hard cock heavy against my thigh. "We need to stop."

"Why?"

"Because I'm about to strip you naked, and being arrested for indecent exposure isn't where I want our night to go. I hear conjugal visits aren't a thing in holding."

I swallow, kissing him again, quickly, briefly, because I don't want to be separated. I grip his shirt and ask, "Where do you want this night to go?"

"Same place you do. With me buried inside your ass."

My legs tremble. "My place is closer."

"It is, but the wait will be worth it."

"Why?"

"Because I want to fuck you in my bed so hard my sheets will smell like you for the rest of the week."

"Oh, shit."

Sanden smirks. "So your place or mine?"

"Yours. Definitely yours. But just saying, you'll be returning the favor in my bed. And soon."

Twenty-Two

SANDEN

R emy squirms in my passenger seat. Traffic is a fucking bitch because of the rain. You'd think people in Seattle would know how to drive with a little drizzle, but no. When the rain comes out, so does the incompetence.

"You know, this wouldn't have been an issue if you'd told me from the start what your plan for the end of the night was," I point out.

"What would you have planned for our date if you knew it was leading to sex? Actually, don't answer that." He squirms some more. "This car ride is already uncomfortable enough as it is."

I can't hide my smile because the moment is surreal. That I'm the one with Remy. Turning him on. Taking him out on a date. A few months ago, I'd convinced myself this wasn't ever going to be a possibility, and now it's here, I'm in a bit of disbelief.

I thought I'd never have the chance to make him happy—*anyone* happy. I always thought I didn't deserve to live a happy life when it's my fault my sister didn't get to have one at all. And maybe that guilt is still there, maybe I never asked Remy out because I believed I didn't deserve a happy ending, and just maybe, I'm letting us happen now because part of me knows he'll go back to Eman eventually. Or he'll get over Eman by using me as a rebound, and then he'll move on.

Because I deserve to suffer.

I've watched Remy with someone else for three years, and once he's done with me, I'll have to see it all again.

Even with those possibilities looming over my head like huge clouds of doubt, I'll still go through with this.

The brief moments of pleasure we've had between us have been just that: brief. Too brief.

I'm going to milk him for all he's got. Figuratively and literally. I want to draw out every wave of cum. Every ounce of pleasure. I want to take it from him and give it back.

Out of nowhere, Remy kicks his legs and flails around in his seat, sending up a frustrated sigh before yelling and pointing at the car in front of us. "Nice turn signal, fuckface."

Not going to lie, road rage Remy is adorable.

"I love how impatient you are for me."

"I'm not being impatient. The people in front obviously can't drive."

"What about the people in front of them?"

"Them either. I told you my place was closer."

I'm not laughing. I'm not. Out loud anyway.

By the time we make it through all the terrible drivers—every citizen of Washington State, according to Remy—I'm pulling up to my apartment block and hitting the clicker on my remote for my garage door.

My street is filled with apartment buildings, each with single-car and very narrow garages lining the road one after the other. The need for car spaces means it's a tight fit when I get my car inside, and then Remy, still being impatient, pushes open his door so fast that all I hear is the crunch of metal hitting the wall.

I wince.

"Oh, fuck," Remy whispers and then turns to me, eyes wide. "I'm sorry, I'm sorry. I'm so fucking sorry."

The very real panic in his eyes kind of scares me because it's just a car.

"Hey," I soothe and lean over to take his arm, but he flinches. "It's okay. It's only a dent."

"I'll pay for it."

"No, you won't. I want to keep it."

He narrows his eyes at me.

"Every time I see it, I'll remember that you were so excited for my cock that you broke my car."

His shoulders release some of the tension, and he couldn't look more relieved. I purse my lips, though, because this reaction only adds to the bigger picture of exactly what Remy has been through.

"Can I ask you a question?"

"Can you do it inside when we're both naked?"

"Hmm, how about we compromise? I'll ask inside before we get naked."

"Deal." This time, when he moves to get out of the car, he does it slowly, and when he closes the door, he bites his lip.

I join him on his side and check out the damage. "It's not even that bad. Can barely see it."

"I still want to pay to fix it."

"It's honestly okay." I put my hand on his shoulder, and this time, instead of pulling away, he leans into the touch.

"How can you be okay with this? I dented your *car*."

"It's only a car. It's not like you totaled it or thought it was thirsty, so put Coke in the engine. It doesn't affect the way it drives. It's only a dent."

Remy's lips part, but no sound comes out.

Before he can argue again, I open the door, grab a marker from the glove box, and draw a smiley face on the dent. "There. It's an improvement."

The wide-eyed, awed look Remy gives me makes my heart stutter.

"Come on. Let's go upstairs." I link my fingers with his, and we walk up the three flights to the top floor.

My apartment isn't much in terms of space, but my living room, dining area, and kitchen are open plan, so it doesn't feel like a shoe box.

Remy tries to drag me through to my bedroom, but I pull him back and take him to the couch.

"Oh, right. You wanted to ask me a question. Is this going to be like a whole sex preference thing? Kinks?"

I internally groan. "I wish. This is ... kinda more serious than that."

"I'll have you know, safe words are very serious."

"Remy ..."

His face falls, and he wriggles closer. "Shit. It really is serious."

"I'm not trying to be a dick here, and you can tell me if I'm way off base, but did Eman ever ..." I don't know how to word this without it sounding preachy or accusatory. "Hurt you?"

"When he left, you mean, or—"

"No. Physically."

He blinks at me. Then blinks some more before bursting into laughter. The reaction eases my mind, but I can't get over the nagging feeling that more was going on in his and Eman's relationship. The way he looked like I was going to flip out on him over the car, the apologizing profusely. That's not the only thing I've noticed either.

"Eman? Hit me? No fucking way. I wouldn't stand for that. I'd be out immediately. I wouldn't have agreed to marry him."

"That's good to know. I'm relieved."

"Wait, what made you even ask?"

"I'm being an overprotective jerk. Just ... some things you do make me think you're self-conscious or worried about the fallout of your actions. I thought you were scared of me back at the car with the dent."

Remy doesn't respond for a beat. "Is that all?"

"That, and the yelling at the hockey game, thinking we were going to be embarrassed by you. You have these moments, these amazing moments where your personality shines so fucking bright, but as if realizing you've done something wrong, you shrink back into yourself, and I didn't know if it was a you thing or a—"

"Holy crap."

"What?"

He wraps his arms around himself, staring at my blank TV. "I think you're right."

I frown. "Right about what?"

"Eman never hit me, but he *did* make me self-conscious about nearly everything. If I was too loud, he'd get mad at me for embarrassing him. If I broke something, he'd complain about how dumb I am. Call me an idiot for not taking better care of his stuff. For not thinking. Maybe those things sank in more than I'd realized, and now I'm ... now I don't even know who I am anymore."

"Emotional abuse is a real thing," I say softly. "I've seen the way he gaslights you. Manipulates your thoughts."

Remy looks so damn heartbroken. He buries his face in his hands. "How could I have not seen it before now? For three years, I let him treat me that way, and I thought it was, what? Love?" He slumps back against the couch, looking up at the ceiling.

"Should I have not said anything?"

"No, I'm glad you did because it opens my eyes that bit more."

"I wish ..."

His eyes meet mine. "Wish what?"

"I wish I hadn't worked so hard at pushing you both

away. Maybe if I'd seen that kind of manipulation going on, I could've pointed it out to you before the wedding."

Remy sits back up, slowly, and then he cups my face with one hand. "I guarantee there would've been nothing you could do. You have to remember that Eman was feeding me all these lies about you, and if you'd come to me before the wedding and said Eman was emotionally manipulating me, I would've assumed Eman was right. That you were in love with him and trying to ruin my happiness."

"I'm so disappointed in myself," I murmur.

"Why?"

"I promised I wouldn't be helpless again. That I wouldn't sit back and watch someone else suffer, and—"

His second hand holds my other cheek, and he forces my face up to meet his gaze. "You didn't know. Fuck, *I* didn't know."

"I still could've—"

Remy shakes his head. "No. You've already done so much for me in a short amount of time. The honeymoon, opening my eyes to how I'd been treated for so long, but the main takeaway I get from this is that you had the opportunity to look the other way. When it came down to a choice between sex or making sure I haven't been a victim of something, you made sure I was okay first. I ... I've never met someone like you. You make me feel things. Things I've never felt before."

"What kind of things?"

Remy leans in and kisses my cheek. "Warm."

"Clearly, you haven't been wearing enough layers." I lift my neck, where he works his lips down to my collarbone.

"Ignoring your snark. But you also make it easier to be myself." He kisses lower until he gets to my shirt. "I'm comfortable around you."

"So sexy. You make me feel like I'm an old pair of shoes."

He chuckles against me. "Are you going to let me compliment you at all? You compliment me all the time."

"Yeah, I never learned how to take those."

Remy stands and holds out his hand. "Then let me compliment you all night. While you fuck me."

"Geez, way to pressure a guy."

"Oh, I'm not going to compliment your bedroom skills. I'm just planning on throwing in random niceties here and there."

"This is the kink you needed a safe word for, isn't it?"

"No, and if you keep talking, I'm going to gag you."

"Okay, that's the kink you—"

Remy's hand slaps over my mouth. "No more talking."

He removes his hand, only to drag me through the apartment to my room.

"Take off your clothes," he orders, and I go to open my mouth, but he cocks his brow at me, and I think better of it.

Reaching back, I pull off my shirt and toss it to the side. My jeans and shoes and socks go next. Remy undresses too, and I can't tear my gaze away from him. His lean muscles, small waist, miles of bare skin on display.

"Fuck, I need you to kiss me," I say.

Remy smiles. "And I will. You wanna know why?

Because your mouth is very pretty. Your big, plump lips are hot."

"Is the weird complimenting thing starting already?"

"Yup." Remy slowly stalks toward me. "And this." He palms my junk over my underwear. "Is the hottest cock I've ever had the privilege of having in my mouth."

I think he's starting with the easy ones. Complimenting a man's dick? What's not to like about that?

"I want it in my mouth again." Remy drops to his knees and takes my boxer briefs down with him.

I'm so hard for him, but part of me is cautious. I don't want him to think that I manipulated him into this. "Remy. You need to be sure—"

His gaze flicks up to mine as he wraps his fingers around my hard length. "I am. Because with you, I know you have my best interests at heart. That's the type of man you are." He runs his tongue from my base all the way to my tip on the left side of my cock. "You're selfless." Now the right. "Caring." This time, he closes his mouth over the head and runs his tongue under the mushroom ridge.

I shudder from the sensation, and my legs buckle.

"You make me feel *safe*." He tries to take me in his mouth again, but nope, nope, nope. I can't. I grab him under his arm and yank him to his feet.

"Why are you taking my fun away?"

"Because if you keep doing that, I'm going to blow my load. And I want to be inside you when that happens."

Remy's face lights up, and fuck, I'd do anything to keep that happiness on display. He still has his underwear on, so I tug on the waistband.

"You take these off, and I'll get the supplies."

I move to my nightstand and pull out lube and a condom, and when I turn back around, Remy's up against my wall, arms crossed over his head, and his ass sticking out.

I accidentally drop the lube along with my jaw, and he laughs. Then the fucker wiggles his fine ass at me.

I'm like a moth to a flame. I pick up the lube from the floor and snap the cap open, dribbling it on my fingers as I close the distance between us. I cover his back with my front, my hard cock digging into his ass cheek while I trail my slippery fingers down his crack and press them against his hole.

With my free hand, I reach up and cover where his are above his head.

He turns, and I lean forward, resting my ear against the wall so we're nose to nose. I push a finger past his tight ring of muscle, and his ass opens around it.

His lips quirk. "Your blue eyes are amazingly bright. And blue."

"Now I think you're just stating facts. Have you run out of compliments already?"

My finger inches deeper, and I love how his eyes flutter shut.

"Nowhere near done with the compliments. Like, fuck, one finger isn't enough." Remy pushes back on my hand.

"Was that a compliment or a criticism?"

"Compliment. It means I want more of you." His eyes open again, and he pins with me with his hazel gaze. "All of you."

Physically, emotionally, he has it. Every part of me.

Twenty-Three

REMY

Sanden fucking Masters has no idea what he does to me. My neck and cheeks are flushed with heat as he slowly fucks his finger in and out. It's enough that I feel it, but it's a frustrating type of sensation. A tease of the amazing, promising things he has to come while being nowhere near enough to fill my need.

His second finger strokes my rim before pushing in with the first. I relax my muscles, arching my back more to take him easier. This moment, when I'm being stretched open, prepped, my hole spread to its limits, is one of the things I love most about sex. I've been doing this for long enough that if the guy I'm with knows what he's doing, it doesn't hurt at all.

And Sanden knows what he's doing.

He hasn't dropped eye contact, a softer version of his messy smile makes my body feel all fluttery, while his dark eyes stoke the need in my cock. He's so hot, but it's not only his features. It's the way all that goodness inside spills out of him that turns me to jelly.

"Gone quiet," he taunts.

"I'm fighting with myself over what to say next. I don't want to say the wrong thing and go too far."

"What do you mean?"

"Some of the things I think about you sound obsessive, even to me."

He leans in, the smell of his cologne making my head swim, and runs his tongue around the hinge of my jaw, all the way up to my ear. "I've obsessed over you for years, Remy. Never hold yourself back with me."

I tremble, a lusty laugh leaving me as he shoves both fingers forcefully inside me.

"Sometimes I look at you, overwhelmed by how good you are. By how I could ever believe the lies about you because deep down, you just ... you make me happy. Your energy, being around you, I crave it. More than I've ever craved anyone. I want to be near you, Sanden. Always near you. Close. And not even sexually, which, hey, I want that too. But I'm not used to that being the second thing I think about when it comes to a man I like."

"I guess we need to have more sex, then."

I laugh again, rocking back onto his fingers, and rub my nose over his. "Tell me you don't know what I mean. Tell me all you want is sex when you look at me."

His gaze pings between both of my eyes. "I ..."

"Do it."

Sanden's rasp is throaty and raw. "It hasn't been like that since we first met."

"See?" I tug his lip between my teeth. "Even if you'd lied, I wouldn't have believed you. But you can't, can you? Lie to me?"

"You've got me wrapped around your fingers."

I squeeze my hole. "Technically, I think I'm wrapped around yours."

"I need you wrapped around something else."

"I'm ready whenever you are."

Sanden's grip on my hands tightens, which sends ripples of pleasure right to my balls. The conversation we had on his couch really opened up a bunch of things I'll need to think about, but the main one was that I'd unknowingly given Eman control. He'd *taken* it, even. But here, with Sanden, I want him to take control. I want to give it to him. And I think that's the difference.

With Eman, I had no power.

With Sanden, even with him in control, if I needed him to stop, I don't doubt for a second that he would.

He pulls out his fingers and moves to stand behind me, then runs both hands down my arms, my sides, until they settle on my hips. A heavy exhale rushes from him. "I never ... never thought ..."

"What?"

"That I'd ever have you like this."

I spin in his hold, and Sanden immediately crowds me into the wall. The intensity in his stare, the way he's standing over me ... I reach for his hand not covered in lube and move it until it's settled over my throat. His eyes hold the barest hint of uncertainty, but I tilt my head back more, giving him access, and the next second, his fingers close around me, thumb pressing up under my jaw. Not enough to restrict my oxygen, but enough to hold me in place. My legs shake as Sanden forces a meaty thigh between them and closes his mouth over mine. The kiss is hot and deep, all tongue and teeth, and I can barely catch my breath. I don't want to. This light-headed, floaty feeling is unraveling every muscle in my body.

Sanden's fingers sneak back into my crease and play with my entrance, and I almost sob with want.

"Need you."

He grunts, releasing me and scrambling for the condom. He tears open the packet and rolls it down his length before grabbing the lube and coating himself with it. That perfect, swollen cock, all shiny and ready to go, has me gripping the base of my own. No way in hell am I going to be coming the second he's inside me.

Sanden grabs my hip and flips me back toward the wall. His teeth find my ear, and he growls, "I'm going to fuck you here, then when you're close, I'm going to fuck you over every inch of my bed. And you're not going to come until I've finished with you. Understand?"

"Yes. Now, grab my throat and say all that again," I whine.

Sanden moans, releasing my ear and dropping a soft kiss between my shoulder blades. "You ready for me?"

I shove my ass back toward him.

"I'll take that for a yes."

"Apparently, you're a magical mind reader too."

"No magic. Your body is telling me what it needs."

"Which is?"

His hand wraps around my throat as he presses the blunt head of his cock to my hole. "For me to fuck you until you beg."

Nrgh yes. That's exactly what I need. I tilt my hips back further as Sanden pushes inside. Inch by inch, he splits me open, makes my knees weak, and even with the stretch, my dick stays achingly hard.

To my complete surprise, he doesn't start out slow. His hips set a punishing pace, thrust after thrust, driving me into the wall. His hand stays around my throat while his other wraps around my chest, keeping me close enough every one of his grunts brushes my ear. I keep my forearms planted on the wall to stop from going face-first into it and to give myself leverage to push back into him.

Just like I'd predicted, he's going to ruin me. From his tight hold to his raspy praises to the way he brushes my prostate on every thrust, it doesn't take long to get me close. Achingly close.

But the second I reach for my cock, Sanden pulls away from me.

His chest heaves under his heavy breaths, and when I glance back over my shoulder, frustratingly empty, Sanden points to his bed.

"On your back, ass over the edge."

I smile at his bossiness and follow directions. Then I lift my legs, peel them apart, and reach between them to hold myself open. "Like this?"

He groans. "If you could be not sexy for, like, two seconds, that would really help me out here."

"Don't you want to see my hole?"

"See it. Finger it. Eat it. Fuck it. There are way too many things I want to do with your hole, and I hate that I can't do them all at once."

"Wow, way to sound like a quitter."

"Yeah?" A spark hits his eyes as he lines up his cock again. "We'll see who's begging to tap out by the end."

He slams back inside, my body swallowing him whole, and it's sheer relief to be filled again. Sanden holds my hips as he fucks me, and I keep my hands on my thighs, holding myself as open as I can for him. I'm not sure which is driving me the most wild. How it feels as he pounds into me, or the sight of him, sweat at his temples, arm muscles bulging, mouth slack, and eyes shrouded in pleasure.

I'll never get the image out of my head.

The way he feels as he owns me. Knowing he's wanted this for years only makes everything so much *more*, and the pressure building in my balls is almost too much.

I've leaked a puddle of precum onto my abs, and I watch as Sanden releases his hold on me with one hand and runs his fingers through the mess. Then he lifts it to his lips and sucks his fingers inside.

"Ah, shit." My body bows off the bed as I try to hold back my orgasm, try to back away from the incredible way he's making me feel.

Sanden abruptly pulls out again.

"I'm torn on whether I like you or hate you right now," I snarl.

He slaps my ass. "Turn over. Lie across the bed."

I scramble to do what I'm told, wanting this to be good, wanting him to see that I'm the best fuck he's ever and will ever have. I want to be worth it. I'd hate for him to walk away from sex tomorrow and regret all the years he's had feelings for me.

Not that I think he would. He agreed that this wasn't just sex to him, and it feels horrible to say when I was a hairsbreadth away from getting married, but I've never realized there was a distinction. Never believed there could be a line between romance and sex, and when the line shivers away like Sanden's doing to me, it's explosive.

Sanden presses me onto my front, then blankets me. Legs twisting with legs, abs to my back, one hand linking with mine and pinning it to the bed, while the other covers my throat again. Then he slides back into me.

"Fuck, you feel so good," he moans into my ear. "I want to fuck you on every surface of my room, but I don't think I'm going to hold out."

"Next time, then."

His hips snap forward relentlessly, pushing my cock into the sheets and creating a delicious kind of friction that I lean into. I thrust into the mattress, keeping pace with Sanden, reaching the dizzying levels of a high where my limbs go numb and my brain wipes.

But right before I can shoot, he pulls out *again*.

I almost fucking sob. "Sanden, please!"

"Not yet."

He's true to his word. He fucks me on his drawers, then his nightstand, up against the window, and on the floor.

Then he drops onto the bed, sits with his back against the headboard, and pats his thighs. He looks as wrecked as I feel.

My cock is swollen and desperate as I straddle his hips and sit in his lap. Sanden angles his cock at my hole as I lower myself until I'm completely impaled.

I rock back and forward, loving the slow, aching pleasure.

Sanden shudders.

"You good?"

He tugs me down into a filthy kiss. "It's time for you to come, and it's time for you to finish me off. Bounce on my cock, Remy. Let me watch you."

The challenge goes to my head. I hold the top of the headboard, stretching my body out to make my lean muscles more obvious, and then I move, pace gradually building until I'm sure he's not going to slip out and get hurt.

And finally, like this, on top, I can take what I need—which is hard and fast and as deep as he can reach. My thighs work overtime, strain under the pressure, and once I set my pace, I don't let up. His cock is pegging my prostate, sending tingles through my whole body, and the steady *whack* of my cock against my abs is only turning me on more.

Sanden's arms wrap around me, mouth closing over my neck and sucking. I tilt back, give him more access, and he runs open-mouthed kisses over my skin. *This* is what sex is supposed to be like. *This* is everything I never knew I was missing.

Someone being with me. Wholly. Completely. Like this, there isn't a single other person who matters in the world outside of us.

"I'm right there," he rasps, taking hold of my hips again and thrusting up into me. His moves are erratic, wild, and I clamp down around him as tight as I can. "Ahh, Remy," he cries, then slams inside me again and stills, burying himself deep inside.

I don't even have a second to imagine him not wearing a condom and flooding my hole with his cum because Sanden wraps his hand around me. He jerks me hard and fast, hand tangled in my hair, gaze locked on mine.

"Come for me, sweetheart. Cover me in it."

His low tone does it for me. The uncontrollable waves of pleasure finally take over as my cock twitches in his hold. One, two, three times I shoot. From his belly button to his chin. I tremble my way through it, wishing for it to last, to stay in this amazing fragment of a moment forever.

It's over way too soon.

When he finally pulls out of me, I'm completely boneless. Wrung out, sore, completely goddamn satisfied.

I bury my face into his neck, trying to resist the urge to smile. "Did that live up to your expectations?"

"Every single one of them. And then it created so many new fantasies I don't think I'm ever going to be able to let you out of my bed."

"We have all night. Why don't you tell me about them?" I card my fingers through his hair. "I want every sordid detail."

Twenty-Four

SANDEN

Nothing beats waking up sated and achy from an entire night of strenuous fucking. What's even better is when the other person is still there, in your arms, snoring his cute little head off. Eman was an idiot for letting Remy go, and I think he knows it now, considering the missed calls I've had from him, but since I've blocked him on social media, he can't touch me there. It makes it easier to forget about him and focus on this. Remy.

I kiss my way up his shoulder, spooning him from behind, and he pushes back against my morning wood.

I chuckle into his neck. "You can't be ready to go again."

"No, but you are."

"I can ignore it. I just want to hold you."

"You know what I was thinking?" Remy rolls onto his back and turns his head to face me. "That I'd love to be able to not have to fuck around with dealing with condoms every five minutes."

"Excuuuuse me. I lasted way longer than five minutes each time."

Remy laughs. "You know what I mean."

"I do, and I agree, but have you managed to get to the doctor yet?"

"I'm actually really nervous about going to get tested. Which is kinda bullshit because I don't buy into the stigma that STDs are dirty or shameful, but for me, if I do have something ..."

"It confirms he cheated."

"I don't think I'm ready to face that reality. I'm still in denial, and sometimes it's nice to live there."

I lean up on my elbow. "Want me to go with you? I'll get tested too. It's been a while for me as well." Even though I haven't actually been with anyone but him since my last test, so it's kinda moot, but if it makes him more at ease, I'll do it.

"That sounds like such a romantic date."

"It is if you think about it."

"Getting blood tests and dick swabs together could be considered romantic, I guess. At least someone will be touching our dicks. Even if it's not each other."

"But when we both get the all clear, think of how easy it

will be to flip over and go for round two and three and four without having to find condoms."

"I guess it also means that we're agreeing to be exclusive." Remy bites his lip.

"Exclusive doesn't have to mean serious. I know you're not ready for that. It's just agreeing that for the foreseeable future, we're only sleeping with each other until one of us decides it's not going to happen anymore."

I hope that moment never comes, but I'm leaving that in the hands of Remy. He's the one going through big changes, revelations, and having to grieve the toxic relationship he had with Eman.

It would be understandable for him to have trust issues after that kind of emotional manipulation. I'll have to keep telling myself to be patient, even if I want to jump in head-first and deal with the consequences later.

He's giving me everything he can right now.

I still find it hard to believe he'd find me end goals anyway. All this good doesn't happen for me. I'm not sure if that constant expectation for it to fall apart will ever go away.

"I appreciate you so much," he whispers. "You're so patient and caring and ... you're everything I'm not used to."

I brush his messy hair off his forehead with my hand. "And one day in the near future, you won't take those traits as something miraculous. It's basic respect, Remy. And you deserve that. No, you deserve even more than that."

Remy sighs. "You deserve someone who isn't so fucked-up."

"You say that like I'm not fucked-up."

He rolls to his side to face me and cups my cheek, his thumb running over my bottom lip. "We're a matching pair."

"I would say that's the most romantic thing anyone has ever said to me, but I fear that might mean I'm admitting a therapist would have a field day with us."

"You mean your fire department–appointed therapist doesn't already?"

Ugh. I hate the mandated therapy sessions after a large trauma scene in the field. I've learned all the right things to say to get me signed off and then push down my real feelings. If I get too invested in a job or am on the scene of a house fire ... anything that brings me back to being that helpless teenager, the floodgates open, and there's no pulling me back from that kind of despair.

"Sanden?" Remy cocks his head.

"Sorry. You just reminded me I need to schedule a session for an incident a few days ago."

"Oh, I get them out of the way as soon as I can. Get in, get it done."

"Smart. I have a problem with dealing with those situations on my own that by the time the deadline to get signed off comes up, I have to go back and relive it again for the shrink. So I often go through the emotions twice."

"It's not the most efficient way to do things." Remy smiles.

"Eh. I'm efficient in other things." I move on top of him, kissing him, grinding on him.

"So, so efficient ..."

Despite thinking he can't go another round, I manage to get another load out of him. Our cum mixes between us, and when we've come down from the high, he lets out a loud, long breath. "We need to go to the clinic. Like, today."

Yeah, we do. The idea of going bare with him, coming inside him, is more than I've ever dared to dream about.

"Let's shower and go."

🔥 🔥 🔥

Bloods, swabs, and a safe-sex talk later, we're leaving the clinic.

I nudge Remy. "How was it for you?"

"Amazing. Best date ever," he deadpans.

"Did the doctor you go to get handsy as well?"

Remy stops dead in his tracks. "What?"

I laugh. "I'm joking, but if I wasn't, would you march back in there and defend my honor? That might be adorable."

"Well, no, but I'd be calling whatever medical police they have."

"Medical police?"

"You know ... the medical board thingy. The people who make sure doctors are being good doctors."

"Should I be nervous that you're an EMT and can't remember what the Medical Commission is?"

He snaps his fingers. "That's the one. Sex makes me dumb. So really, this is your fault."

"I'll take that blame and wear it like a badge of honor. I could wear a sign: Sorry Remy can't hold a conversation, I just made him come."

"Aww, my momma would be so proud of me," he jokes, but then his face falls. "Shit. Uh, I mean. Sorry. I didn't mean to bring up my parentals."

"Why? Because mine are so crap? Actually, they're not really crap. They have every right to—"

Remy wraps his arms around my waist. "No, they don't. They have no right to cut you out of their lives. They left you, a teenager, to look after an entire house. They lost a child and abandoned the other. It makes no sense."

I hug him. "I appreciate you trying to make me feel better, but if I broke down every time someone mentioned their loving parents, I'd be in a permanent state of depression. As much as thinking about my parents can bring me down, I've accepted there are much better guardians out there. And you're lucky yours are amazing."

"So if I ever do something like that again, I shouldn't point it out and make it worse?"

I kiss the top of his head. "Good plan. What are we going to do for the next however long it's going to take to get our results?"

"Hmm, lunch, and then take me back to my place so I can get some fresh clothes?"

"I'm telling you now, if you're taking off your clothes to put on new ones, we're going to have to go buy more condoms because I won't be able to resist."

"Give my poor dick a break. I'll close myself in my bedroom and lock it."

"You might have to. You're too damn irresistible."

I swear he blushes, but I can't be sure because he kisses me hard, right out here on the street.

I break from him and slap his ass. "Let's get you fed and then fresh before I maul you right here next to my car."

"We could get the romantic trifecta, then. Morning sex, STD exam, arrested for indecent exposure."

"What can I say? I like giving my partners an adventure."

Now that we've got his apprehension over this morning done with, all I need to do until those results come in is distract him any way I can.

The thing is, even if his results come back negative for everything, that still doesn't mean Eman's not a cheater. And with everything I'm realizing about their relationship —how toxic it really was—the more I'm convinced he did cheat that night he didn't come home.

I'm not going to try to convince Remy of that though. Whatever will help him get through this rough patch, I'm gonna do.

After a relaxing, flirty lunch, we head for his apartment.

He has a carefree smile on his face, his shoulders aren't holding any of the past month's tension, and he looks like the Remy I first met three years ago.

I swear I'm staring more at him than the road at this moment, and while that's not safe, it's like I can't help it.

I do manage to park safely, and the second we're out of the car, I hold his hand all the way up to his apartment.

Our eyes barely break from one another, which is probably why he's struggling with his keys.

"You know what, maybe I don't want to lock you out of my room after all," he says.

He leans up on the tips of his toes and kisses me as he turns the lock in the door.

I like this side of Remy.

No, I love it.

So much so it's hard to associate the Remy I've seen the last few years with the one dragging me inside his apartment and taunting me with promises of more sex than I've had in a really long time.

I haven't been waiting for him or anything because I was certain he was going to be married and out of reach forever, but ... just going through the motions of being Eman's groomsman, wedding planning, going to their engagement party, the whole thing maybe got to me more than it should have. I wasn't interested in anyone else, and I even lied to myself that once they were married, I'd get over it and get back out there. Date. Be with other people.

To go from that to what we have now, it's such a one-eighty that I don't know how to take it. I want to embrace it all, but I'm not blind to the issues we face.

My long history with Eman.

His toxicity.

Remy recovering and dealing with the trauma Eman left behind.

There are so many obstacles Remy and I will have to face, but it's still early. We're in this amazing bubble of affection and passion, and for now, that's enough for me.

That's all I'll focus on until the other shoe finally drops.

Him.

Me.

Sex.

Twenty-Five

REMY

It's so easy to get lost in Sanden. His easy smile, his caring nature, and not to forget the amazingly hot sex. But there's something heavy, weighted between us that I'm not sure about.

Ever since he pointed out Eman's past behaviors, more and more things keep popping up in my memories, and I realize there were a lot of red flags I missed.

When you read about or see abusive relationships, you think of beatings and hidden bruises. You don't think about the subtle things. A minor insult here, casually mentioning things like, "You're lucky to have someone like me who puts up with your embarrassing personality."

He always made me feel small in private, but publicly, he knew how to play the doting boyfriend and fiancé.

There's a lot to unpack when it comes to Eman's and my relationship, but while I'm with Sanden, it's easy to push it all down.

He makes me forget, he puts me in a good mood, and unlike Eman, Sanden knows how to be affectionate and the perfect gentleman behind closed doors as well as in public. Except when I ask him to not be gentlemanly at all. Then he's all about bringing me pleasure. And even that is different than it was with Eman. Eman and Sanden are both toppy with that dominant streak without going too far, but comparing the two—which I know I shouldn't do, but I can't help it—Eman was greedy. It was about his pleasure, and I was kind of an afterthought. He'd get me off, sure, but it's Sanden's priority. Eman made it feel like a duty or a chore to do afterward. Like I was part of the cleanup process. Which, come to think about it, was always on me too.

I know I need to stop thinking about him. I really do because it's not healthy to obsess and analyze every second of our relationship in the last three years, but I can't help it. My eyes are being opened more and more every day, and it's like I'm watching my life as a movie. I don't recognize the main character as myself.

There's a knock on my door, and when I open it, Sanden's there, fresh off his night shift and still in his uniform. Since becoming a wearer of that same getup, I've lost that fantasy of a man in uniform.

But this man?

He *is* the fantasy.

"Hi." He enters my apartment and drops a kiss on my

cheek, but it's not enough for me. I bring our lips together softly.

Nope. Still not enough.

My tongue pushes past his lips, and he finally loses his cool composure, turning us and pinning me against the wall while he dives in. A moan leaves him and then a happy sigh.

"As much as I'd love to continue this, I'm dead on my feet," he murmurs and pulls back.

"Rough night?"

"The worst."

I touch his arm gently, letting him know I'm here for him. "What happened?"

"We had one call out. *One.* And it was a false alarm."

I burst out laughing. "Oh no. Poor you!"

"You know how it is though. On those quiet nights, an hour feels like five, so if you think about it, I just did a shift that lasted over one hundred hours."

"You're dramatic when you're exhausted."

"Yep. Feed me coffee and give me cuddles."

"Okay, I'll let you be dramatic if that's the worst you'll ask of me."

"You got any plans today?"

"Other than waiting on you hand and foot until you're unexhausted, no."

"Pfft. After coffee, I'll be back to my golden retriever self."

I cock my head. "Hmm, nah. I see you as something like a German shepherd myself. Heroic. Protective."

"Either way. After I'm caffeinated, let's go do something. Something that'll have my adrenaline pumping that my shift failed to give me."

"What will it be today? Bungee jumping? Skydiving? All of the above?"

"What if we go out on Lake Washington? Hire a speed boat and do donuts in the water?"

I smile. "Why does that sound like hell and fun at the same time?"

"We don't have to go. What would you like to do?"

Even him asking is something I'm not used to. It's unsettling, and the need to keep him happy rises up swift and strong. "Let's do the boat thing."

"Okay, and then you can pick what we do next time we manage to get some time off at the same time."

"We really need to talk to our captains and get them to give us better rosters."

"I've heard bribery works."

"Bourbon and chocolates?"

"For yours, maybe. Cap is more like a cigars-and-tequila kind of guy."

I shake my head. "Because the smoke we inhale at work isn't enough for his lungs?"

"Doesn't bother me. The sooner he kicks the bucket, the quicker I'll make captain."

Of course he has his sights set on that. He'd be damn amazing at it too. "Aim high, but maybe without wishing death on those in your way."

"Where's the fun in that?"

I might not know the answer to that, but I do know Sanden makes my life a whole lot funner.

🔥 🔥 🔥

Dating Sanden is so ... indescribable. And the fact I can't come up with words to describe what an equal, respectful, and all-consuming relationship is like, only drives home how much Eman manipulated me all those years.

Ever since our date out on the boat, we've alternated picking what we do. Whether it's going on an adventure, opting for a night on the couch, or hitting up Pike Market Place for actual good street food than the two-star Yelp tour he tried to take me on.

I'm always with him, and I don't actually want to be anywhere else. When we're not together, I can't settle. Anxiousness vibrates under my skin.

I'm desperate for him. Always.

There's something about him that soothes me. Settles me, somehow. At the same time, the need I have for him only grows. The station and Sanden are my entire life at this point, and I can't bring myself to care about anything outside of that bubble.

None of my old friends have reached out, making me think they've taken Eman's side, and if that's what they want to do, I can't change it. All I can do is surround myself with the happy bubble of Sanden and ignore what opinions are being posted online.

After another amazing date that we cut short because we can't get enough of each other, we enter my apartment, mouths all over each other, hands exploring ... And then, out of nowhere, a throat clears.

"You mind? You're interrupting the game." Eman's voice makes us freeze.

We pull apart to find him sitting on *my* couch, watching hockey, his feet up on the coffee table and a scowl on his face.

"What are you doing?" I bark.

"I live here."

"No, you fucking don't. Get out."

"I have every right to be here."

I swear I hear a growl come from Sanden beside me, but I've got this.

I put my hand on Sanden's shoulder before I step in front of him and then face Eman. "You lost the right to that when we broke up."

"When you left me, you mean?" Eman snarks.

My jaw clenches hard, but I still bite my tongue.

"You know that's not what happened." I'm surprised I'm able to keep my tone calm because I'm anything but calm. "Get out of my house."

Eman winks. "Name's still on the lease, babe."

Seeing Eman sitting there, watching his favorite sport, in his favorite spot, a flood of familiarity comes over me. I almost ask if he wants another drink.

And then ... the automatic slip back into a subservient, domestic role makes me rage. Is that how I always was? Without question? The memories of fetching him snacks and beer rattle through me. His complaints that time I bought the wrong flavor of mixed nuts. The way he'd point out, every single time, that he chose to stay home with me instead of going with Sanden to watch the game live because he felt bad for leaving me.

A hundred little comments exactly like that one.

"What exactly are you trying to achieve?" I'm pissed as hell, but I don't want him to know he's getting to me. It's what he wants.

And he doesn't deserve any emotion from me.

"I'm *trying* to watch the game, but you're being insufferably loud."

"So go somewhere else and do it."

He pauses the screen, jaw ticking for a second before he turns to me. He doesn't even glance Sanden's way, just fixes me with that *watch yourself or we're going to have trouble* look. The look that immediately curls my stomach and makes me want to shut up.

"Where do you get off assuming that you can leave me, fuck around behind my back, and then kick me out of my own damn home? I'm not going anywhere."

I force nonchalance and cross my arms. "Good. Neither am I."

"Even better."

"But you'll be paying half the rent."

Eman scoffs. "Good luck with that, precious."

"You're not being a freeloader anymore. You want to be my roommate, you can cough up the cash."

I'm purposely not looking at Sanden because I barely feel in control as it is. All my energy is going toward not breaking down and crying over how fucked-up this is. Stress tears are the worst, and they're trying to come in hot.

"Freeloader?" Eman stands and stalks forward, and from the corner of my eyes, I notice Sanden shift closer. "We were partners. We shared everything. You don't get to make claims now that it's over and *he's* in your ear. You're a big boy, Remington. Stop twisting the truth to make yourself look innocent. No one believes it."

"W-what do you mean?"

He sneers and unlocks his phone before handing it over. There, on the picture of Sanden and me smiling and happy in Hawaii, are hundreds of comments that I've been ignoring. Right up until now where I can't. They start out warm and complimentary but then take a serious turn after Eman's comment.

Good to see you're enjoying OUR honeymoon with YOUR side piece #heartbroken

"Hashtag *heartbroken*?" I spit. The calm I'd been forcing snaps, and I fling his phone at the wall. "Fuck. You. Fuck you and your lies and everything I went through when I was with you. Get out of my fucking house before I call the cops, and then get out of my fucking life."

I'm blind with fury when he smiles and slowly retrieves his phone. "I'll be sending you the bill for this."

"I will do literally anything to get you out of my fucking life."

He chuckles, finally glancing Sanden's way. "Are you happy? Listen to him. A feral puppy. You've succeeded in turning another man against me." Eman claps. "Well done, you."

Sanden groans, long and drawn out. "You are so goddamn pathetic. You had the greatest man ever, and you fucked up. You treated him like shit and threw him away. What the actual hell is wrong with you?"

"Remington didn't think he was being treated like shit when he was screaming my name. He's a real vocal bottom."

I launch at him but barely get far when Sanden's arms close around me.

"Don't do it," he warns. "He's looking to press assault charges. Trust me, I want to rearrange his face too, but he's not worth it."

I'm shaking with the force of staying in place.

Sanden presses his forehead to my temple. "I've got you, sweetheart. You're okay."

His warm voice helps.

But calming down is even harder when I know Eman's the one in the wrong, and there's literally nothing I can do about it. He's going to win. He's going to move in here and take over, and my only choice is to move out. To *give* him this place. And ... and ...

My molars grind together as I nod.

Sanden slowly releases me.

"Oh my fucking God," Eman mutters. "Maybe you didn't work so fast after all. I knew you were screwing now, but I never believed you were doing it behind my back. I've gotta say, Sanden, I thought you outgrew that in college. Guess not." His cold eyes turn my way as he softens his voice. "How can't you see it, baby? He's in your head. He's twisting your thoughts against me, after we were so happy."

"You might have been happy, but I wasn't."

"That's a lie. We had three years together. No one stays

that long if they want out. No one accepts a proposal if they don't plan on spending their lives with someone."

"The scary part is, I *was* planning on that. You had me so fucked-up that I actually thought what we had was love. I was a wreck every day, waiting to see if you'd be angry or affectionate, constantly on eggshells and second-guessing every single choice I made. I *knew* something wasn't right, but I couldn't put my finger on it, until now."

"The only difference between then and now is that Sanden's got his hooks in you—"

"No, the difference is that I've seen what a good man looks like and what a monster looks like, and it makes it a hell of a lot easier to see through your shit. It is *so* lucky I never actually loved you because it'd make walking away a whole lot harder than it already is." Fuck these intrusive tears. "But I am. Walking away. And there is nothing you can ever do or say that will get me back—"

"Remy—"

"*I'm not finished.* You want to move in here? Fucking do it. But I'm not going anywhere. And neither is Sanden. You can lie in your bed, listening to us fuck all night if you want to. You can sit in that armchair while we cuddle together on the couch. You can sit at the fucking breakfast bar while we talk about work, and you can watch us and you can be as pissy and fucked-up as you like, but as far as we'll be concerned, you won't even exist. We'll be fucking in an empty house and cuddling in private and sharing our days with each other. From now on, you're invisible to me. You mean nothing. You want to stay here? Fine. I wish nothing but goddamn misery on you for every second you're under this roof."

Then I grab Sanden's hand and pull him into the bedroom, slamming the door closed behind us. Eman tries to follow, but Sanden blocks his entry, and when he gets the door closed again, he flicks the lock.

And it's lucky he does because Eman loses it.

I flinch as he pounds on the door so hard the hinges rattle.

"Are you fucking kidding me? Open the goddamn door, Remy!"

"Leave me alone."

"Open it! It's my bedroom, asshole!"

"Go away!"

Both fists hitting the door and making it bow sends my heart rate skyrocketing.

"Look at what you're making me do!"

"He's not making you do anything," Sanden snaps. "Get the hell out."

"Come out, baby," Eman says. "Come out and we can talk about this. You've embarrassed me enough. I'm sorry I lost my cool, but I miss you so much. My life isn't right without you. I need you, ba—"

"Stop calling me baby!" I pace closer to the door. "It's over. Stop playing these fucking games."

Eman lets out a noise half between a roar and a scream. He hits the door so hard it shakes, and I scramble back away from it.

"I'll kill you! I'll burn this whole fucking apartment block down, is that what you want, huh? If you think I'm letting you two make a fool of me, you're wrong! Do you hear me, assholes? Count those last fucking breaths!"

The shouting and banging get so loud it consumes me. It takes over the room, makes it impossible to think.

Sanden's coiled for a fight, but I can't let it happen. He's right. Eman will press charges. He'll play the victim.

When that's always been me.

I'm done being forced into a role I never wanted.

Full of dread and the sensation that everything is about to change, I grab my phone and call 911. The dispatch officer who answers is someone I've spoken to before but have never met.

"Tammy, it's Remy from Station 21. I need the police dispatched to my residence for a domestic disturbance. My ex is here, and he's made death threats against myself and Sanden from Station 40."

"Remy, crap. Okay." She kicks into protocol, asking me questions, which I do my best to stay calm and answer, even as Eman is trying to kick the door in. Sanden pushes the dresser in front of the doorway, and my gut leaps into my throat as the bottom of the door splinters.

Fuck.

My adrenaline is pumped up to a thousand.

Do I think Eman would actually hurt us? I have no fucking clue. Half an hour ago, that answer would have been a solid no, but then if you'd asked me if he'd flip out like this, it would have been a hell no as well.

"A car has been dispatched," Tammy says. "I'll wait on the line. Let me know if anything changes."

"I've called the police," I shout. "They're on their way."

"Fuck you!" Eman shouts. "I'm not the one in the wrong here! You gonna tell them how you drove me to this? All the shit you did wrong? You're mine, Remy. You said yes to marrying *me*. And now you're making out like *I'm* the monster. I'll fucking kill you both!"

There's another loud *thud* that makes me jump, but a moment later, the faint sound of sirens reaches us.

"You actually called them?" Eman yells, hitting the door again. "You're so fucking dramatic. All I wanted to do was talk to you. If you'd just faced me like a man, you could have avoided all of this. Now look at the mess you've made. You want them to arrest me, Remy? Will that make you happy? To finish ruining my life?"

Sanden leaves where he's holding the dresser and pulls me into his arms. I didn't even realize tears were spilling onto my cheeks until they soak his shirt.

"Don't listen to him," Sanden says. "None of this is on you. None of it."

I use all my energy to keep my breathing even. "Yeah, I know."

"Keep reminding yourself of that."

Eman curses again, but I block it out. Cling onto Sanden. Remind myself it'll all be over soon. A few minutes pass, and Eman's completely silent.

"Is he gone?" I ask.

Sanden squeezes me tighter. "If he's smart, he will be. But we're waiting for the police before we go back out there."

I close my eyes, breathing in Sanden's scent and letting it settle me. Focusing on him and only him. My nerves are all on edge, and I'll never be able to convey to Sanden how much I need him here. Right now and every time before this.

Because if I hadn't had him boosting me up, I don't think I would have stood up to Eman to begin with. That first dinner, we probably would have worked things out, and the idea of that future is more terrifying to me than being barricaded in my bedroom.

I can't imagine what it's like for the people who don't have the support I do.

All I can hope for is that it might finally be over. I might finally have gotten through to him.

I just want to move on.

Twenty-Six

SANDEN

Hopkins and Roscoe from the East precinct, guys both Remy and I have worked alongside before, take our statements.

Eman fled before they were able to gain access to the building, so he's long gone, and seeing as he didn't actually physically hurt us, the most we could ask them to charge him with is damage of property to the door he was trying to rip off its hinges to get to us.

In the moment, I was prepared to do whatever necessary to keep Eman away from Remy, and I never felt in any real danger, but now that the dust has settled and adrenaline is no longer taking over, I can't help but sit back and wonder how the fuck Eman became this person.

He's always been conceited, narcissistic, and mildly annoying, which is why I started distancing myself from him, but this violent, insecure, emotional manipulator is a new side to him. Or maybe it was always there, but I'd never witnessed it.

They say in situations like Remy's that it escalates slowly. At first, those small, minor issues with control seem like a quirk or a minor flaw, and then the next moment, you're not going out to see your friends or family, shutting everyone out until the only people you have is your partner and their friends. You're alone.

It's lucky for Remy that the fire department has close bonds—within his team and even with ours, silly rivalry be damned.

But the weight of his situation with Eman is finally burdening us with heavy shit I don't think either of us is equipped to deal with.

"We'll file the report and send you the link to add it to your restraining order application if you should file one," Hopkins says to me.

Remy checked out about ten minutes ago and has been staring blankly at his TV, which isn't even on anymore.

"Thanks. Would he qualify for a restraining order?"

"They lived together, and one party has made death threats, so yes. A temporary one will be issued after you file, and then you'll have a court appearance in about two weeks, where the official restraining order will be issued. Here's a card with all the links on it."

It's surreal having a colleague, someone I've saved lives with, had after-work drinks with, be professional toward me, but their unemotional detachment from the situation is what is needed.

"What about living arrangements?" I ask. "They're both on the lease, and that's what the fight was about. Eman trying to move back in."

"He's the respondent in this case, so Remy has every right to stay here and keep Eman from the apartment by having a locksmith change the locks."

I scoff. "He nearly kicked a door in. I don't think changing locks will stop him."

"It's possible. I think until that temporary restraining order is in place, it might be an idea for him to stay elsewhere."

Remy, obviously having been listening to this all, turns his head toward us. "I don't have anywhere to go."

"Yes, you do. You can stay with me as long as you need to."

"That's moving too fast, don't you think?"

"Only until the restraining order comes in. I'm not asking you to move in with me permanently."

Remy stands on shaky legs, and all I want to do is console him, but he flinches when I go to touch him.

Fuck.

He glances around the apartment like it's tainted now with Eman's threats. "I ... I don't think I want to stay here now anyway. He can have the apartment."

"In that case, we can wait with you while you pack up your things," Roscoe says, "or you can call one of us to come back with you when you're ready to collect it. In my experience, it's better to get out as much as you can now—

at least the valuable things. Anything he can sell, set on fire, or damage."

One look at Remy, and I know that's not going to be a possibility tonight. He looks wrecked. But I still give him the choice anyway.

"What do you want to do?"

"I don't want to move in, but—"

"Stay with me as long as you need," I say again.

"In that case, I'll grab a bag of clothes, my laptop, chargers, things like that."

"I can help."

Me helping turns into me going to fetch everything Remy points to or directs me to because as soon as we're back in his room, his legs buckle, and I have to guide him to the bed. He sits on the edge while I collect his belongings, but with every item, every piece of him I put into a duffle bag, he seems to withdraw even more.

He needs time to process, and I'm trying not to coddle him or baby him or be condescending in any way. I just want to be here for him. Protect him.

I don't want to be his savior because after witnessing him stand up for himself, I know he's strong enough to push through, but I want to be his support. I want to help lift him up and get his life back together.

"You can stay with me as long as you like," I remind him.

He nods.

I hold out my hand for him. "Come on. Let's get you out of here."

At first, I think he won't take my offer, but then his palm slides into mine, and he stands.

Before we walk out, he says, "I know we said we could be a fucked-up pair, but I didn't have this in mind when I said it."

I actually laugh. "At least he hasn't stolen your sense of humor."

"No. Just our friends, now the apartment, and any dignity I had before I was with him."

"Again, not on you," I soothe.

His voice is small when he says, "No matter how many times you say that, I'm not sure there'll ever come a time where I believe it."

My heart fucking breaks for him.

🔥 🔥 🔥

By the time everything's over, we get Remy's things, and head for my place, we're both exhausted. We fill in the restraining order info online and send it off, I ask if he wants dinner, but he says no, and then we end up going to bed without eating. I hold him all night, even if neither of us sleeps well, and as much as I want to ask how he's doing and what's going on in his head, I'm trying to be the supportive silent type. He'll talk when he's ready.

At some point, I must fall into the deepest sleep of all time because I don't even stir when Remy gets out of bed. I wake to him gone, and mild panic claws at my throat.

It's an overreaction, I know that. He's probably getting

breakfast. But after witnessing Eman's rampage yesterday, I think it's safe to say I'm on edge too. I'm worried about Remy's safety. I'm worried about his headspace. He thinks Eman's actions are his own fault, but they're not.

He's too unforgiving of himself. He's the victim. He should never be the one to get the blame, but I of all people know how easy it is to fall into that pattern.

I get out of bed and find Remy out in my living room, drinking coffee and looking out my window. "Hey," I say softly, not wanting to startle him.

He turns, and his beautiful smile is a shadow of his usual one. "Morning. I made you coffee too, but even me holding it under your nose didn't wake you."

"Uh, thank you?"

"I also called my cousin Wren. He said I can go stay with him."

"Huh. Yeah, of course." I'm trying not to be insecure about how fast he wants to get out of my place, but it must show on my face because he puts his coffee down on the dining table on his way over to me.

His eyes are soft, and the gentle way in which he cups my cheek makes me want to melt into it.

"Don't get me wrong. The idea of staying here indefinitely is really damn appealing, but I think that's why I have to go. My instinct is telling me to stay here, where I'm safe, but that can't exactly be trusted when the last three years of my life aren't what I thought they were. I'm confused, and I have a lot to figure out. I can't do that here. For something so new, something that's developing in the midst of trauma, it will be best for us if I don't live with you so soon, even temporarily. It would feel like I'm bouncing from one serious relationship to another, and I worry that's setting us up for failure."

I understand it, one hundred percent, but if he's not here, I can't protect him. Despite that knee-jerk reaction, I know he's right. "It's probably the smart choice." I pull him in for a hug, and unlike yesterday, he doesn't hesitate. "How are you holding up? Yesterday was—"

"Intense," he finishes for me. "But I was up most of the night, analyzing everything, every part of our relationship, every controlling move, which is why, when I woke up this morning, after calling Wren, I called the fire department's mental health department to see if they had counseling available outside of work-related things. They're going to get back to me."

I can't hold back my surprise. "That's actually a really good idea."

"All my great ideas come to me when I have little sleep. I think it has something to do with work. The less sleep we get on shift, the harder we work."

I purse my lips. "Uh, that might be something to bring up with the therapist."

Remy laughs. "You're probably right."

"When do you move into Wren's?"

"Today." He looks nervous to say the word. "He said he'll be home after four."

I grip Remy's hips, determined to be supportive. "So we have all day to hang out?"

Remy's hands roam over my chest. "If hang out is code for sex—"

"You don't have to."

"Oh, no, sorry, I should rephrase. What I meant to say was, hang out *better be* code for sex."

"Only if you want to, and if you're okay with me. You don't think I'd ever—"

Remy presses against me, chest to chest. "My feelings toward you haven't changed. You still make me feel safe."

Good. Because if I ever became a problem for Remy, I don't think I could forgive myself.

Twenty-Seven

REMY

By the time I'm settled in the spare room at Wren's place, I finally let it all hit me. The last twenty-four hours have drained my energy, and the only way I got through today was by creating a sense of control by putting plans in place and accepting all the affection Sanden wrapped me in.

But now I need more plans beyond where I'm going to live and setting a date with the therapist. Now, I have to think about things like restraining orders and court dates. It feels easier to stick my head in the sand and ignore it all. Needing a restraining order makes me feel like an even bigger victim than I realized I was.

It was bad enough having to tell my parents. They're both lawyers, and Dad said he'll represent me, but admitting to them that I let my relationship with Eman get that far before I realized what he was doing was embarrassing.

I can see why men are less likely to come forward in a domestic violence situation, but reminding myself that it's the emotional damage Eman caused that's letting that insecurity get to me helps. It's what manipulative people do, and it was his goal all along.

Would Eman have followed through on his threats and moved to physical violence?

I ... I don't know.

The uncertainty is maybe the worst answer I have for that question because it makes my decision so much harder. If it was a solid no, the restraining order wouldn't be needed, and if it was a yes, the added judgment that comes with people knowing I had to take that step would be worth it.

Really, the whole thing would be so much easier if people didn't have opinions about things that weren't their business.

Guess that's another thing to add to my list to unpack.

My sleep that night is shit. I keep being hit with flashes of Eman's face, his voice, that room. I roll over for Sanden so many times, on instinct, and I'm hit with a fresh wave of panic every time I remember he isn't here.

I'm bleary-eyed when I get up, and a stress headache is building behind my eyes.

"Morning," Wren calls happily from the kitchen. "How are you feeling?"

"Terrible." But I smile to soften the words. "I just need a few days to distance from it."

"I bet." He slides a coffee across the breakfast bar to me. "And I know you're dealing with a lot, but I want to stress that I meant what I said. The room's yours as long as you need it. There's no such thing as overstaying your welcome with me."

"I really appreciate it." I take a sip of the coffee that's slightly more bitter than I like, but hey, I'm not really in a position to complain.

Wren stares into his mug for a moment before he shifts on large feet. "I want to apologize," he says suddenly.

"What for?"

"For not, I dunno, coming around more, I guess? I always felt something wasn't right about that guy, but I could never pin what it was."

I slide into the stool across from him. "Yeah, I guess we kinda grew apart over the last few years."

"And that's my fault, in a way. Whenever I came over to hang out, Eman always made it very clear I wasn't welcome there."

"How?"

"That's the thing." He squints like he's trying to think. "It's not something I've ever been able to put into words. It's why I didn't say anything, because it sounds petty even to me."

"I like petty," I say, thinking of Sanden. "Try me."

"Okay, like, he'd always put himself between us. Physically, I mean. If we were sitting on your couch watching a game, he'd call you into the kitchen and then take your seat. Or he'd pout until you sat with him. Sometimes he'd answer the door when you weren't around and not say a single thing to me. Just sigh, like it was a real inconvenience to see me. One day, he even said—and it wasn't even in a shitty tone or anything—that texting first would be a good idea because you guys were on the way out. And I dunno why I didn't believe him, but it's not like I could say that without sounding bad, you know? So I left, and then every time I texted you to meet up, you were busy."

A distinct memory comes back to me.

"Who's that?" Eman asks, crawling over my body.

"Wren. He wants to grab lunch." My fingers hover over the keypad to give him a time when I notice Eman giving me his puppy dog eyes. "What?"

"It's nothing. Don't worry."

"Tell me."

Eman buries his face in my neck. "I was going to surprise you by taking you to that cocktail bar you've been talking about." He climbs off me, pressing his fingers to his eyes. "There goes Wren, ruining my chances to spoil you again."

I see the image of him walking off, that same tightening hitting my gut now as it did back then. I had two choices: cancel on Wren or deal with Eman being mopey and disappointed for the next few days.

I'd canceled.

We'd gone to the bar, where we met up with two of Eman's work friends, and I'd been frustrated the whole time at their constant work talk. I'd gotten drunk and loud, and Eman had been pissed with me for days after that anyway, for embarrassing him in front of his colleagues.

"You have nothing to be sorry for," I tell Wren. "I've been blaming myself, but it was all Eman. Whether it was intentional or just a fucked-up part of who he was ... It doesn't help for either of us to blame ourselves."

"But—"

"Seriously. It's fine. I've got some stuff to work out, but I'll be okay. I know I will."

"I'll take your word for it." He moves to the sink to rinse his mug. "I'm off to work, but bring in anything you need to. This is your home now."

"Thanks."

"Got plans today?"

I sink in on myself. Sanden's back at work, and I'm on nights. Opposite shifts is going to be a nightmare because every part of me needs him, and it's not an option. "Sanden's working, so probably nothing."

He takes a step toward the door before pausing. "He's a good guy."

"He is."

"But you used to catch up with Tig a lot ..."

"He's got a baby now. He never wants to go out."

"Right, but ... we drifted apart because of Eman. Maybe it's the same thing. And what about your other friends? Before you met Eman, you were always taking short vacations by yourself. Meeting up with friends on days off. Trips to the beach, shit like that. I ..." He shifts again, obviously uncomfortable with all of this sharing. "You were kinda the person I always wanted to hang out with because you were ... you were just *fun*, okay?"

"Hopefully, I can find that again."

He heads to his room to get dressed.

While I face an entire day of nothing.

Around lunchtime, I cave and head down to Station 40. Thankfully, Sanden's having a slow day because I really needed to see his face. When I'm around him, things settle. I feel safe, like I can never get enough of him.

We eat together, and he fills me in on his day, while I let him know I have my first therapist appointment.

He eyes me from across the table. "You doing okay at Wren's?"

I nod. "Yeah, we had a good talk this morning. He reminded me of the things I was missing about myself."

"I'm glad you have him."

"If Eman had his way, I wouldn't."

Sanden's jaw tenses. "I don't think I want to know."

"You really don't."

The next few days are hard, but even on back-to-back shifts, we make it work. Every second we're not at our stations, we're together. Whenever I'm bored, I text him, and whenever he has a Station 40 story, I'm the first person he calls.

We try not to talk about Eman much, which is a nice change. Sanden doesn't deserve being in his shadow, but as much as I know that, Eman haunts us both anyway. The memories, the restraining order, the lingering knowledge in the back of my mind that I'm moving on too quickly.

I said if anything started between us that I wanted to be sure.

And I am.

When it comes to him. Sanden is the best person I know. He makes me feel incredible, like I can handle anything.

It's *me* I'm not sure about.

When I'm not around Sanden … I don't think I've ever reached so low. It's like swimming against the tide every time I take a minute to stop and assess my life, and the thoughts of how the hell I got here hit me all at once.

I want fun Remy back, but I'm beginning to worry he doesn't exist anymore.

I'm on the couch in Wren's small living room, zoned out as I process having an official court date, when a giant *clank* makes me jump out of my skin. I whirl around, heart in my throat, and find Wren staring at me, hand frozen over where he's dropped his keys on the counter.

"You okay?" he asks.

"Yeah. Sorry. You startled me."

His eyes scan the dark room, lingering on the blank TV screen. "Whatcha doing in here?"

"Thinking."

"Dangerous."

"Yup."

He approaches me cautiously, like he's afraid of scaring me again, and rubs his jaw as he takes the spare armchair. "I wasn't expecting to see you here."

Discomfort settles in my gut as I realize that maybe his offer of me staying as long as I wanted wasn't a genuine one. That maybe, after living with me, he's had enough. "Sorry. I can start looking for a place tomo—"

"What? No. I mean that you're never here. If you're not working or sleeping, you're with Sanden."

"Oh." I relax back into the couch. "Yeah, he's a great guy."

"He is … And you know I approve of him and like him as a person."

Something about his tone is off. "Why do I sense a 'but'?"

"'Cause you're a smart guy?" Wren grins. "Look, it's not my place, but I'm worried about you."

"I told you, I just need time, and I'll be okay."

"Yeah, and I believe you …"

"I'm sensing that 'but' again."

He chuckles. "Don't hate me for saying this, but you and Sanden have gotten attached really quickly. Through some pretty heavy shit. And I worry that maybe you haven't taken the time you need to process everything."

Ouch.

That out-of-control spiral threatens to sweep over me again.

I run a hand over my face, all out of words for him. The problem is that Wren's hit on the exact same doubts that I've been having myself, and hearing them vocalized like that … I push the rising panic back down again. That's *my* issue. Not Sanden's. I need to figure out a way through.

"I get that" is all I can say.

"I feel like a dick for bringing it up, but I don't want to see you hurt again."

"Yeah, I know."

But it seems he's not done pushing. "You can ignore me if you want to, it's your life, but when you go to your appointment next week, it might be worth mentioning. Just … see what he says about your new relationship. Maybe I'm being protective."

"I will."

Wren opens his mouth, but whatever he wants to say next is drowned out by his phone going off. He glances at the screen, and whatever he sees there makes him do a double take. He scrambles to unlock it, and after reading his message, he falls into a stunned silence.

"Everything okay with you?"

"Huh. Yeah." He locks his phone and sets it down again.

"That was about as believable as me being okay."

Wren gives his head a shake like he's trying to knock his thoughts loose. "My, uh, dad died."

My eyes almost shoot from my face. As far as I was aware, Wren didn't know who his dad was. He and his mom lived with us for a while when we were younger, but I was too young to remember it. The only memories of Wren's dad being mentioned was Dad saying how the no-good excuse for a man ran off on his sister.

He shakes it off. "Anyway, where were we? I love you and want to protect you and all that lovey crap."

"Dude. Your dad *died*. Are ... are you okay? Do you need anything? I didn't realize you found out who he was."

Wren shrugs. "Mom only told me a few years ago. Apparently, he's been giving her child support all these years, so whenever she told me I was her miracle growing up, making me think she was the goddamn Virgin Mary, it turns out it was some married rich dude who wanted nothing to do with me but still put me through school and college. He was never anything more than a sperm donor to me anyway."

"Wow." I tilt my head back to look at the ceiling. "Is it possible I'm a walking bad luck omen? Just spreading drama everywhere I go?"

Wren laughs. "No offense, cuz, but I don't think you get to take credit for death. No matter how badass you are at work."

A smile slips onto my face. "I guess I'm not the only Porter going through some shit."

"Again, no offense meant, but I'll take some dude I didn't know dying over ..." He waves a hand my way. "All of that."

"I'm a mess."

"You sure are." He gets up and ruffles my hair. "But it's temporary, and you're a strong guy. Three years is a lot to move on from, so give yourself permission to be a little messy. The rest of us are here for whatever you need, but unfortunately, you're going to have to do the work yourself."

He's right. But at this point, I'm aching for direction. When Sanden's around, I don't have to think about all that, but when he's not, I'm so ... untethered.

Therapy can't start soon enough.

And I really fucking hope I get some answers.

Twenty-Eight

SANDEN

When they say something went up in flames, it doesn't really do the literal meaning justice. A failed relationship. A plan. These are minor things compared to what I have to face when I'm staring at a house that is on the verge of collapsing. "Up in flames" doesn't describe how quickly the fire licks at timber and catches so fast that it basically signs a death warrant to anyone in its path. It doesn't paint the full picture that when walking through a burning house, the smoke is so thick we can't see anything through our oxygen masks. And it doesn't invoke nearly as much adrenaline, fear, and panic as it does when discovering you're too late.

Despite this callout being the worst we've seen in a long time, despite looking at the fresh burns on someone who's already passed, I breathe calmly, my oxygen mask making each breath sound like I'm Darth Vader. The house creaks, and while we got the all clear to enter the house, I know we don't have long before it will collapse from the pressure.

The heat is intense, but knowing we didn't get here in time is almost crippling.

Gabe, who's checking the next room, is suddenly beside me. "All clear. We— Oh shit."

"Let's move," I say, going into professional mode. I pick up the body, a woman, age undeterminable, to bring her out, even though I know it's too late. Will we work on them? Try to save them? Of course. But sometimes, you just know. "Clear a path for me," I order Gabe.

We go back the way we came in, every creak of the floorboards below us threatening to give out at any moment.

The closer we get to outside, the more my heart races, and when we make it outside to applause from everyone being goddamn nosy, I almost tell them all to shut the hell up. Because what we did here doesn't deserve applause.

We failed at the one thing we're supposed to do: save lives from fires.

The team's job of search and rescue is complete, less than ten minutes after we arrive. But it's ten minutes too late.

She didn't wake up when her smoke alarms went off. She didn't wake up when her skin started to burn. She's been gone for a while. Smoke inhalation. Exactly like ...

I swallow hard.

Cap and Gunderson have started on the flames, the engine's hose blasting its way into the house, while Gabe and I place the victim on the gurney for the EMTs—not Remy because he's on his first day off of four—to take the body to the hospital.

Even though there's no pulse, and she's long gone, it's protocol to try to save anyone we pull out of a fire until a doctor can legally declare them dead.

The same way they did with—

Fuck.

Gabe and I take our masks and helmets off and head for the truck. I throw my helmet in the cab with so much force I'm surprised I don't break something.

Tears stream down my face, and Gabe knows not to approach me. This reaction is normal for me when we lose someone. Especially like this.

Though he doesn't know why.

No one knows why.

Except for Remy.

Autopilot kicks in, getting me through the next few hours of putting the fire out and filling in reports about it.

When it kicks over to 6:00 a.m. and Gabe asks to go to breakfast to debrief, I say I just want to go home.

But I don't. There's only one place I want to be—only one place I feel like I could go, and that's to Remy's.

Because he knows.

He understands.

And even though I've only been to Remy's new place once, my body carries me there, my brain somehow focusing on weaving through traffic until I'm on his cousin's doorstep.

I'm barely holding it together when I knock, but I pull it tight when Wren opens the door.

He looks surprised that I'm here so early but steps aside to let me in. "He's still asleep."

"Thanks. I had an exhausting night, so I'm gonna go join him."

Wren frowns, his eyes soft, which makes his hair that's shaved on the sides with a mess of length up top seem like a part of him wanting to look tougher than maybe he really is.

Or maybe I'm reading into that one look. I'm too tired to fucking dwell on it.

I make my way down the hall to where I helped Remy move his boxes last week, strip down to my underwear, and slip into bed next to him. He doesn't stir until I wrap my arms around him, but he settles just as quickly.

The only problem is that now I'm covered in his warmth, his support, I can't hold back the tears. Not the controlled streams of salt water that fell from my eyes while on the job. I'm talking body-racking sobs that are like a runaway freight train. It's impossible to stop and doesn't go unnoticed.

Remy rolls over, cracking his eyes open. "Sanden? What's wrong?" His hazel eyes fill with concern.

"Bad shift," I murmur.

"They're the worst. Anything I can do?"

"Just ... hold me." I kiss him softly, but his tongue

pushes past my lips. "Mm." I break my mouth from his. "Or we could do this."

Remy rolls on top of me, his morning wood grinding against me, making me hard. "I figured you wouldn't want to talk about it, but if you do, you can talk my ear off while you fuck me."

The thing is, for the first time ever, I do feel like I have someone to talk to about Billie. Someone who will be supportive and not tell me to "get over it" like he who shall now remain nameless after the shit he's put Remy and me through. But also fucking Remy. Bare.

I'm in a constant need to be closer to him, and that's about as close as I can get.

"Get the lube," I rasp.

When he moves off me and opens the drawer on his nightstand, I shuck off my boxer briefs.

He tosses me the lube, and while I oil up my cock, Remy gets rid of his underwear too.

"How do you want me?" His whispered words are full of want, but his question is unanswerable.

"In every which way, but I probably only have the energy for you to ride me."

Remy smiles. "We'll do every which way another time."

He climbs back on me, straddling my waist while grinding his cock against mine. It's nice and slippery from the lube, and I grip his hips to keep this going a little longer before I'll prep his hole. It feels so good. So amazing. Having him close to me, his warm skin on mine.

This is as healing as talking would be because his closeness fills me with comfort.

Remy's hands trail over my chest, his fingers pinching my nipples.

I arch into his touch.

"Sanden." He sounds so tortured. "I need you. Make it so we both forget."

"I want to get so lost in you I can barely remember to come up for air."

"I need you inside me."

I feel around the bed for wherever I put the lube and cover my fingers in it. When I press against his hole, he shudders on top of me, the shiver of lust coursing through him and shooting into my balls. Watching Remy fall apart is one of my most favorite things in this world.

He's one of my favorite things. The most important person in my life.

I can never let anything happen to him.

I work him open as quickly as possible, and he helps by sinking down on my fingers as far as he can go. I want to be inside him. I want to surround him, take care of him, and own his body.

"I'm ready," he breathes, and I pull my fingers free.

Remy reaches behind him, gripping the base of my cock while he lowers himself. I fill him up at an achingly slow rate, but I want to make sure I don't hurt him. I'm also thankful for the pace because going bare with him is always so damn intense. The sensation of his ass around my cock is amplified, and the thought of spilling inside him drives me fucking wild.

But most of all, this connection, the notion of filling

him up yet being the one who feels full, is something I've never had before.

We're one, and he takes me away from the pain. The traumas, past and present.

A small, fleeting thought of it not being healthy tries to invade my mind, but I push it away because Remy rises up and then slams down on my cock faster. Harder.

His hips rotate, and I flex my ass to thrust up and meet his every move.

We're in sync, so lost in each other, the rest of the world blurs. I can't tell if the banging on the wall is Remy's bed moving or Wren trying to tell us to be quiet, but there's no stopping me. Either of us.

Remy's moans fill the room along with our harsh breaths, and as we pick up speed, chasing that finishing line, our skin flushed, pleasure rising fast, there's absolutely no stopping the orgasm that racks my body.

I unleash inside his ass and almost pass out from the rolling waves moving through me.

Remy keeps going, bouncing on my cock and milking every drop from me, but it's obviously not enough for him.

I try to reach for his dick so I can jerk him off, but my arms are Jell-O. He takes matters into his own hands, stroking himself hard and fast until he tenses on top of me, my softening cock still inside his ass, though slowly inching its way out.

His cum splashes against my abs and chest, and he collapses on top of it.

We breathe heavily, and I run my fingers down his back and up again.

"That was ..." He gasps to get air. "Amazing."

"It's always amazing with you."

He lifts up. "Ditto." Then Remy brings our lips together for a searing kiss that I never want to end.

Eventually, it does, and Remy rolls off me.

"Water. Going to get ..." Another deep breath. "Water."

"I'll get it for you." I slip out of bed and put my underwear back on, as well as my pants, but use my shirt to wipe down my cum-covered skin.

Remy smiles at me. "Always taking care of me."

"Not true. That—" I wave my hand toward the bed. "—was all you."

When I exit Remy's room and close the bedroom door behind me, I can't help laughing—and blushing a little—at Wren on his couch, eating cereal, while wearing noise-canceling headphones.

I hurry to the kitchen to get Remy's water, but as soon as I pull a glass out of his cupboard, I turn to find Wren there, arms folded, noise-canceling headphones around his neck now, and a cold look on his face.

"I'm sorry about the noise. We, uh, got carried away."

"Yeah, that's not why I'm angry."

"Oh. Umm, have I done something wrong?"

Wren deflates and runs a hand over his hair. "Yes? No? I don't know. All I know is Remy isn't in the right headspace for this mess." He waves his hand over me from head to toe.

Well, that definitely wasn't a compliment. "Thank ... you?"

He grunts. "This is coming out wrong. Look, I like you. All

those times I met you through Remy and Eman, you seemed genuine, a much better match for my cousin than that loser, but ..." Wren glances back toward Remy's bedroom. "I'm not trying to overstep here, but I really am worried about him. He's not dealing with this Eman mess. I keep asking him about the court date coming up, and he says he's fine, but I don't think he is. And you ... you turn up looking like someone died—"

"Someone did die," I say through gritted teeth. "We were too late to the scene, and so we lost someone we were supposed to save."

"That makes my point even more relevant. You came here, put that burden on him, when he's already going through so much as it is."

"I didn't even tell him what happened."

"No, you had sex with him instead, and that is what I'm trying to say. I fear you guys are really codependent for a new couple. You're barely apart unless one of you is working, and when Remy can't be with you, he just ... switches off. Instead of dealing with shit, you're drowning in each other. It's not healthy."

My own fleeting thought of the same thing while I was fucking Remy comes back to the front of my mind.

And as much as I don't want to admit that he might be right, I have to face facts.

The timing for Remy and me has never been perfect, but maybe we're pushing something we're both not ready for.

Instead of dealing with the fire that took my sister's life, I push down every incident, every work scenario that reminds me of Billie, and now, with Remy, it's really easy to push the unresolved grief away.

Wren's right.

Remy and I are drowning in each other, thinking we can make each other float, but eventually, one of us has to let go, or we'll both get hurt.

Twenty-Nine

REMY

Sanden took a long time to fall asleep, so as soon as he drifts off, I creep out, hoping he'll manage a few solid hours. We didn't talk much after sex, but I could tell by the way he clung to me that something wasn't right, so I throw myself on the couch and pull out my phone to punch out a message to Gabe.

Me:

What happened last night?

Surprisingly, he texts straight back.

Gabe:

House fire. DOA. It messed us all up a little.

My heart sinks. Those are the worst kind of jobs to get, and now that I know what Sanden went through with Billie, his panic this morning makes sense.

I tuck my knees to my chest, chewing on my thumbnail, replaying the look on his face as he climbed into bed. He'd been crying, his face was pale, but we didn't even talk about it. I distracted him with sex, and while I know that would have helped me, I don't think I made the right call.

I'm not even sure I'd know what the right call is.

Feet shuffle behind me, and I turn to look back over the couch as Sanden enters the living room. His eyes are bleary with sleep, and he looks wrecked as he drops down next to me, hand sliding over my thigh.

"You should go back to bed," I tell him. "You've barely been out of it for an hour."

"Can't sleep," he croaks.

I jump up to grab him some water and then curl up beside him again. "I asked Gabe what happened. I'm so sorry."

"Thank you." He draws a measured inhale and finally meets my eyes. "I spoke to Wren this morning."

Uh-oh.

"He said he's worried about you."

"Of course he's worried about me, but I've told him plenty of times I'll be fine."

Sanden's quiet again for a moment. "That should be me though."

"What?"

"Worried about you."

"Where have you been? That's literally all you do."

Sanden shakes his head. "It's not the same. I've been telling myself you'll be okay too, but I don't think it's that simple."

"That's why I'm seeing someone. To help."

"A shrink isn't a magic fix."

I swallow slowly, studying the side of his face. "What are you saying to me?"

"I ... I don't know." He leans forward, pressing his fingers into his eyes. "I'm so out of my depth here."

"You've been perfect," I mutter.

"Yeah, but I think that's part of the problem." His cautious eyes find mine again. "No one's perfect, Remy. And we're having fun now, but eventually, we'll fight. It's inevitable. It's a part of being in a relationship, but how would we even navigate that? How do I hurt or upset you knowing the pain that you're already in? How do you tell me when there's something you're unhappy with if you've built me up into this perfect human when I'm just not? I don't want you to feel like you have to go along and keep the peace like you did with Eman."

My bottom lip starts to waver, but I trap it between my teeth. "We have a lot to work out," I say meekly. I'm afraid though. Afraid to say the wrong thing. Because everything Sanden's saying mirrors the doubts I've been having, but I still don't have a solution.

"We do." His hand closes over mine. "Can you say something? I don't want to upset you, but I'm terrified if we keep going without having this conversation that I'm going to lose you."

I blink to clear my eyes. "I ... I've been worried too. Mostly about me and how fucked-up everything got. About how quickly we moved on. I've tried to shove the thoughts down and tell myself that once I have this therapy appointment, they'll tell me what to do and that I'll immediately be over the Eman shit."

"Yeah. Maybe."

"But after this morning, I'm a bit worried about you too."

Sanden's blue eyes look watery. "Sorry that I put that on you."

"That's the thing though. You should be able to. But we've been so focused on what Eman did to me that we never stopped to think how he affected you as well. He was the only person you had to talk to about your sister, and he used it against you. Now that you don't have him, I'm it. I'm not strong enough to help you with that guilt. I hope one day I can be, but I also hope that one day you won't need me to be. It kills me to see you putting what happened on yourself, and I kinda think you need to talk to a professional too."

He tries for a grin, but it's weak. "The couple who head checks together stays together?"

"Something like that ..."

We're quiet for a long time, but I know what I need to say next. It's something I've avoided thinking about, even though it really is the only move for us.

"We ..." I swallow again, but my throat is thick and

sticky. "We started this thing really quickly, and I ... we ..." I force myself to inhale.

"It's not our time," he whispers.

The words almost break me, but I force myself to not be a dramatic idiot. This hurts, probably more than it should, because my rational brain knows it's the right call, but every instinct I have is telling me I won't make it through without him.

And hello, red flag. Perfect timing.

I clutch hold of him tighter. "I know you're right, but I think I'm in love with you. How do I make the right call here?"

He flinches like I've hurt him. "And that's all I need to be sure. When I've dreamed about you loving me, you didn't need to think. You just ... did."

"I'm *sorry*."

"No, sweetheart. I know that it's coming. You can't right now, and that's okay." A shadow of his beautiful, crooked smile crosses his face. "I've waited over three years, and I'll wait ten more if I have to. You're worth it, and you need this. And I will always give you what you need."

"So it's ... like we're hitting pause?"

"Yeah." His thumb brushes my cheek. "Pause. We've both got a lot of shit to work out, and once we do, we can try this thing again. For real this time."

"Third time lucky?"

"Exactly."

I hate it, even though I know it's the only choice. My voice is barely audible. "What if it takes months?"

"Then I'll consider myself lucky."

"You think it could take *longer*?"

"It could."

"Fuck." It's really hitting me what we're agreeing to. This isn't a few days. Or a few weeks. I'm facing an undetermined amount of time without him.

"Yeah. Fuck is right."

"W-well, we can still be friends, right?"

He opens his mouth, pauses for a second, and then sighs. "Let's see how things progress. I'm *always* here if you need me. Always. And things won't change at work. But I think the whole point of this is that we work out how to rely on ourselves before each other. So, that needs to be our focus, and if we can manage friends in there, then fuck yes. You know I'm in."

"Okay."

Sanden leans in and leaves a lingering kiss on my lips. "It's going to suck, but we're doing the right thing."

"I know."

"Just ..." He flinches. "If you change your mind about us, that's okay, but give me the heads-up so I'm not waiting on you forever."

There's no way that will ever happen. I need him. And even after I work on myself and feel more like me again, that isn't going to change. I don't want it to. I want that need to feel healthy instead of desperate.

"Same for you," I say. "If you meet someone and they're good for you, don't hold yourself back."

His eyes are practically laughing at me, and I know he's having the same thoughts I am. That it's impossible. That no one else will compare. But neither of us knows what's going to happen in the future, so he doesn't deny it either.

"I better go."

"You can stay here and sleep if you want to."

Sanden slowly untangles himself from my grip and stands. "Not a good idea. And I doubt I'll be sleeping anyway."

I know what he means. I sense a lot of overtime in my future.

"I don't want to say goodbye," I admit.

"Yeah." He scratches the side of his face, slightly angled away. "But that's not what this is."

Then why does it feel so final?

🔥 🔥 🔥

"I'm glad to meet you," Dr. Herber—Colin—says. We're in his comfortable office, sitting in chairs across from each other, with a table between us. It's all navy and wood tones, and even though I've been a high-strung mess about this, I'm calmer than I've been all week.

"So how does this all work?"

"That's up to you. There's no set structure. We're simply here to have a conversation."

"Aren't you meant to voodoo my brain and tell me how to get better?"

His smile is friendly. "I wish it was that easy. My role here is to help you work through your thoughts, confront some of the ones you've been avoiding, and then offer some perspectives you might not have considered."

"How much time do you have?"

Colin laughs. "As much as you're willing to pay for."

And I'm not sure what I was expecting, but he's not as stuffy as I pictured.

"I was left at the altar over a month ago by a guy I didn't realize had been manipulating me for three years, and then I went on the honeymoon with one of his friends, who's also a guy I work with, who's *also* the one I had a crush on when I first met my ex, and is *also also* the one who was with me when my ex went off the deep end and threatened to kill us both. So. Yeah."

His eyes soften, like he can tell I've been dying to spew all that at him. "That's a lot to unpack."

"Which is why I'm here."

"We'll get to your ex in a moment—"

"Which one?" I ask.

He tilts his head. "You have more than one?"

"The manipulative dipshit, and the greatest person I've ever met and the reason I'm so eager for this thing to work."

"So the new guy is the reason you're here?"

"I need to get better so I can be with him."

"Tell me about him."

Where the hell do I start? "He's safe and kind. He hasn't said it, but I know he loves me, and I'm pretty sure I feel the same way."

"Okay. And when you talk about being better, what does that look like?"

I try to pin it down. "Well ... not so fucking confused

would be a start. The thing is, I didn't even notice the stuff with Eman going on. It was so subtle and gradual, and all of a sudden, I have no friends, I'm scared of confrontation, I don't even know how to have a single goddamn unassisted thought. And then Sanden and I jumped into things quickly, and I so desperately wanted to be ready for him that I ignored the fact I wasn't. I couldn't support him when he needed it. I can't ..." I force back my frustration. "I wasn't ready. I knew that. But it took him being the one to admit that things weren't working for me to face it. I want to be brave like he is."

Colin nods for a moment. "You've made some really good points I'd like to highlight and a couple I want to push you on. First, knowing you weren't ready and ending things before they could develop in an unhealthy direction—no matter who brought it up first—is a real positive, whether it feels like it or not."

"We wanted to make sure we didn't ruin things. That we'd have another chance."

"That's a fantastic first step from you both."

He's right. It doesn't feel like it. These last few days without Sanden have been the worst.

"Wanting to be a support for your partner is also a healthy goal, so long as you understand that you can't be their only support. It also can't be the only foundation a relationship is built on."

I'm worried that's all we were. Or at least, all we were becoming.

"There's a few things I want you to think about. The first is that when you spoke about Sanden, you said he's safe. Your past relationship has left you feeling *un*safe, and now that you've found someone who embodies what you need, that's what you seek from him. You also keep saying things were fast. It's important to remember that time is only a unit of measurement. Plenty of people move from one healthy relationship to the next in short time frames, and that's okay. If you had come out of your relationship with Eman and been ready to see someone else, there's no reason you and Sanden couldn't work out. It's not the time that determines whether you're ready. It's you. Some relationships need space to process. To heal from. That could take a day or a year. There's no rule. The good news is that you're self-aware and solution focused. It may only take a few sessions of working on what you went through with Eman to be on the right track to getting your old self back. But there's no pressure either way."

"That sounds good."

His expression tightens. "The next question is going to be harder."

"Okay."

"What happens if you put in all this work, if you get to that place you're aiming for, where you feel like you, where you're ready to commit to Sanden ... and he's no longer an option?"

I'm shaking my head before I can stop it. "He said he'd wait."

"This is a hypothetical, Remy. And an important one. Who are you doing all of this work for?"

My thoughts immediately spin to Sanden and our relationship and wanting to be better for him.

I know the answer Colin wants though. It'd be simple enough to give it, to lie, but I'm goddamn doing this thing right.

"I don't know."

He smiles. "I can work with that."

Thirty

SANDEN

"The outcome was less than ideal," the fire department–appointed therapist says. It's not the same person each time, which is annoying, but I've played this game before. I know how to get around their baiting tactics. And James "can call me Jim" Geoffry is definitely good with tactics.

"It was. The unfortunate thing in this instance was that it wasn't reported quickly enough because the sole person inside didn't wake up to the smoke alarms. It wasn't until the neighbors woke and called it in. In an ideal situation, everyone would have smoke detectors that immediately call the fire department."

"So you're saying you'd rather have more false callouts

from someone burning their toast than spend your time chasing real fires?"

This new guy is good.

"No. I'm saying if that's what I have to do to save one more life, then it would be worth it."

"After facing death the way you did, do you have any feelings of failure or low self-worth?"

Yes. "Nope. Same shit, different day, if you know what I mean."

His blank expression doesn't change.

"I'm not trying to be blasé about death. I know it's a very real part of my job, but I've learned how to deal with it and move past it. If I got hung up on every death, I think I'd be completely ..." Disconnected to it. Like I am.

I let out a sigh because I've been doing it for so long I haven't actually realized how much I disassociate when it comes to death anymore.

"Completely, what?" Jim asks.

I don't want to tell him. "I'm trying to think of a word that means crazy but without being ableist about it. The bottom line is I've learned how to accept death. Not everyone can be saved."

I hold back my tears because this last job hit me harder than others. House fires and casualties always do. But I've always bounced back.

I'll bounce back again.

Because if it's a difference between having the opportunity to save other lives or having to hang up my suspenders forever, I have to push forward.

I owe it to Billie.

"I'm going to sign off on you returning to work," he says, and I mentally high-five myself. That is, until he keeps talking. "But I do want to have a few more sessions with you."

"Umm, why?"

"While I admire your eagerness to get stuck back into the job right away, I feel there's a disconnect between you and the heaviness that comes with death. It's nothing major. I just want to make sure you're dealing with those feelings in a proper manner."

My smile is tight. "I am."

I'm totally not.

My mind goes back to the breakup that wasn't a total breakup ... the step-back conversation I had with Remy. Even his name brings thoughts of longing and growing resentment. The resentment isn't toward him but Eman.

The whole DOA on the job is icing on the shit cake, and I want to move past it. Shove it down with all the other crap I have buried.

"Let's schedule a time on one of your days off next week anyway. To be sure."

Damn it. How dare the fire department hire a competent shrink for once.

"Sure. No problem," I say anyway.

We stand and shake hands, and when I walk out to my car, I check the time. If traffic isn't too bad, I can still make it to the courthouse.

I know Remy and I need space, and I know turning up for him at this restraining order hearing goes against that, but Remy still needs support. Even if it's just a friendly face in the room.

When it comes to him, I can't shut off my protective instincts. I thought I might have been needed as a witness, but apparently, the 911 call is enough to push the restraining order through. On it, you can hear Eman threatening to kill us. I was asked if I wanted a restraining order too, but honestly, it's probably in Eman's best interest to take one out on me because if he tries anything, I'm bigger and stronger. Sure, jail won't be fun, but it might be worth it in his case.

It'd make sure Remy was safe for good.

I've gone back and forth on showing up out of the blue, but while Remy has admitted that he needs to be more independent and to make his own choices, on his own, that doesn't mean I can't be there for support.

Or maybe I can't be, and that's the point.

I want to be a shoulder he can lean on, but there's a difference between him wanting it and needing it.

He has depended solely on Eman for the last three years, and look where it's gotten him. I'll go, I'll hang in the back, and maybe if I time it right, I can enter with the crowd and go unnoticed.

Great plan.

Except for one thing.

Restraining order hearings are not like trials you see on TV and movies.

Nope. It's a judge, two lawyers—Remy's dad being one of them—and Remy and Eman. Oh, and that court reporter or dictator person. The person who writes down everything that's being said.

There are seats in the back of the small courtroom that is modern and not at all like TV and movies either, but they're empty.

Fuck.

I slip into one of the seats, not even sure if I'm allowed to be here or not.

Thankfully, Remy hasn't turned around, but Eman notices me.

I'm tempted to wave at his scowling face, but I don't want to draw the attention of everyone else.

The lawyers give their cases. Remy's dad plays the 911 call, and Eman's lawyer defends it, saying the words were empty threats coming from a man who had found out his ex-fiancé was having "relations" behind his back. He actually says relations, and it sounds every bit as creepy as you would expect.

For a brief second, fear shoots through me that the judge will take Eman's side. He got a good lawyer, that's for sure.

But then when it's Remy's actual turn to speak, he stands and clears his throat. I know this isn't what I'm supposed to be focused on, but damn, his ass looks good in those suit pants.

At least by staring at his ass, I'm not preoccupied wondering if we made the right call by taking a step back. All I want to do is march up to him, sweep him into my arms, and then never let go.

But he has things to deal with, and I have stuff I should deal with but know I probably won't.

I don't even know where to begin unraveling my baggage, and I'm scared once I start, once those floodgates open, there'll be no stopping them. And then I won't be any help to Remy.

Messy people don't belong together, but I want to belong with him.

He might've been hesitant to begin, but up there, as Remy finally speaks, he finds his confidence. "The death threats were an escalation of Mr. Faile's many manipulative behaviors. After being with him for three years, I realized he'd driven all my friends and family away, stripping me of a support system. He belittled me, made me feel inadequate and that I was lucky I had him because no one else would deal with my antics."

I couldn't be any prouder of him than I am right now.

"Through therapy I am now receiving because of the threats he made against me—"

"Oh, come on. That's a bit dramatic, isn't it?" Eman says.

Moron. But also thank you to him, because he just proved Remy's point.

Remy ignores him and keeps talking, and my heart fucking swells with pride. "It's not the death threats on their own that is alarming. It's the textbook red flag behavior of an abuser."

Remy's dad pats Remy on the shoulder, and when Remy turns to him, I must catch the corner of his eye because our gazes meet.

His eyes are soft, giving off longing and regret, before turning back to the front.

It's a relieved sigh from both of us when the judge agrees in Remy's favor. That maybe the attack on us wasn't ever going to be followed through on, but that it's important that it can't happen again.

While the judge explains the rules of the protective order, I slip out again and start heading for my car. I came to be moral support, but Remy fucking killed it in there.

He's really doing it. He's working to make himself better, and I'm ...

I'm still lying to therapists and not owning what I did. What I continue to do.

Remy's voice comes from behind me before I've even left the courthouse steps. "Sanden, wait."

I turn to see him rushing after me, and damn, his front looks just as good as his ass. He should find a job where he has to wear a suit every day.

"You came," he says softly.

"I did. I didn't know if I should, but—"

"I'm happy you did. You didn't need to, but I'm thankful you care enough to."

The urge to cup his face and hug him is strong, but I hold off. We're doing this to be mature and shit. Even if the way he looks at me makes me want to say fuck it all.

"I will always care, Remy."

He stares at his feet. "Do you think ... can we go for coffee?"

I bite my lip because as much as I want to, I can't. "I actually have somewhere I need to be."

"Right. Of course. I didn't mean—"

"I'm not lying. I would have coffee with you. You know, doing the whole friends thing. But there's something I should've done this morning, so I need to go do that now."

"O-okay. Thank you again. For being here. It means a lot."

"Wouldn't have missed it. I thought you might have needed someone to lean on, but you really didn't. You kicked ass in there."

He grins up at me. "Thanks. My therapist—"

My gut sinks. Not because he's doing what he said he would and that it's working. It's because I haven't yet started working on myself. "I'm sorry. I really do want to hear all about it, but I do need to go." I touch his shoulder, and even that small contact hurts. "We'll catch up, okay?"

I turn and walk away in a hurry, holding on to the sudden courage I have to go back to the therapist's office.

He's probably with someone else now, but I'll wait. I'll wait as long as it takes to go in there and spill my guts out. I'm terrified to take this step, but it's more than time to do it. If Remy can be brave, I sure as shit can be too.

I drive there, park very crookedly, and charge through the doors to his offices.

I'm running on the same adrenaline I get on a job, and I know from experience I need to follow through before I crash. With the way my heartbeat is loud in my ears, I don't have long.

Jim's receptionist tells me he's at lunch, but when I tell her it's an emergency, she glances at the closed doors to his treatment room and then back at me. "Let me call and see if—"

"That's okay. I'll only be a minute."

I stalk toward the doors, hold my breath, and push my way through.

The shrink is at his desk, downing a sandwich.

It feels rude barging in, but I need to let this out.

Now.

"I lied."

He looks up at me, confusion across his face, and that's when I let myself crumble.

"I've lied about so much. Why I became a firefighter. Why I still do it. But most of all, I lied when I said I was okay." Tears hit my cheeks. "I'm *so* not okay."

Thirty-One

REMY

I'm nervous and unsettled as I pull up down the street from the café. It's been a long, long month without Sanden. Other than the brief moment we had outside of the courthouse, I haven't seen him at all.

I thought it would be easy.

I thought that knowing I'm doing this so we have a real shot would make the process fast. Smooth. Bearable.

But I underestimated how much I miss him. All of him. His bright and easy laughs. His laid-back personality. The way it's so easy to be me around him. Surprisingly, as incredible as the sex with him is, it's not even in the top five things I think about when it comes to Sanden. Which just goes to show I'm head over heels for him.

I force myself out of the car with the mantra that this is

fine. We're going to try for friends. Friends has to be easier than all of this nothingness. It *has* to be. A whole month of being untethered from the one man who grounds me has been a complete mindfuck.

I hadn't realized how much I needed him until we took that step back, and I have no doubts it would have ruined us in the long run, even if it felt incredible short term. It's been like going through withdrawals. The high of seeing something I want to tell him about, followed by the crushing low of remembering he's not there.

Over and over.

Every fucking day.

Even reminding myself that I'm doing this for *us* doesn't help. If I'm never better, there is no us. Sanden said he'd wait, indefinitely, but saying and doing are two completely different things. When we'd made those promises, had that talk, I'd assumed it wouldn't take much to undo what Eman did to me. Colin made it seem like it was a surface-level, rip the Band-Aid off and let it heal type of thing.

Instead, my wounds are bleeding all over the place.

I laugh under my breath at that imagery. If this shit was physical, I'd be able to fix myself up. A gaping wound is nothing. Mental fuckery is a whole other beast, and I still find it impossible to believe that through words and actions alone, Eman turned me into a totally different person.

A needy person.

An insecure person.

A person who doesn't feel whole.

I'm working on it, I remind myself. And until I'm all

better, I'll be Sanden's friend. Then he won't be able to forget about me.

I push through the door to the café and look around, breath catching when I spot Sanden in a booth at the back. There are already two coffees on the table, and I know that he's ordered for me, even without having to ask.

Only the closer I get, the more I realize Sanden looks exactly like me.

Lost.

"Hey ..."

He smiles up at me, hands tight around his cup, but it's a shadow of the smile I love. "I was getting worried you weren't coming."

"I had to find a parking spot." And had to force myself from the car when I found one.

"You look good."

I snort as I drop into the seat opposite him. I *don't* look good. He doesn't either. He's got bags that match mine, hair that he's definitely been dragging his hands through, and a whole demeanor that's just ... not Sanden.

Fuck.

Have I turned him into an entirely different person too?

This whole time I've thrown myself into therapy, into forgetting Eman, into being driven to get to Sanden again, I didn't stop and think about how it was affecting *him*. He's got his own issues, and sitting around waiting for me to decide to do this again can't be helping with that.

"It's good to see you," I try, but the words catch in my throat.

"You too." His stare roams over my face greedily. I'm

doing the same to him. Matching up all his features with my memory of them, holding back from reaching over. From cupping his face. From pressing my lips to his.

I can't even sit here without needing him. That's proof enough that this isn't going to work. All my instincts are pushing me to ask why he's been avoiding me at work, why he hasn't messaged me, what he's been doing in our time apart. To fill him in on Eman and therapy and my fear that I'm never going to change.

But those are the things we're trying to avoid. Me leaning on him too much. Taking too much.

And without those things to talk about ... I can't do it. I can't sit here and ask him about the weather and Gabe and the hockey game on the weekend.

I can't make small talk.

Not with him.

My eyes sting, and I hurry to look down at my coffee before he can see.

But he sees.

Of course he sees.

"Remy ..."

"I'm fine."

"Hey ..."

I glance up at the soft tone and find all the love and affection in his eyes that I'm used to. I see the man who'd willingly give me everything if I put an end to this and lied. Told him I'm better.

What if I'm never better?

What if I have to sit here one day, looking at Sanden

and a man who actually deserves him? How the hell will I survive that?

How the hell do I ask him to wait when that's exactly what Sanden deserves? His person. A *whole* person.

Fuck.

This was a stupid idea.

"I can't do this," I whisper.

He immediately pulls back. "It's hard. I get it, but—"

"No, I really, really can't. Any of it. I don't ... I still need you. I can't be here."

Then before Sanden can say anything else, I jump up from my chair and leave. Colin's question comes back to me, the one he first asked that I didn't have an answer for. The one that caused me more pain than I'd let myself feel in the moment.

What if I do all this and Sanden isn't there waiting for me?

And if I'm not doing it for him, how the hell do I do it for myself?

Thirty-Two

SANDEN

I read over the text message Gabe sent earlier today. I'm parked outside the firehouse, urging myself to go in and get this over with.

Dude, when are you coming back to work? Your work husband misses you.

It brings elation and also dread. It's good that he misses me because I fucking love working with Gabe, but when the department put me on a sabbatical because of all the shit I've unleashed upon my mental health, I knew I'd eventually have to tell my crew everything.

I've put it off for a few weeks, doing my usual brush-off when Gabe has called or messaged checking in on me. He knew it had to be something big for me not to get cleared to return to work. But it has been easy to say the therapist is being thorough and I'll be back any day. Lies, lies, lies.

I've been sent to a clinical psychologist outside of the department to get the help I need before I'll be assessed again, so I can't even answer when I'll be back at work. Or ... if I will be.

Not going to lie. My life is a nightmare at the moment. I don't have work. I don't have Remy.

He couldn't even sit through one coffee with me. It doesn't give me hope for this time-out to come to an end.

What if, when he is ready for a relationship, he realizes he can't have one with me? Too many memories of Eman. Too much hurt.

Eman broke him, and I can't be the man to put him back together. No matter how much I want to be.

Jim encouraged me to come to the firehouse today. To let my people in on the hurt I carry around. I'm not sure how it will help. I'm not sure how any of this will help. Because opening old wounds, bleeding all that trauma, it's doing nothing but wearing me down.

Physically, mentally ... Even if Remy were to turn up and give me everything I want, I'm not in a place where I can take it.

The idea of ever being happy again is a foreign concept, but I'm assured it's a process.

Life has to break me before it can fix me.

Apparently.

Well, here I am. Broken.

Alone.

If I get anything out of today, I hope it's that I'm not so

damn lonely anymore. The two people I've spoken to about my issues surrounding Billie are unavailable. One by choice, but Remy ... I don't choose to be away from him. I need to be away from him.

We're not good for each other the way we are now. Codependent, reliant, needy. It's not healthy.

It's these thoughts that have me getting out of my car and heading into the station.

After so long away—the longest I've ever taken off, which isn't saying much because before this, my week in Hawaii was the longest vacation I've had in ten years—I'm welcomed back with cheering and whistling from the rec area upstairs.

I take a bow before jogging up the stairs.

Gabe practically tackles me, Rina fist-bumps me, and Cap, who's in the kitchen pouring himself a coffee, nods my way.

"Are you back? Please tell me you're back. Rina is a terrible partner. She doesn't shut up," Gabe cries.

Rina flips him off, and I laugh.

"Hey, I know how that feels."

And now my work husband is hitting me.

"That's assault," I complain.

"The assault is on my sanity," Gabe grumbles.

I rub the back of my neck. "Speaking of mental health, I have an announcement."

"You are coming back! Yes." Gabe fist pumps the air, but before everyone can get excited, I cut off their hopes.

"I'm not coming back."

Gabe looks like I punched him in the gut. "Ever?"

"No. I will be back. But ... I don't know when. Can we all take a seat? I have some things to say."

We move to the sitting area, where there are two long leather couches for them to sit. I sit in my armchair—I might not be lieutenant right now, but no one steals my chair—while Cap takes his armchair opposite me.

Then we're all there, waiting for me to talk, and I can't find the fucking words.

Telling them all why I'm the way that I am, telling anyone, is fucking daunting. I feel naked and exposed. Raw.

I swallow hard and force out words. Any words. Hopefully, I can ramble until I get it all out. "As you all know, I wasn't cleared to come back to work yet. I ... I've been keeping things from the department. From you all. And I know that's not fair on you. It hasn't even been fair on myself. I've always needed to be the best, to save all the lives, and be looked at like some fucking hero because the truth is ... I'm not. I'm far from it."

"What are you talking about?" Gabe asks. Out of everyone, I know my secret will hurt him the most. Not that he'll blame me for Billie's death like my parents but because I didn't feel close enough to him to tell him. Didn't trust him enough.

But it has nothing to do with that. I've never trusted me.

I don't trust that I'm doing a good job. I don't trust that I've made up for my past mistakes. The biggest trust issue I have with myself is that I can't promise to never lose another person. It's an impossible ask to promise that, yet I still feel like a failure that I can't.

"When I was a teenager, I was looking after my sister, Billie. We fell asleep and woke up to a house fire. I got out. She didn't."

Everyone here has seen those fires, the aftermath, and what that all looks like. They get it. Which is why, when they all wince at the same time, I already don't feel so alone.

"I became a firefighter so I could save others as some sort of karmic justice for letting my sister die." I hold up my hand as all their mouths open at the same time to refute that. "And I know, with my firefighter brain, that it wasn't my fault. But I can't convince my conscience of that, no matter how I've tried. Which is why I pushed it all down. Ignored it. Pretended it didn't exist. But ... I can't pretend anymore."

"So every house fire," Gabe says. "Every DOA ..."

"I push them down too. This, plus the stupid time-out I have going on with Remy, it's all boiled over, and I'm dealing with fifteen years of unresolved emotional trauma."

Gabe groans. "You really are never coming back."

I know he's joking, and I'm thankful for it because this serious moment needs a shred of light. "And for that, when I do come back, I'm asking for a new partner."

"You wouldn't dare."

I grin. "You're right. I hate that you are, but you're right."

"Aleks and I are there for you whenever you need."

I nod. "I know. Thank you. I've done this whole thing practically by myself, so letting people in is really difficult for me. So thank you to you all for listening."

After a round of hugs from everyone, I'm thankful I

got through it without crying. Or throwing up. It could've gone either way.

I'd love to say that I'm all cured and feeling light as I walk away, but it's not that easy a fix.

The weight on my chest still tries to pull me down, but I'm not going to let it.

I'm taking steps. The right steps.

That's all I can do for now.

I might not be able to have Remy in my life for the moment, but that doesn't mean I don't have anyone.

Thirty-Three

REMY

For the first time headed to a job, I'm nervous. Well, I wasn't nervous, but now we're approaching a house that had a tree blown onto it with an engine from Station 40 pulling up, I'm *nervous*.

It's been weeks since I've seen Sanden. After our coffee date, the distance between us made me feel raw and untethered. Sitting across the table from him, not being able to touch him, to tell him how I feel, was torture. It still hurts. It was way too early for the friend stage.

But now there's a very real chance I'm about to come face-to-face with him, considering Gabe's the first one to climb out of the engine.

I get out of my ambulance and approach. "Sorry, guys. This one's on us."

"Nice try, Remy. But we were here first."

"Were you though?" Tig asks, scratching his chin.

"First one to the door gets it," Rina challenges, and she and Tig take off at a sprint. I laugh as I watch them, then realize ... Rina isn't normally on their crew.

I try to be subtle as I glance around. "Sanden off sick?"

Gabe spins toward me. "What?"

"Normally he's with you, so I thought, well, I'd say hi, but—"

"He didn't tell you?"

Worst-case scenarios fly through my mind, everything from him being injured to leaving town. "Where is he?"

Gabe averts his gaze. "He wasn't cleared to come back after that house fire."

"He *what*? Why?"

"Ah ... I can't say."

"Sanden's never had an issue with it before."

"Yeah, well, uh." Gabe's having issues finding words. "He's got some things he's kept quiet about."

"Did he tell you what things?"

"It's not my story."

I narrow my eyes, trying to read Gabe's face. "Do you know ..."

"Do *you*?"

We talk at the same time.

"Billie—"

"His sister—"

Gabe's sigh of relief rushes from him. "You *do* know."

"He told me a while ago. After that big car accident we were all called out to."

"He didn't tell any of us before now. He went in to have a meeting with the shrink, came back out on mandatory leave, told the whole station about his sister and that he had a bunch of things he had to sort through before he came back."

"Wow." I'm ... I'm in awe. I have no idea what prompted him to take such a big step, but I'm so goddamn proud he has. Just like I told Colin, brave as fuck, that man.

"I can't believe he was carrying that around with him," Gabe muses.

"Alone," I add. "I'm so glad he's finally let it out."

"Me too. I can't look out for him on a job if I don't know what I'm looking out for."

And even though I hate that Sanden's off work and probably bored as fuck, I'm smiling. That was a huge step for him, and I can only hope that it means he might be heading toward peace.

"So ..." Gabe gives me the side-eye, and I know what's coming. "Can't believe you guys broke up."

"Is that what he told you?" Because yeah, it's true, but *ouch*. I've been trying to avoid talking about it at all, which admittedly is easier when you don't have any friends to talk to. I'm lucky I have Wren and Tig, and I'm hopeful some of the people I used to be friends with will come around.

"Actually, he said you were both in time-out and then turns into a kicked puppy literally every time you're mentioned."

"We're ... taking a break."

"Yikes."

"Thanks for the confidence."

"I just don't understand. You both seemed so into each other. Outside of me and Aleks, you were the cutest couple I knew."

"Yeah, but how many couples do you know?"

"A lot, I'll have you know. But ... they consist of manchild hockey players and my ridiculous best friend, so I admit the bar wasn't high."

"Doesn't sound like there was a bar at all." I'm keeping my voice light, careful not to drop into my mopey attitude that kicks in every time Sanden is mentioned. I miss him so fucking much, but the thing keeping me going is that every time I take another mental step, every time I work on the plan Colin and I set out, it's like I'm coming out of a haze. I almost feel good. There's still a lot of work to go, but hell if I'm not on my way.

The tiny chip in my heart that constantly aches for him is less of a misery spiral and more a reminder these days. I'm fighting for us.

"I'm working on myself," I tell Gabe. "Eman messed me up, and Sanden deserves better."

"He deserves *you*, Remy."

"The problem is I don't deserve him. Not yet."

"You know, when I first met Aleks, I had some hang-ups. A super-rich, wildly successful, famous sports star and ... *me*? But he made me realize that there's no score chart. And thank fuck for that because I would have lost big time. All we have is the way we treat each other. That's all you need."

"Thanks."

"Yeah, I just hate to see you both like this."

"Believe it or not, this is what healthy looks like on me."

Gabe looks me over. "In that case, I'm a fan. Let's hope that—"

Before Gabe can finish that thought, my phone goes off in my pocket. I pull it out to silence the alert, but then it vibrates. And vibrates again.

"What's going on ..."

As I watch, notification after notification pops up on my screen in a steady stream.

"You okay?" Gabe asks.

"I have no idea."

I unlock my phone and click the most recent one, but instead of some kind of emergency I'd been expecting, Eman's profile loads.

It's his social media, and the guy looks *wrecked*. He's got deep bags under his eyes, and they're all red like he's been crying. He hasn't shaved, and his hair is a mess.

"Hey, fam. I've backed off posting recently because of some personal shit I've been going through. I tried to keep it to myself—" He lets out a self-deprecating laugh. "—but my life has literally crashed and burned in the last month, and I thought ... if this is happening to me, how many others go through this? Staying silent, simply because I'm a man, creates more of a stigma around others seeking help. So I'm coming on here today to talk about domestic abuse and how it ruins lives."

My jaw drops, and I glance at Gabe before refocusing back on the screen. Is Eman for real? Is he actually owning up to it all? My heart is *hammering* in my chest, and even as I watch, the video is racking up the views.

"Most of you know I was in a loving relationship for three years. We were set to get married this summer, and ... that's when my whole world ended. The lead-up to the wedding was rocky, but I thought it was the usual couple's mess. Remy was constantly telling me I was overreacting, that nothing was wrong ... but something felt off. Then on our wedding day, I took a walk to clear my head, remind myself why I was marrying my man, and by the time I got back to the hotel, my best goddamn friend had made his move. He told Remy he'd been left at the altar, fed him lies so he called off the wedding and had a party instead. This is from that night." A photo of me *attempting* to kiss Sanden pops up on-screen for a few seconds before disappearing. Eman's smile isn't amused. Blood is pounding in my ears, but I can't look away. "In case it wasn't clear, that wasn't me he was kissing. What's worse, they took off on the honeymoon together, and my fiancé went from being mine to my ex-best friend's in less than a week. Sanden's twisted three years of happiness and turned Remy against me. All my attempts to reach out were met with contempt, and then ..." He sucks in a shaky breath. "A month ago, they took a restraining order out on me because I wanted to move back into *my* apartment. They lied, they ran up my credit card on the wedding night, and now they're rubbing their happiness in my face. I'm broke and alone, and the two of them are off enjoying life." Eman pauses, like he's trying to control himself, and my hand is a death grip on the phone. "I've found evidence that the two of them have been seeing each other behind my back. I feel like such an idiot. Remy drove my friends away and left me with no support system. He broke a door in our apartment, which they blamed me for, and two people against one, I didn't stand a chance. I've had to take extended leave from work to sort my life out again ..." He mouths soundlessly like a fucking fish, and watching him on-screen, watching those views tick up, watching him finally get that viral moment he's always goddamn wanted, makes me feel like my head is going to shoot off with rage. "The truth is, I'm a victim. It's not something any man wants to admit, but I'm hoping, if my story helps one person—"

I can't watch any more. I can't ... I *can't*.

That goddamn damn motherfucking dick fuck.

Gabe's mouth is hanging open. "Is he for fucking real?"

I actually scream. "That *fuck*."

"Sanden's gonna kill him."

"*I'm* gonna kill him." More notifications fill my screen, and I make the mistake of clicking on one of them.

@remyport *You're disgusting. Jump off a bridge you piece of shit.*

I almost laugh. It's not happy. More ... I don't even know.

I've worked so fucking hard to walk away from this. To grow, to heal, and here's Eman trying to take it from me again. He can't get to me physically, so this is his next step.

My first instinct is to run to Sanden, but I remind myself why I can't.

He has his own shit, and this is exactly the kind of thing I need to be able to handle by myself. He'll want to support me, and I hope soon I can accept that, but right now, I'd take advantage. I'd lean on him too much. Even though I know it's the right call, it doesn't mean I don't hurt.

It doesn't mean I don't ache to be wrapped up in his arms.

"What are you going to do?" Gabe asks.

I switch off my phone. "Ignore it."

"That healthy?"

"The thing is, I know why he's doing this. He wants my attention. He's trying to hurt me. To control me. So the best thing I can do is ignore him. He doesn't get to take from me anymore."

"Wow. Remy." Gabe pulls me into a hug, and while it helps, it's not Sanden.

I miss him so fucking much.

"Anything I can do, let me know."

"Thank you." I mean it. But I'm determined to be strong. To prove to myself I can handle it and that I don't have to constantly run to another person. I'm confident in my decision to block out Eman's noise and keep focused on the path I'm taking. To ignore the toxic feeling that he's won.

Now let's hope that sticks.

Thirty-Four

SANDEN

"I don't see how this is going to do anything," I mutter to myself as I stare up at a block of apartments that now sit where my childhood home used to. About ten years ago, they demolished all the old houses on the block to put up this monstrosity, so the neighborhood doesn't even look the same.

But apparently, to push past my fear of inadequacy and my sense of debt, I have to open up the old wounds that I've been covering with duct tape for years, just hoping it'll hold.

I've taken EAP counseling leave and continued seeing Jim, the fire department shrink, and he thinks I need to let go of Billie. Because no matter how many times I save a life, none of them will ever fill the imaginary debt I hold over my head.

I have a new mantra, which to me sounds kinda hokey and narcissistic, but it's simple to remember: It wasn't my fault.

It's not my fault Billie died.

It's not my fault the woman on my last job died.

And it's not my fault that Eman had three years of manipulating Remy.

I don't owe him anything. I don't owe anyone.

Jim has asked me nearly every session if I even want to be a firefighter, and every time, I have the same answer for him. "It's not a want. It's a need."

He says it's going to take a while before my brain catches on that, no, it's not actually a need, and I can do whatever I want with my life.

The thing is, though, I can't imagine doing anything else. And maybe that's because my brain is taking too long to catch up to where I'm aiming to be. I can't yet separate my sister's death from the reason I love my job.

Being here now, where she died, there's no lingering guilt. There's no real connection to Billie at all, thanks to the changes in this neighborhood.

That might be a good thing or a bad thing, but I'm here to say goodbye to her, so I'll see what I can do. Do I have a sudden delusion that doing this will set me free of everything?

No.

But I've squashed it down long enough.

I feel like a moron, standing on the side of the road and

talking to an apartment building, but I'm even more concerned that a licensed professional deems this as mentally healthy.

"I don't know where to start, so I'm just going to say it. I'm sorry your death broke up our family. I tried to be strong for our parents, but they blamed me. I blamed me. The logical firefighter side of myself—oh yeah, by the way, I became a firefighter. Ironic-ish, am I right?—but as I was saying, that side of me continually tells me that what happened to you was a tragic accident. I've carried around the guilt and the shame of it for so long it destroyed that fun-loving big brother you once had. But I'm working on it, okay? For a long time, I wished I could trade places with you—that you were the one who was supposed to live—but as I get older, I realize that your death put me on my future path. If there is a god, maybe this was His plan all along. I need to start thinking about it that way instead of a curse He bestowed upon me. A debt."

A middle-aged couple walks by, giving me a weird look.

"I swear my shrink told me to do this!" I call after them, which only makes them huddle together and walk faster.

"I need to wrap this up, little sis. I guess all that's left on my conscience is I'm sorry. Even though it wasn't my fault, I'm sorry I couldn't save you. I didn't have the chance. I wish I did, but ..." Tears pool in my eyes, but I try to shake them away. "I will always love you. Uh ... I guess that's it."

And even though I hang my head low when I walk away, I'm lighter than I have been in a really long time.

I might even make it to the Fireman Ball later tonight that I was going to try to skip out on.

I should've skipped out on the ball.

Gabe stands next to me. We're both in our dress uniforms by the punch bowl, drinking what I hope has alcohol in it because Remy's walking through the entrance with Tig.

I wanted to tell him when we had coffee that I was going to therapy, but he didn't give me the chance. And while I'm not delusional that one talk with my dead sister will suddenly make me a well-rounded, adjusted adult, I can at least acknowledge that I have issues. Therefore, I'm totally a well-rounded, adjusted adult, yes? That's how it works?

"How's the grown-up time-out working out for you both?" Gabe asks.

"I miss him," I admit. "He wasn't even mine for that long, but ..."

"You should go talk to him. At least see how he's doing with all the ex-boyfriend drama."

My head swivels so fast it almost falls off. "There's been more drama? Did Eman break the restraining order? Why didn't Remy tell me?"

"No, the online shit. You haven't seen it?"

"I blocked Eman after the honeymoon when I posted photos of Remy and I enjoying Hawaii. We were both being petty back then. Ah, good times. When pettiness was our only priority instead of the state of our mental health."

"Uh ..." Gabe looks like he doesn't know whether to laugh or give sympathy.

"Dr. Jim says it's okay to laugh."

Gabe's hand touches my upper arm. "Sanden, tell me. Can you see Dr. Jim right now? Is he here with us?"

I shrug out of his grip. "No, but that's what he told me when he instructed me to talk to my dead sister. In public. Where people could see me."

Again with the unsure look. "Okay, I'm unsure how to deal with this Sanden."

"Because I share now?"

"Yes. And I can't tell if you need a hug or a shoulder to cry on."

"I'll never say no to one of your hugs."

The moment I say that, Gabe's boyfriend comes back from the bathroom.

"Or one of Aleks's." I wink at Aleks. "I missed you, boo."

Aleks laughs.

Gabe does not. "Just for that, I'll leave you two to pretend you're each other's soul mate, and I'm going to go talk to Remy. Because unlike other people standing here, I'm not in a grown-up time-out with him."

Damn. Hitting me where it hurts.

"Haven't seen you with Gabe at the arena on game nights lately," Aleks says, and I get the impression he's fishing for me to spill all my dramas.

"I've been 'working on myself.'" I use air quotes and all.

"Eww."

"Yeah, that's what I said. But apparently, looking after

your mental health is good for you? Doesn't sound right, but whatever."

Aleks smiles. "Seriously though. Are you okay?"

I actually feel confident in my answer for once. "I'm on my way."

"Good. Because you're one of my good-luck charms. I need you in those stands."

"Aww, what are soul mates for? I'll be there whenever I can. Which, lately, is always because I'm still on sabbatical."

"How long for?"

I shrug. "I think I'm ready to go back, but the fire department still has to sign off on it."

Movement on the dance floor catches my eye.

"That motherfucker."

"Who?"

"Your boyfriend and my work husband."

Aleks follows my gaze. "Well played, Gabe." He turns to me. "I'm going to go pull my man away from your man because this whole joking about being soul mates bit is our thing."

My gut reaction is to do it too. To march right out there and pull Remy away from Gabe, but ... it's not really my place to do that. Not at the moment.

Aleks takes a few steps but pauses. "Come on. You said you'd still be friends."

Eh, fuck it. It won't hurt to check in. Plus, Gabe never did end up telling me the Eman update.

We both hit the dance floor, making our way through couples dancing, and approach Remy and Gabe, who are laughing. Probably at us, but oh well.

"Excuse me," Aleks says, bodychecking them both and somehow landing in between them. "Oops, how did I get here?"

Gabe smiles at his boyfriend. "It's a real mystery."

Aleks whisks Gabe away, leaving Remy and me standing in the middle of the dance floor.

He looks good. Happy.

There are no bags under his eyes, and he seems lighter. Stress-free.

He puts his hands up in the dancing position. "How about it?"

I step closer to him, put my hand on his hip, and join my other hand with his. It feels like coming home.

We sway to the slow song, just staring at each other.

"Hi," he eventually says, and I chuckle.

"Hey."

"How have you been?"

"I've been better, not going to lie, but I'm good. I will be good."

"I heard about the sabbatical."

"I heard about Eman being a dick. Though, specifics were left out."

Remy shakes his head. "Nope. We're not doing that. When we were together, we constantly talked about Eman and my issues. It's one of the reasons we broke up—"

"Are on time-out," I correct.

"Same thing. I want to know how you're doing."

"My therapist thinks I'm ready to go back to work but not able to stop sessions yet. I'm waiting to be assessed by the fire department shrink."

"That's good. That's a decent step."

I nod. "It is. I've still got a ways to go, but more and more every day, I'm able to tell myself that Billie's death wasn't my fault, and each time I manage to do that, I believe it a little more."

"Good."

"Now, can we talk about you?"

Remy glances away. "Eman went viral painting both of us as the perpetrators in ruining his life, so that's been fun to deal with."

I stop swaying. "He what?" And okay, maybe that was a bit too loud, but what the fuck?

"Played the victim card. I've had messages to kill myself, that I'm the worst type of human to ever live ... Have you not got anything? He names you. Though, he tagged my profile in the actual video, so ..."

"Nah, he wouldn't have been able to tag me. I had him blocked everywhere. And we didn't share any real friends. Only you. Are you handling it all okay? You shouldn't have to put up with that."

"I'm actually doing surprisingly well? I think therapy helps."

"Who'd have thought?" I snark, but every bone, every muscle ... everything inside me deflates with a moment of weakness. "I fucking miss you, Remy."

"I fucking miss you too," he says.

I lower my head next to his so we're cheek to cheek as we slowly dance. I want to find a way for us to be together now. I know I said I'd wait for him, but it's so fucking hard.

It was one thing to want him when he was with Eman,

knowing it would never happen between us. It's a whole other thing knowing we want each other but have things we need to work out first.

"I was thinking ..."

I pull back to meet his gaze. "Thinking what?"

"That ... that I'm ready. I mean, if you haven't already moved on and—"

My heart thuds loudly in my chest, making my body vibrate with every damn beat. "What ... what are you saying?"

Remy takes a deep breath. "I know we both still have a lot to work on, but Colin's given me the tools and insight on how to do that without becoming too attached to you. I was thinking, maybe we could ... start dating again? Dating. No sleepovers. Go slow."

It's a scrap, but fuck if I'm not going to take it.

"I'm in, but I have one question."

"Shoot."

"This no-sleepover rule ... does that extend to sex or only sleep because sleeping over means serious relationship, and we're not there yet? Like, what are the rules on restroom quickies at a work event?"

Remy's face lights up, even tinges a light shade of pink. And then in the next moment, he's dragging me off the dance floor and toward the bathrooms.

Thirty-Five

REMY

My grin is wicked as I tug Sanden into the bathrooms and shove him into a stall. Those sweet eyes, his crooked smile, that sexy fucking uniform he's wearing. And he wears it well. His muscles fill out the suit, and I ache at how much I've missed them. I want to run my hands over his entire body, but that's going to have to wait. We don't have long, but I fully plan to show him exactly how I'm going to take care of him from now on.

Because I'm finally capable.

I think I'll always have doubts about myself and relationships in general, but Colin and I both agreed that I'm in a good place now. I can recognize those intrusive thoughts and head them off before they become a problem, but more importantly, I feel like a whole person again.

And this whole person wants to be filled to the brim.

I back Sanden against the cubicle wall, hands on his chest, faces so close his breath puffs against my lips. I'm so blindingly hard, but I give myself this moment. This fractured second to memorize his face and let myself *feel*. The relief, the warmth, the comfort. He's still safety and always will be, but I see so much more of him now.

Sanden's big, rough hands cup my face. "What if I lose you again?"

"Not happening," I growl, pressing closer against him.

He laughs, that deep, sexy laugh that I've missed. "I'm serious though. It's been torture without you."

"Yeah, I felt the same." My fingers trail up to his neck, seeking skin. "And no relationship is guaranteed. All I know is that you were right. We needed that time apart because if we didn't, we would have imploded. Guaranteed. And I wouldn't have been okay. Now, if we don't work out for whatever reason, it will gut me, but I'd make it through. Because you don't make me a person." I nuzzle his jaw. "You just make me a better one."

"Ooh, Remy got wise."

"Yep. And now talkie time's over. Plenty of time for us to do that later. I need you to remind me what I've been missing."

He doesn't need any more convincing than that. I think we'll both be a little raw from our time apart for a while, but I'm going to show him every day that he's it for me. I'm going to put in the work and make him happy and give him everything he needs because I have zero doubts that he plans to do the same for me. No more constantly taking. From now on, partners. Always.

Sanden's mouth meets mine in a bruising kiss, sending my entire body to jelly. He tastes like want and relief, and the sheer contentment that flows through me at being here with him almost makes my head spin.

I break our kiss to trail needy kisses along his jaw, down his throat, then grunt with frustration at the collar of his dress uniform getting in my way.

"Want you naked," I whine.

He squeezes my ass and rocks his hard length against mine. "You're coming home with me after this, and we're going to spend hours naked. For right now, make me come because I've needed you so damn much."

I drop to my knees, scrambling to open his pants and pull out his cock. He's so hot and hard in my hand, veins straining against silky skin. Sanden wraps his hand around mine, and the other grips my hair.

"Stick out your tongue."

My mouth drops open, and Sanden hums in satisfaction. He slaps his thick cock against my tongue, my cheek, my lips before pushing inside.

"Suck, Remy."

I moan as my lips close around him, and I'm hit by his taste, so familiar and intoxicating. Everything I've dreamed about in our time apart. His thrusts are rough, uncontrolled, and it's a struggle to keep my eyes on him, but I can't look away. All that beautiful man towering over me, eyes locked on mine, this growing awareness between us that we were always meant to be. Inevitable. No matter the setbacks, we were made for each other.

It's why we couldn't settle into being friends. We were never friends. This attraction, our feelings, like our bodies have always known what it took our brains too long to figure out.

I pull off him with a gasp, and his hand trails from my hair to cheek.

"I need you inside me," I beg. "Please."

"I ..."

And like I can read his mind, I know what he's thinking. He doesn't have any condoms. Neither do I, even though I knew there was a high chance our night was going to lead here. That's how much I trust him.

I laugh and push to my feet, lips pressing briefly to his.

"You're ridiculous if you think I've been with anyone since you."

The smile that breaks across his face is full of relief. "I couldn't even think about another man. My brain wouldn't believe that we weren't together."

"My last good orgasm was when your cum was dribbling out of my ass, and I want to feel that again."

Sanden's arms wrap around me, and he spins us until I'm slammed face-first into the wall. His hot breath ghosts the shell of my ear as his hands work open my pants. "Brace yourself, sweetheart. I have a lot of cum to fill you with."

He shoves my pants to my ankles, then spits in his hand and rubs it over my hole. My whole body relaxes, opens for him, as he fucks me with his fingers.

"Do it," I say. "I can take it."

"Oh, fuck."

His fingers disappear and are replaced by his blunt cock-head. I bear down, ready, desperate. So hungry to be filled by him the feeling overrides everything else.

He's not gentle, and it's perfect. With one hard thrust, he fills me. The stretch burns but doesn't hurt, and the second he draws back, I rock my hips forward, ready to bring us back together. Our bodies meet hard and fast, me matching every thrust, my ass alive with the feel of his bare skin inside me.

It goes beyond missing him. It goes beyond sex.

It's this connection I've needed, and now that I have it again, I'm never letting him go.

Neither of us bothers to be quiet, and the fact we're at a work event has totally left my mind. I don't care. None of it matters.

Not in this moment anyway.

"You feel so fucking good," he says, voice strangled with emotion. "I will never get over being able to have you. Never."

His words shiver through me, lighting up in my gut. Sweat prickles along my back, under my jacket, my skin growing overheated and tight. My nipples tingle with my shirt dragging over them, and Sanden's pegging that place deep inside me that makes me see stars.

A garbled kinda prayer leaves my lips because my brain is officially offline.

I love this, and I love him.

It's not a question anymore.

Then Sanden releases my hip with one hand and settles

it over my throat. My eyes roll back, and the tingles race from my ass to my spine before settling in my balls. His grip isn't tight, which makes the feeling of being claimed so much better. He doesn't need power or control, just the gentle reminder he's there.

My hand shoots to my leaking cock, and I jerk off with purpose. "I'm so, so close."

"I've got you, sweetheart. I want you to go first this time, but I don't know how much longer I can hold back."

I arch my back more, vision swimming, hardly able to catch a breath. "Harder."

He pounds into me, over and over, and unlike the grip on my throat, his hold on my hip is bruising. I feel wrecked, used, and so unbelievably wanted as Sanden mouths along my ear and against my hairline, grunts loud and harsh. He doesn't let me go, and it's perfect.

The arm I'm bracing against the cubicle wall buckles as my orgasm hits me. Wave after wave of pleasure courses through my body, tensing every muscle as I milk my cock through it.

"Fuck, yes. So tight," Sanden says before finally unpeeling himself from my back and straightening. It only takes a few more seconds of him fucking me before he cries out, and I get that glorious sensation of him unloading inside me.

I sink against the wall, dopey smile in place.

His sweaty body follows me.

"I needed that," Sanden sighs into my hair.

"Me too." I reach for his arm around me and bring his hand to my mouth so I can kiss his fingers. "But as much as I hate to say this, we really need to get back out there."

"Fuck."

"It's a miracle no one came in while we were going at it."

"We got really, really lucky." He presses a lingering kiss to my jaw. "You still wanna come home with me tonight?"

I snort and straighten, nudging him off me. "Yes. But still no sleepovers. I know things are going to be rocky while we settle back in, but I meant what I said about you being it. I'm in this for real. Boyfriends. Partners. The whole thing. We're restarting it slowly, but that's because I'm serious about you. No mistakes this time. Slow doesn't mean unsure. It's how we can look after ourselves and each other."

"I like that." Then with a cheeky grin, he drops, grabs my pants and underwear, and yanks them back up again. Sanden closes in, hand snaking around me and slipping between my ass cheeks. He rubs the material against my hole, soaking up his cum. "And since you're coming home with me, you get to sit in this all night."

"Only if you promise to clean me up later."

He lets out a gravelly hum and dips his mouth to my ear. "I'll lick up every last drop."

"Deal. Can we go now?"

Sanden laughs and draws back, cleaning himself off and fixing his clothes. "We've still got dinner and everything to go. What were you saying about going slow and patience and everything?"

"I'm not so good with the patience thing."

He leans in and kisses me. I melt against him, never wanting this to end.

But we've already been more than lucky with not getting caught, so I reluctantly pull away again. His hand closes over mine as we leave, and my heart trembles.

I'm smiling so big by the time we step out of the bathroom—and almost run headfirst into Gabe.

"*Finally.*" He huffs.

"Ah ... what do you mean?" I can't look at Sanden, or I'll break into giggles.

"Everyone thinks this bathroom is out of order." He pins us both with a look. "I hope you washed your hands."

Then he stalks away, and I can't hold it in. Sanden and I collapse against each other, laughing.

Hey, if this is the start of our forever, our lives are gonna be awesome.

Thirty-Six

SANDEN

"Fuck!" Remy hisses.

I wake, bleary-eyed as I take in our surroundings. My apartment. Sun shining through the blinds. Fuck knows what time it is. "Urgh. We already broke our no-sleepover rule."

"Colin will be so disappointed in me."

I can't tell if he's being genuinely distraught over that or is being dramatic. We're working on not much sleep and a whole lot of cum dehydration. That's a thing, isn't it?

"Come here," I murmur and pull him against me.

"No, I need to get up and go home. I'm already fucking this up." He tries to slide out from underneath my grip, but apparently, he really is freaking out over this.

"I have a question," I say, more awake now.

"What is it?"

"What was the rule against sleeping over again? Like, is it to make sure we're not jumping into anything too serious too quickly?"

"Yes. And sleeping over leads to more sleeping over, which leads to practically living together, and—"

I pat his hand. "The thing is, we were so wrecked from all the fucking last night, and the ball, and the emotional shit we put out there. I think sleeping over was the right decision, otherwise, I would've worried about you getting home safely. What if ..." I think about it. "Okay, what if we make a deal that we're only allowed to sleep over at each other's places twice a week and never two days in a row. People who date sleep together, Remy."

He bites his lip. "True, but I'm worried about making it a habit and losing myself in another relationship."

I sit up and cup his cheek. "Then we won't let it happen. It might not be the typical way people navigate a new relationship—having rules in place—but I think we're both mature enough to know that we need to put our mental health first. I don't want to spend time away from you, and I don't want to go back to not being with you, but I want to make this work. Like you said last night. Boyfriends, partners, all of it. And eventually, we won't have to have all these rules in place. It's only now while we're both in vulnerable places. We can lean on each other. We just can't depend on each other. Not yet."

Remy nods. "That ... That's actually a really good idea."

"Stick with me. I'm full of good ideas."

Remy grins. "Yeah, like what?"

I lean in and kiss him softly. "Like that."

"Mm, that is a good idea. No, a great one." Remy slowly climbs on top of me, straddling my waist and pushing me back down.

"I would've thought you'd have no cum left by now."

"I don't. I need to feel your skin on mine." He rests either hand by my shoulders and stares down at me with a lazy smile on his face.

He's so goddamn gorgeous he lights up every bone in my body.

I could stay like this forever.

And as if thinking that sent up a warning sign to the universe for us to slow right back down, Remy's phone goes off.

He groans. "That's probably Wren trying to find out where I am." He reaches over the side of the bed to pull it out of his pants pocket on the ground. "Yep." He answers. "Hey."

His cousin is so loud I can hear him say, "Oh good. You are alive. Thanks for letting me worry for nothing."

"Sorry. I had planned on coming home, but then ..." Remy stares down at me again. "I kinda—"

Okay, now that Wren has calmed down, I can't hear his actual words, but Remy laughs.

"Yes, I fell on Sanden's dick. Whoops, I slipped. Oh noooo." There's a pause. "I know what I'm doing. We have a plan." Now he frowns. "What? When?"

"*What's going on?*" I mouth, but he doesn't even give a clue.

"I'll look now. Thanks." Remy ends the call and stares at me with wide eyes.

"What is it? What happened?" Before I can freak out, his lips quirk.

"You know that video that went viral of Eman's sob story?"

"God, what is it now? You had a love child with some woman while you were engaged? You stole all his clothes? What?"

He climbs off my lap and flops down beside me. "According to Wren, he's gone viral again, but for all the wrong reasons. He told me to check out the drama."

Yeah, I'll believe it when I see it.

And then Remy loads it up, and I do.

Holy shit, this is amazing. Someone has stitched our 911 recording over the top of Eman's whining, and there are thousands of comments and shares about how Eman is obviously the real abuser. I don't know where or how they got the recording, but I also don't care.

I never believed in karma until this moment because no one who's ever wronged me has had it blow up in their face before. Until now.

Remy's scrolling through the comments so fast I barely get to read them, but then one of them makes us both pause.

I blink at the screen and then blink at it some more.

Remy's just as frozen as I am.

Wait, this guy's wedding was supposedly in August? I met him at a bar in July, he fucked me and then left. I didn't even get off.

That's followed by a string of cheating accusations against Eman.

"You can't believe every comment," I say quickly.

"I know, but I think I do with this one. When we got tested, I was actually expecting for something to show up, so when it didn't, it was almost like ... almost disappointing because I wanted that proof to shove in his face. Which is petty and irrational and—"

I nudge him. "Hey, we like petty."

He chuckles. "We do, and the thing is, even if this comment isn't true, I still feel like it gives me validation that my suspicions were correct. I should have listened to my gut when it was telling me the night he didn't come home a week before our wedding, he cheated on me, but I thought it was pre-wedding jitters or something. The whole thing has turned me off ever getting married."

My heart sinks because while it's way too soon to even be thinking about that kind of thing, I would want nothing more than to have Remy walk down an aisle where I'm waiting at the other end. After Eman, I wouldn't make him wait around. I'd be there at fucking dawn so he'd know I was going to show up.

That I would always show up for him.

"I think we should celebrate our new beginning. We're together, we're both getting the help we need, and Eman's social media dream is imploding as we speak."

"What do you have in mind?"

I reach for my phone and call up Gabe.

He answers with "Why did they let me drink so much

last night? I'm hungover and not coming in to fill in for whoever else has called in sick."

Our teams both lucked out in having the ball fall on our rostered days off, and there are usually always a few who claim they can't make it in the next day, but my phone has been eerily silent.

"It's not that. Aleks has a home game tonight, doesn't he?"

"Yeah, and it's his fault I drank so much. I was all woo, you can be designated driver because your coach will kill you if you turn up hungover tomorrow."

"Sure. His fault. Let's go with that. Anyway, I'm wondering if you're taking anyone to fill those season tickets of yours."

"Nah, I wasn't even going to go myself tonight. Too sick, and hockey is slow and boring as it is."

"You are a disgrace to the Crosby last name, and you should be stripped of it immediately."

"Ugh, you sound like Aleks."

"It's because we're soul—"

"Don't fucking say it."

I laugh. His little jealousy act is so cute. Especially considering as much as I admire Aleks for his athletic ability, he in no way compares to Remy. *No one* compares to Remy.

"You should come with me and Remy tonight, then. We're celebrating."

"What are we celebrating?"

"Our new start."

"Oh, good. You two finally got your shit together? I'm in."

We make arrangements for tonight and end the call while I hold Remy close.

"Want to scream your lungs out at a hockey game tonight? You know you want to."

"I really do, but I want to do anything with you. Everything."

I squeeze his shoulder. "We'll get there. There's no rush to this."

"I think that's what I like about this arrangement the most. In the past, I've always thought that relationships needed an end goal. They had to be heading somewhere and getting there as soon as possible. Like, marriage and a family was the only way to have a happily ever after. But it's not. You've made me realize that having a partner isn't about end goals. It's about making each other's life *fun*. It's going through experiences together. Growing together. And there's no time frame on when or how we have to get there."

"It's the journey that counts."

"Exactly." Remy's hazel eyes meet mine. "And I'm so glad I get to spend my journey with you."

"I couldn't agree more."

Epilogue

REMY

Five Years Later

Being in Hawaii brings back a billion and one memories. Eman's amongst them, and I haven't thought of that guy in a while, not since he deactivated his social media accounts, then packed up and left Seattle.

But without him, I wouldn't be here. Or … maybe I would have gotten here a lot sooner than I have. Who knows?

Sanden pops up out of the water and flings droplets

from his hair everywhere like a dog. I laugh and splash him back, but then he gathers me up in his arms.

"What are you thinking about so hard over here?"

I grin. "Remember the last time we were in this pool and I said you were a hero type?"

Sanden tries to duck back under the water, but I hold tight.

"*Mister* Medal of Valor."

"You're such a dick." He's smiling though, even with his cheeks tinged red. We both know he's proud of the award but hates all the praise that goes with it. And I get it, but Sanden deserves all the recognition.

He's everything I ever thought he was and so much more. I can't believe the mistake I almost made all those years ago because there's no one else I'd want to spend my life with.

"We're heading to the bar," Gabe calls out. "You both coming?"

Sanden's about to follow him when I grab his arm.

"Actually, we'll catch up."

I could kill Gabe for the unsubtle way he's looking at us, but Sanden doesn't seem to pick up on it. They might be work husbands, but Gabe and I have gotten really close. Aleks too. Every off-season, the four of us plan a trip together somewhere and try to catch up once a week if all of our schedules line up. I have friends outside of Sanden, which was one of my main priorities, but those two feel like family to me.

"You don't want more Sex on the Beach?" Sanden asks.

"I only order that drink so you can make that dad joke."

"Which is one of the many, many—" He presses his lips to mine. "—*many* reasons I love you."

"Hold that thought."

Sanden eyes me, lopsided smile in place. "What have you done?"

"Nothing. Or at least ... nothing *yet*."

"Okay?"

"You know how I've always said I never want to get married again?"

"Yeah." He drags a hand back through his wet hair. "What of it?"

"We live together."

"Yes."

"We have Rex and Bumrag." I could still kill Wren for training our dog to only answer to that name.

"Remy, what's going on?"

I let out a shaky breath, suddenly way more nervous than I thought I'd be. "I love you."

"*Remy.*"

"Marry me." The words come out so fast I realize a second too late I forgot to pull out the ring.

"W-what? But you said—"

"I know. But the more I thought about it, the more I realized how stupid I was being. I kept saying I wouldn't let him control my life anymore, but this was the one last thing he still had a hold over. The bad memories. The fear of being left again. But I'm not afraid anymore. You make it impossible to be."

Sanden's mouth is hanging open, and he moves

through the water closer. "Are you serious? Because I don't need it. I swear. All I need is you."

"Yeah, I know." My perfect, perfect man. I reach into my swim trunks and pull out the ring I hid there earlier. "This is how serious I am."

"Holy shit."

"So ..."

His hands find my waist, and he tugs me against him, mouth claiming mine. "If you even need an answer to that, I'm going to have to do better at this whole relationship thing." His nose runs along my jaw to my neck. "You don't need a ring to own me, sweetheart. But I sure as fuck want to wear one for you."

Sanden blows a raspberry on my neck, and I squirm away, laughing.

"You don't need to be better at relationships," I assure him.

"Clearly, I do."

I shake my head as I slide his ring on. "Actually ... I might have already registered. And I know I've sprung this on you, but ... well. We're here. And the sunset is absolutely beautiful."

"What are you saying?"

"We both have to go in and pick up the license. Gabe is already registered from when he performed his best friend's wedding—"

"Is this why your parents are here?"

I give him a sheepish grin. "Are you mad?"

"You invited Mom and Dad and our two best friends. You planned this, knowing how happy it would make me.

The only thing I'm mad about is that we have to pick up a damn license and I can't be your husband sooner."

"We've waited for so much more in our relationship, I think you can be patient for a few more hours."

"Fine," he grumbles. "But we're getting you your Sex on the Beach, and then we're *actually* going down to have sex on the beach."

"Excuse you, sir, I'm an *engaged* man." I bat his chest. "But I refuse to have sex again until I'm doing it with my husband."

Sanden all but pulls me from the pool. "In that case, let's get this show on the road!"

I laugh and slow him down, wanting to look at him one more time. "You make me so happy," I whisper.

"That's literally all I've ever wanted for you. And now I get to make you happy for the rest of our lives."

Thank You

Thank you for reading *Up in Flames*.

This was Eden and Saxon's first joint venture outside of hockey, and we're happy to announce it is just the beginning of our extended Sadenverse.

If you missed Sanden's work husband, Gabe, and his HEA with hockey star Aleks, read their book here: https://geni.us/foolish

To stay up to date with our releases, join our Pucking Disasters Facebook group.

Come be a disaster with us: https://www.facebook.com/groups/puckingdisasters